We
of
Deceit

Chris Longmuir

To Willie

Enjoy

Chris Long

B&J

Published by Barker & Jansen

Copyright © Chris Longmuir, 2022

Cover design by Cathy Helms www.avalongraphics.org

Edited by Helen Baggott

Web of Deceit is a work of fiction. Names, characters, places and incidents are the product of the author's imagination or are used fictitiously. Any resemblance to actual events, locales or persons, living or dead, is purely coincidental.

ISBN: 978-0-9574153-9-3

DEDICATION

This book is dedicated to UK Crime Book Club in grateful thanks for all their help and support.

1

Thursday

He flicked back the sleeve of his jacket to look at his watch, but only two minutes had passed since he last checked. The revellers had long since gone and Teasers looked forlorn with the unlit neon sign above the door. How much longer would he have to wait?

As if sensing his impatience, one side of the front door opened and the first of the girls came out. He slid down in his car seat and balanced his camera's long lens on the dashboard, firing shot after shot as more girls emerged. It would be hit or miss whether the photographs turned out. But he'd set the camera to a slow speed and the early morning sky was lighter now than it had been earlier. He crossed his fingers and hoped for the best.

Their voices drifted through the air, too faint to distinguish the words, but he listened and watched as they strode along the street. Confidence radiated from them, and it was plain they saw no reason to be nervous. He supposed it was the confidence of numbers. Would they be afraid if they were on their own?

His target glanced over her shoulder before turning to say something to her friend. They laughed and continued walking, their voices floating back to him until they vanished out of sight around a bend in the road. Had she noticed his car? Did she suspect?

He switched on the ignition and inched the car along the street, slowing to a stop when they came back into view. Laughter drifted back to him, and he waited until they reached the corner. After they rounded it, he put the car into first gear and drove to the junction. He didn't want them to see him, so he waited again. In this fashion, he followed them until they

1

arrived at the block of flats where they lived. Flats they rented from their boss, Tony Palmer, a perk provided to the dancers who worked for him.

He parked his car at the end of the street and continued to watch until the last lighted window faded into darkness. This was the fifth night he had followed them home, but there was no sign of Palmer. Tony's reputation for visiting his dancers after hours did not appear to be warranted, and he had nothing to report back. He waited a further hour before returning to his hotel.

Tony Palmer stood in front of the one-way mirror overlooking the club. It took up an entire wall in his office and he often stood there watching the action below. But after the departure of the girls, the clubroom always took on an air of desolation. At this time of night, there was nothing to see except for empty tables and the detritus left behind by customers.

The bar was directly below. This area of the room was masked to him, although he knew Marlene would still be there tidying up and making sure everything was ready for the next evening's entertainment.

Unwelcome thoughts crept his mind. This used to be the place which confirmed his success and bolstered his ego. This office, with its antique leather furniture, mahogany desk, expensive artwork, adjoining bedroom, and en suite bathroom, spelt out to him how far he had come since his days working on a market stall. But it was all ash now, ever since his daughter had been left to die in Templeton Woods. The mad man responsible had changed Tony's life forever. It made him wonder whether his success had been worth it. What good were money and power when he had been robbed of the most important person in his life?

He rubbed his face and gave himself a shake. Brooding on it wasn't doing him any good and it wouldn't bring Denise back. Turning his back on the mirrored wall and his office, he padded down the stairs to the clubroom below.

Marlene looked at him as he slumped on a barstool.

'You look like shit.' She poured him a whisky and laid it in front of him. 'This'll cheer you up.'

He gulped it down, even though he wasn't in the mood. 'I think I'm past that stage.'

She refilled his glass. 'You know, brooding about it won't bring her back.'

Marlene always knew what he was thinking.

'I know, but it creeps up on me. One minute I'm all right and the next I get pulled back into the depths.'

'How's Madge coping?'

'To tell you the truth I'm not sure. Her doctor prescribed medication for her and I think that takes a lot of the pain away. But she's not like she used to be. She doesn't laugh much, and she's turned into herself.' He missed the Madge of old, vibrant, funny, and always laughing. She had changed but so had he. It was to be expected, he supposed.

He laid his glass on the bar. 'Speaking of Madge, I'd best get home. I don't like leaving her alone all night.'

Marlene picked up the glass and submerged it in the sink behind the bar. 'Yes, Madge needs you just now.'

He knew she was thinking of the days when he would shack up with a dancer and stay out all night. But those days were gone and each time he looked at a dancer, it reminded him of Denise, the daughter he'd lost.

Not that Madge noticed any change in his behaviour. Or at least he thought she didn't. She was so consumed by her grief, he doubted whether she even noticed he was around.

Brian was waiting with the car in the small parking area at the side of the club. He got in, slumped in the back seat, and closed his eyes.

'Take me home.' He didn't hear Brian's response or register when the car rumbled into life.

Angel laid a restraining hand on Candace's arm after the outer door slammed shut and the other girls clattered upstairs to their flats. She waited until they were on their own before she whispered, 'Did you see the car following us again? It's been

3

there all week.'

Candace nodded. 'It's scary. But he can't do anything if we're all together.'

Angel tightened her grip. 'I'm sure it's me he's after.'

'Why would you think that?'

'You know why. Besides, I have this horrible feeling of being watched all the time. I'm sure Kevin's behind it.' She thought of her empty flat on the second floor. Why hadn't she agreed to share instead of insisting on her own place? 'I'm scared of being on my own in case he comes for me.'

Candace frowned. 'D'you want to kip in my flat tonight?'

A flicker of hope flared in Angel's chest but just as quickly died. She shook her head. 'I don't think Linda would like that. You know how she feels about me.'

'She wouldn't mind.' Candace sounded unconvinced.

'You know it wouldn't work. Linda doesn't like to share you with anyone. Because we're friends, she seems to see me as some kind of threat.'

'That's rubbish.'

'Is it? Have you seen the way she looks at me?'

Candace frowned. 'You're overwrought. I'll come upstairs with you and stay for a while.'

'No. I don't want to spoil things between you and Linda.'

'I don't care. I'll sort it out with her after.'

A door clicked shut when they passed it on the first landing. Angel stared at it, sensing Linda standing on the other side, but Candace guided her past the door and up the next flight of stairs.

'Give me your key.'

Angel rummaged in her shoulder bag, produced the key, and handed it over.

The room was in darkness, and Candace reached to flick the light switch.

'No!' Angel grabbed Candace's arm. 'Don't switch on the light. He's probably watching.' She strode to the window. 'That car is still there. Kevin's behind this. I'm sure. When will he ever let go? Every time I think I've escaped him; he always finds me again.'

'That can't be Kevin down there. If it was, he would have been up here by now. You know that.'

Angel frowned at her in disbelief.

'It's time I did something about him because he's not going to let up. He won't stop until either I'm dead or he is.'

'That's wishful thinking. What on earth can you do to stop Kevin from doing whatever he wants?'

'I'll think of something.'

Worry lines creased Candace's face. 'I don't like to leave you alone. I'll stay with you tonight.'

'No,' Angel said. 'Linda will get worried. You'd best go back downstairs. I'll be all right.'

After Candace left, Angel returned to the window to continue staring at the car below.

'I thought you weren't going to come home.' Linda's voice sounded petulant.

'Why would you think that?' Candace closed the door and reached over to stroke Linda's cheek.

'You were with her. I saw you going upstairs.'

'We were followed home again, and she lives on her own. I only wanted to make sure no one lurked in her flat.'

'You never worry about me in that way because you care more about her. Nothing I do pleases you, although I keep on trying my best. I even dyed my hair blonde because I know that's what you like about her.' Linda's voice wobbled, and she turned away.

Candace reached out and pulled Linda into her arms. 'Don't be silly. You're the one I'm living with. But Angel is like a sister to me. She's been my friend since we went to school together and I can't ignore her.' She ran her fingers up Linda's back. 'I don't care what colour your hair is, and I don't want you to be a clone of Angel. I'd love you if your hair was pink, green, or tartan, although I preferred it when it was brown, the way it used to be.'

'Do you mean that?' Linda raised tear-stained eyes and looked at Candace.

'Of course, I do, silly.' Candace tightened her arms around the girl.

'Should I change it back to brown?'

'I'll help you pick the shade the next time we're in town. Now, come on, it's time we went to bed.'

Candace waited until Linda fell asleep before rising to peer out the window. But, although the car had gone, the worry remained.

2

Friday

Angel narrowed her eyes against the morning sun shafting through the window onto her face and rolled over in bed. Once her eyes adjusted, she stretched her arm out from underneath the sheet to check the time on her phone. She'd slept later than usual, and the morning was almost gone. Sweat trickled down her back. Dundee was in the grip of an unusual heatwave.

Fully awake after she stepped out of the cold shower, she scrubbed herself dry with a towel that had long since lost its softness. After pulling on an azure tee shirt, a deeper blue cotton skirt, and high-heeled sandals, she peered out the window before leaving her flat. The car from last night was gone. She breathed a sigh of relief, grabbed her shoulder bag, and left.

Police Headquarters in West Bell Street wasn't too far to walk, and she welcomed the opportunity to stretch her legs. The breeze teased the ends of her hair, flicking strands over her face, while the hem of her skirt swirled around her legs.

Noise and fumes from speeding traffic on her right contrasted with the peace in the park on her left. She ignored the temptation to turn off the main road and wander through its leafy paths. Her safety was more important than a dalliance in more pleasant surroundings.

Cars whizzed past her in their eagerness to play Russian roulette at the roundabout, each one trying to outdo the other, so she walked further along to the pedestrian crossing. Ten minutes later she was standing outside Dundee Police Headquarters, summoning up the courage to go inside.

Up to now, she'd always tried to avoid contact with the police. She'd heard too many stories about their persecution of people like her. Her father, a small-time house breaker, was

7

forever moaning about them. 'Damned cops are always on your tail, and it don't matter whether you did it or you didn't. In their eyes, you're always guilty.'

When she ran with the Glasgow gangs they were always on the lookout for police, and a lot of them had suffered a wallop with a baton. At least that was what they claimed when trying to outdo one another with who was the toughest.

Living with Kevin had reinforced her lack of trust in the police. But that was for a different reason. When they visited her father-in-law's establishments, which was where her dancing career started, they were always on the take and always expected something for them to turn a blind eye. She'd lost count of the number of times she'd had to fight off their advances, although the threat of telling Kevin or his father was enough to dampen their enthusiasm.

But Kara, the wee barmaid at Teasers, had said a cop by the name of Bill Murphy was someone she could trust. He'd helped her out of a hole earlier in the year and he was a good guy. She hoped Kara was right.

'I need to speak to Bill Murphy,' Angel said after she worked up the courage to enter the building and approach the reception desk.

Sweat beaded the brow of the policeman on duty while she waited for his response.

'I'll need more details first.' His eyes bored into her, and she didn't like what she saw.

Prick. He reminded her of the policemen who used to frequent her father-in-law's pubs in Glasgow. But she sighed and told him about the stalker.

'You say this car has been following you for several days? How many days is several?' His voice was harsh, and he seemed uninterested as he scribbled on the pad in front of him.

She wondered why he wasn't using the computer at his elbow.

As if he sensed what she was thinking, he muttered, 'Bloody computers are down today. They've been playing up all morning.'

She looked away. Would he have used the same language

if she'd been someone he considered respectable? She'd seen the way his eyes raked over her when she came in.

'I'll pass it to the duty team. Someone will be in touch.' With that, he turned away from her.

'I was advised to ask for Bill Murphy and I'm not leaving until you've contacted him.'

He sighed and shook his head. 'Who should I tell him advised you to do that?'

'Kara Ferguson. He was involved with something concerning her earlier this year.'

A flicker of interest showed in the man's eyes. 'Where did you say you worked?'

'Teasers.'

He reached for the phone. 'I can't guarantee he'll see you, but I'll give it a try.' Moments later, he turned back to her. 'Detective Sergeant Murphy is tied up, but he says if you leave your name and address, he'll get back to you.'

Angel's steps were faster on the way home and her cheeks burned with anger. No one would come, she was sure of it. The piece of paper would be conveniently lost. What a waste of time it had been to report the matter.

Tony stayed in the shower longer than he intended. Water jets pounded his body from every angle, and he closed his eyes. If only the streams of water could wash away all the filth of his life and make him clean again. He tilted his head allowing the water to mingle with his tears. How had it come to this? A few months ago, he'd been satisfied with his life as someone of importance in Dundee. A man who'd risen from the gutter to prominence in both the underworld and the business community. He had a lovely wife and daughter at home and a succession of glamorous girls to satisfy his other needs. All it took for everything to change was the actions of a mad bastard who left his precious daughter, Denise, to die a lonely death in Templeton Woods.

His biggest business venture, Teasers, was successful, but the joy had gone out of it. The girls no longer attracted him, and he knew he snarled more at his employees now. Even his home life changed following Denise's death. Madge, who'd always been there for him, now relied on pills and walked about the house like a zombie. She was more broken than him and he didn't know how to help her.

The world had become a dark place for both of them. After he'd meted out punishment to Denise's killer, he'd thought the darkness would lift, but it made no difference. Uncertain of Madge's reaction he'd never told her what he did to the man who murdered their daughter. Whether she would have welcomed the knowledge was unclear to him, but he'd always protected her from the violence that was part of his life and he saw no reason to change that now.

Madge appeared to be asleep when he returned to the bedroom, although he was never sure whether she was asleep or simply avoiding having to talk to him. But it wasn't only him. She avoided everyone now. When friends visited she refused to see them, so they no longer came, and the house seemed to have lost all life and felt cold and unwelcoming.

Each morning, Tony couldn't wait to escape to his equally cold and empty office in Teasers where the only noise came from the cleaners clattering their buckets and mops.

Tony shrugged off his melancholy and selected one of his many suits from the wardrobe. He had a business to run, and he couldn't allow his employees to witness his despair. It was a sign of weakness, and there were always people in his line of business who would take advantage of that. Today, he chose to wear navy with a pristine white shirt and silver tie. His choice would ensure he looked smart enough to keep up appearances at the club. With a last glance at his sleeping wife, he tiptoed out of the bedroom.

Since his daughter's death and his wife's descent into melancholy, he'd taken to eating in the kitchen, and this was where he was heading.

Big Bet finished chopping the carrots on the butcher block in front of her before she looked up.

'The mistress still sleeping then?'

She lifted the board and scraped the vegetables into a large pot.

Tony nodded. 'I didn't want to disturb her.'

'Morag lass, put the kettle on while I make the master's breakfast.'

The maid scuttled into the kitchen from the utility room. She avoided looking at him while she filled the old-fashioned copper kettle.

Bet's eyes followed her movements. 'That's fine, lass,' she said after Morag placed it on the Aga. 'You can start your cleaning now. Make sure the breakfast room's done before the mistress gets up.'

'How long has Morag worked here?'

Tony watched as Bet slid an egg and a couple of rashers of bacon onto his plate.

'Best part of a year.' She placed the pan in the largest of the two sinks. 'She's a good wee worker.'

'Seems a bit nervous.'

'She hasn't worked out how to respond to the men who come in and out of the house, so she's a wee bit wary.' Bet ran water into the sink. 'Better that way than the other. Some of them wouldn't need much encouragement.'

Tony frowned. He always made sure the roughest of the men he employed came nowhere near his home. But Phil and Gus reported to him here, and he didn't trust either of them even though they had no interest in women. Brian, his bodyguard, had free access, but he would never do anything without Tony's approval, and he trusted Brian above all others. Luigi, the newest arrival, was here under Tony's protection following the attack on his cousin Georgio. Then, there was Luigi's nephew, Georgio's son, who was only seventeen and preparing to start university in September. He resolved to have a word with Luigi to make sure Fabio understood the staff in his house were under his protection and that anyone interfering with them risked having their hands cut off.

No longer hungry he pushed his plate back. 'If any of them bother Morag let me know and I'll take care of it.' His eyes narrowed. If he couldn't protect his own daughter, he would make damn sure he took care of everyone else under his roof.

Bet raised her eyebrows, the only sign of surprise at his words.

Damn it, if he didn't watch out he'd be turning soft, and he couldn't allow that to happen.

Angel's mood hadn't improved by the time she reached the house. She slammed the outside door behind her and stamped up the stairs. A door on the first landing opened and Candace peered out.

'What's up with you? It sounds like a herd of elephants climbing the stairs.'

'Damned police,' Angel snapped. 'Treated me like dirt when I reported our stalker. They'll do damn all about it if I'm not mistaken.'

Candace shrugged. 'What did you expect? The only time they pay any attention to us girls is if they want a bit on the side. Any other time they ignore us or treat us like prossies.'

'That's what gets my back up.' A scowl marred Angel's face. 'They treat us like streetwalkers, and they're not interested if we get stalked or beaten up. I'm going back to bed so I'm ready for my act tonight.'

She climbed the stairs to the next landing, and once inside her flat strode to the bedroom, stripped off her clothes, and threw herself on the bed. Burying her face in the pillow, she screamed to relieve her tension before rolling over and closing her eyes. Her act at Teasers was demanding and she would need all her energy to perform tonight.

3

Tony Palmer's photograph stared down at Bill Murphy from its position at the top of the whiteboard. Bill scowled. He'd been trying to get something on Tony for as long as he'd been a detective, but the evidence to ensure the gangster's arrest kept on eluding him and it wouldn't be long before Detective bloody Inspector Rawlings would look for a report.

A door slammed at the far end of the room and there she was, striding towards him. His nemesis. Ever since Kate Rawlings transferred from the Forfar office, she hadn't given him a moment's peace. When she first arrived in Dundee it was supposed to be a secondment, a temporary arrangement until Andy Michaels recovered from his heart attack. But Andy had now retired on health grounds, so there was little hope Kate Rawlings would return to Forfar any time soon.

'I see you've been busy setting up a board,' Kate said. 'Talk me through it.'

'Tony Palmer, age 45.' Bill pointed to the photograph. 'Considers himself a businessman, but he's behind all the drug dealing and prostitution in Dundee, as well as running his nightclub, Teasers. I'm sure he uses the club as a front for his other less legal activities. But he keeps his hands clean. Most of the illegal stuff is taken care of by these two men.' Bill nodded towards the photographs of two well-groomed blond men featured below Tony on the board. 'Phil Beattie, age 25, and Gus Jones, age 24. Don't let their looks fool you they're a vicious pair. I'd like to see them locked up. Phil and Gus do all of Tony's dirty work. They keep an eye on the dealers and the pimps and they make sure Tony gets his cut. Phil's an ambitious sod, though, and I have my doubts whether Tony trusts him.'

Bill tapped another photograph on the board. 'This man,

Brian Crowe, is a real thug. He's an ex-boxer with a long record of drug dealing, housebreaking, and violent crime, but he's loyal and he's the one person Tony trusts. I think they went to school together. Tony employed him as his driver when Brian came out of prison the last time and he seems to be staying out of trouble.'

'What about the rest of the names you've posted?'

'They're Tony's employees at Teasers, security staff and doormen. Most of them have records and quite a few have had spells in prison. We're still investigating how involved they are in Tony's other activities. But see this guy here?' Bill pointed at the photograph of a man with dark good looks. 'This is Luigi Modena who came to Dundee a few months ago. He's a relative of Georgio Modena whose nickname is The Italian. Georgio operated a business in Edinburgh which was very similar to that of Tony's, but there was some kind of gang warfare, and a Glasgow outfit took his business over about the time Luigi came to Dundee. The word is that Georgio was badly beaten up and still hasn't recovered.'

'So, what is Luigi doing here?'

'Not sure. But he's working for Tony as a sort of butler. Georgio and Tony go way back and I'm guessing he's agreed to take Luigi out of the firing line.

'Then there's Marlene, who manages the nightclub and keeps an eye on all the staff. Tony trusts her and she's the only one who has access to Tony's office upstairs. Apart from the bouncers and security staff, there are the dancers, and Kara the other barmaid.'

Bill remembered Kara from a previous investigation. Funny how she was now working for Tony when only a few months ago she was in fear of her life from Phil and Gus.

'This Teasers. What type of activities go on there?'

'Apart from the bar and disco on the ground floor, which is open to the public and can get rowdy, there's the nightclub upstairs which is a mite more interesting. It's a members-only establishment, although the rules are lax, and it's reckoned if you want to get in all you need is enough money. It's not exactly a strip club, but they have pole dancers, and the entertainment is pretty near the knuckle.'

'Prostitution?'

'Tony's too fly for that. He doesn't encourage anything on the premises, but that's not to say that assignations don't happen. If they did, Tony would claim no responsibility for them.' Bill tapped his teeth with a pencil. 'We've raided the place several times, but it's always come up clean.'

'I see.' Kate gave one last look at the board before turning and heading back to her office. 'Put everything you know in a report and let me have it before you finish tonight.'

'Yes, ma'am.' Bill stared after her. What was it with her and reports? She always wanted everything in writing. As if there wasn't enough to do.

He returned to his desk and glared at the yellow piece of paper stuck to his computer monitor. Sue must have stuck it there before she headed out. On the point of binning the note, he stopped to scan it when the name Kara caught his eye. Something about a stalker and a reference to Kara. The information was scrappy, and he lifted the phone to dial reception.

'DS Murphy here. I'm looking for clarification of a message that was left for me. It's a bit garbled.'

'I've just come on duty,' the voice answered, 'I don't know anything about it.'

'Check the bloody computer. See what's been logged.'

'Sorry, sir, but the computers are down and all I've got is a pile of papers waiting to be input.'

Bill groaned. Input, what kind of language was that? All these blasted computer terms. Didn't anyone speak regular English nowadays?

'Can you sort through the papers and find the original referral? It's from someone called Angel and it's to do with stalking.'

'Will do.' The cheerfulness of the voice grated on Bill's nerves. 'As soon as I have a moment. I've got loads of people down here needing to be seen to first.'

'Make it a priority.' Bill slammed the phone back into its cradle.

It was late afternoon before the return call came. Bill looked at the clock before scribbling down the details and shoving the piece of paper in his in-tray. It was too late to do anything about the referral today. But he didn't like the sound of this one and made his mind up to visit the woman. He'd make a point of doing it tomorrow even though it was his day off.

4

'I know where you are!' Angel stared at the text message on her mobile phone. He'd found her again.

The phone slid from her fingers and balanced on the edge of the bed before tumbling to the floor. She burrowed deep under the duvet, clasped her arms around her body and tried to blot out the threatening text, but it floated before her closed eyes, taunting her. He could be here waiting for her in the living room, the kitchen, or outside on the landing. Hiding under the covers wouldn't save her and with no clothes on she remained at her most vulnerable.

With tentative fingers, she pushed the duvet back and slid from the bed. The heat of the day had passed, and cool air struck her naked body. She grabbed the thong and bra hanging from the doorknob. She'd worn them this morning, but she didn't have time to hunt for clean underwear. Her tee shirt and skirt lay in the corner where she'd thrown them, and she donned them with trembling fingers. Rummaging below the bed she found shoes and thrust her feet into them.

Her hand closed over the doorknob, but she waited, listening for sounds of movement in the room beyond, before peering out. No one was there. The room was empty. Holding her breath and walking on tiptoes she sidled around the door in case someone was lurking out of sight in the kitchen or bathroom.

'You in there?'

The flap of the letter box rattled. She let her breath out in a rush. The voice belonged to Candace.

'What's up? You look like you've seen a ghost,' Candace said when Angel opened the door.

'He's found me again.' Angel's voice trembled. 'How does he do it? Every time I think I've escaped he still finds

17

me.'

Candace pulled Angel into her arms and stroked her hair.

'As long as you stay in Scotland, he's going to keep tracking you down. You know that as well as I do. You should have gone abroad after you left Edinburgh.'

Angel relaxed in Candace's arms. Tears trickled down her cheeks, and she buried her face in her friend's shoulder until they subsided. 'I had it all arranged. Georgio said he would help me, but you know what happened to him and now he's in no fit state to help.'

Downstairs, at street level, a door slammed followed by the sound of feet in the stairwell. Angel tore herself from her friend's arms, panic reflecting in her eyes and on her face. She pulled Candace inside the flat and closed the door turning the key on the inside.

'Just in case it's them,' she whispered.

The two women stood behind the door listening to the footsteps approaching the flat. When they continued past and up to a higher level, they both let out a sigh of relief.

'You sit down. I'll put the kettle on. You'll feel better after a coffee.'

Angel slumped into an armchair while Candace headed for the kitchen. She reappeared holding a small package. 'Is this what I think it is?'

Angel stared at the polythene wrapped parcel. There was no mistaking it. Nor was there any doubt who had left it and what they wanted her to do. It was Edinburgh all over again. She wrapped her arms around her body to quell the shakes taking hold of her.

'What on earth are you thinking about having this here?' Candace threw the package down on the coffee table. 'There must be about a kilo in there and there's another parcel of the stuff on the kitchen worktop.'

'It wasn't there when I went to bed,' Angel's voice whispered. 'They must have come in while I was sleeping and left it there.' The enormity of what she'd said hit her. They had been in her flat, her home, while she was sleeping, and she hadn't heard them.

Candace knelt on the floor beside Angel and grasped her hands. 'It must be worth thousands of pounds.' She gestured towards the package. 'If we sold it, we'd make enough money to take us to the other side of the world where they couldn't reach us.'

'It's tempting, but I don't know the dealers and wouldn't know where to start. And even if I did how do we know that information wouldn't get back to them? If they knew we'd sold their product they'd kill us.' She lowered her face into her hands. 'They'll want me to set up Tony for a drug bust.'

'What if we tell Tony?'

'Oh, yes. Tell him I've been recruited to set him up for a drug bust. I can see that working out.'

'You only have two options. You go ahead with their instructions to set Tony up, or you go on the run again leaving the drugs behind.'

'Only one problem with that. I don't have the money to run.'

'Can you tap Tony? He's got loads of money.'

'But he's not going to give it to the likes of me.'

'Didn't stop him from hopping into your bed at a moment's notice.'

'I think he regards that as being one of the perks of being my boss.' Angel had no illusions about Tony's need for her. His loyalties lay with his family. She'd only been a pastime to while away a few hours of boredom, to be dumped when he no longer needed her.

'If he won't help you voluntarily, I reckon we take it from him some other way.'

'If you're thinking about that mad idea you had to blackmail him, I can tell you it won't work. And you're forgetting how dangerous he can be. I don't want to end up with cement shoes at the bottom of the Tay.'

'But the way we've planned it, he'd never know.'

'I wouldn't be too sure about that.'

'I've talked to Linda and she's up for it.'

Angel sucked her breath in. 'We don't need Linda.'

'Yes, we do. She's the one with the camera savvy and if

19

things go wrong, she'll be in the frame, not us.'

'But she creeps me out the way she always watches me and copies what I do. Every time I buy something new, she buys it as well, and she's even styled her hair the same way as mine.'

Candace laughed. 'That's because she admires you.'

'I could do without her admiration.'

'We can't do without her if the plan is to work.'

'The plan! The plan! All you've been able to talk about lately is this crazy plan. It might work with someone else, but it won't work with Tony.'

'Why not? You said yourself he's a family man and doesn't want anything to upset his wife.'

'I have to admit Tony worries about her. I think their daughter's murder sent his wife around the bend and he fears she might do something drastic. That's why he always goes home at night now instead of playing the field.'

Angel recalled the worry lines on Tony's face when he talked about Madge. 'We were childhood sweethearts,' he'd told her. 'It would kill me if anything happened to her.'

'I'll make the coffee while you think it over,' Candace said. 'But I don't think we have anything to lose by trying to take Tony for enough money to set you up in a new life somewhere abroad.'

The sound of voices and laughter echoed around the dressing room as the dancers removed their clothes to don scanty G-strings and apply their makeup. It would soon be time for them to perform.

Angel ignored the activity around her and threw the phone from her. It skidded across the top of the vanity unit coming to rest against the mirror, but the voice echoed in her mind. 'Did you think I wouldn't find you?' She stared at the mobile with eyes full of loathing. Would the demands never stop? Would it never end?

After the Edinburgh job she thought she'd escaped them; thought they would never find her in Dundee, but once they had you in their clutches they never let go. Her eyes filled with tears. She'd been fond of Georgio and hadn't wanted to set him up. But you didn't argue with them. And now, although Georgio wasn't dead he might as well be.

The chatter of the other dancers faded along with the sound of music thudding along the corridor, and Angel was back in Edinburgh looking at Georgio's broken body. 'Why?' she'd shouted. 'Why did you do that?'

But Mad Dog had smiled, laid the hammer down, and removed the knuckle dusters from his fingers, before saying, 'Be thankful it's not you.'

Angel shivered at the memory. The man was a psycho.

'What's up?' Candace's voice broke into her thoughts.

'Nothing,' she mumbled. 'I'm a bit off colour, that's all.'

'You do look peaky. You sure you're up for tonight?'

'Of course, I'm not backing out now.' She stared at her reflection in the mirror and didn't like what she saw. But it was too late to change her mind. Besides, Tony was a gangster as well as a businessman and deserved all he got.

The spotlights framing the mirror accentuated the worry lines on her face. It brought back the doubts that plagued her when they first thought of the plan.

There was no doubt in her mind Tony would fight back and she would need to convince him she was as much of a victim as he was.

5

The mobile in Luigi's pocket vibrated against his thigh. The screen showed the caller was Lucy Sampson, his eyes and ears at Teasers. He and Lucy went way back, and she'd followed him from Edinburgh when the trouble with Jimmy Matthews erupted.

'Yes?'

'Thought you'd want to know that Jimmy Matthews and his gang are here and the dancer who calls herself Angel is in a panic. I think he's contacted her. It feels like a repeat of Edinburgh.'

Luigi's hand tightened on the phone. It was as he'd suspected, Matthews had his eye on Tony's nightclub. He'd known that when Angel came to work for Teasers, the Glasgow gangster would surface.

'Got to go,' Lucy said, and the call ended.

Jimmy Matthews. His uncle's voice, as he struggled to speak, echoed in his mind. 'That bugger stood laughing when Mad Dog was laying into me.' The attack had been vicious and life-changing and left Georgio paralysed from the neck down. It was a wonder he could speak at all.

Luigi rammed the phone into his pocket and climbed the stairs to seek Fabio. The boy wasn't in the bedroom they shared but that wasn't unusual. Tony had allocated them both a room when they arrived, but Luigi had insisted that Fabio slept in his room to ensure his safety. His nephew had turned the other room into a workroom where he indulged his passion for electronics and all things digital.

Luigi tapped on the door and entered to find Fabio sitting in front of a computer, a serious expression on his face and his fingers jabbing at the keyboard. Rows of letters and numbers scrolled up the screen. Fabio probably knew what they all meant, but it was gibberish to Luigi. He was no slouch with computers himself, but he didn't even try to understand what Fabio was doing. The boy had always been a genius with electronics.

'I need you to monitor the security system while I'm out.'

'You're going out?' There was a hint of surprise in Fabio's voice.

'Yes. Jimmy Matthews is in Dundee with his gang. They're at Teasers and I want to check them out.'

'What will you do?' Fabio pushed a lock of black hair away from his face and his lips tightened.

'If I get a chance, I'll stick a tracker on their car so I can keep tabs on them. You got one handy?'

'Sure.' Fabio rummaged in a cardboard box behind the computer. 'This one should do the trick.' He handed over a small square box. 'It's magnetic, you can stick it anywhere. The battery will last for almost a month. If you still need to track them after that it'll need to be replaced.'

Luigi stuck it in his pocket and turned to go.

'What will you do after you've attached it?'

'Nothing for the moment. Just watch and plan what we do next because you and I know they'll be back. This time they'll be reconnoitring, but the next time they'll mean business and we need to be ready.'

Fabio nodded and closed down his computer. 'I'll keep an eye on things here until you get back. But watch out for Mad Dog.'

'You don't need to worry about me.' Luigi's eyes were bleak as he thought of what Mad Dog had done to his cousin, Georgio. 'I know I wouldn't stand a chance in a standoff with him. We need to be more subtle. But I will get him, and he'll pay for what he did to your father. You have my word on that.'

Fabio's face darkened. 'Count me in. You can't do it on your own.'

Tony stared through the one-way glass on the mirrored wall which overlooked the clubroom. Business was booming. It was a Friday night, and the place was full. Angel, the principal attraction, was an asset to the club although she didn't appear to enjoy mixing with her admirers.

Over the years Teasers had grown into an exclusive club limited to those with the ability to pay the membership fee. Tony was proud of it, and this was where he spent most of his working life. It attracted a lot of custom because of its reputation as the best nightclub in Dundee. And admission to the clubroom on the top floor was the most sought after of all.

Anyone could frequent the disco and the bars on the floors below, but only members could access the delights of the top floor. Membership, however, could be applied for at the door and was easy to obtain provided the potential member had sufficient money.

Tony didn't regret what he'd spent redesigning the place. This room was now the most sumptuous of any in the building. The colour theme was red. Red carpets, red velvet curtains, red plush chairs, and a massive glitter ball in the ceiling. In the far corner of the room was the large semicircular stage backed by floor to ceiling mirrors and a central silver pole flanked by two others at opposite ends of the stage. Scattered around the room were several other smaller circular platforms each with its own pole. Teasers could always guarantee club members a good night out with entertainment by the most attractive dancers and hostesses in Dundee. But it wasn't a brothel although Tony turned a blind eye to whatever the girls got up to when they weren't working, and he had, from time to time, sampled their charms.

All eyes turned from the dancers on the circular platforms when the red velvet curtains on the main stage began opening to reveal the star turn. Angel lay on the stage to the left of the central pole. Tony held his breath. Waiting in anticipation for Angel to perform.

The music, a slow sensual rhythm, increased in tempo until Angel writhed in time with the beat. Her body arched and her arms moved sinuously in the air. As the music pulsed through the room, she pushed her shoulders from the floor and, in a dramatic surge of energy, bent her head to meet her knees and swung her blonde hair forward to flow over her face. Her hands continued to caress her body, taunting, and teasing the watching men. She lifted her head, pouted her lips, and stroked her skin before reaching to grasp the shimmering silver pole. Pulling herself upright she walked around it, each step more erotic than the last, before she embraced the pole and swung herself off the ground, her legs and body arching, and stretching into sensual positions that seemed impossible. Behind her the mirrored wall reflected her movements, making it seem as if a multitude of Angels were performing.

As he watched her dance, Tony experienced the usual surge of desire. It would be so easy to invite her up here and spend the rest of the night with her as he had done many times before. But he worried what Madge would do if he didn't return home after the club closed. His wife was teetering on the edge of a depression, and he would never forgive himself if she did something stupid because of his actions. She was more important to him than any dancer even one as inviting as Angel.

The performance ended and Angel slid down the pole coming to rest on the stage in a sitting position. She bent over her raised knees allowing her hair to flow over them. Tony released his breath and mopped his brow with a white handkerchief. No other girl in his employ had this effect on him and he was sure he wasn't the only one to feel this way.

He smiled with satisfaction as he scanned the room noting the effect Angel had on her audience. His eyes settled on a group of men sitting at a table beside the door and a frown gathered between his brows. What was Jimmy Matthews doing in his club? His territory was Glasgow, although there were whispers he was intent on expanding his business interests to other areas. His recent foray into the Edinburgh nightclub scene was evidence of his ambition.

Tony tightened his jaw and clenched his fists. Forewarned was forearmed. He'd be ready for Matthews if he made a move on Teasers.

6

Angel, reluctant to rise and leave the stage, remained with her head bent over her knees after the music stopped.

But Tony liked his dancers to traverse the length of the clubroom when they finished their acts. That was why they had to walk between the tables to reach the dressing rooms. 'Give the punters their money's worth,' he'd say. 'They've paid for the pleasure.'

It was also profitable for the girls and on a good night Angel could pick up well over £500 after each dance. Money she needed. Money she intended to set her up in business and bankroll her future. That was why she smiled at the men, stroked their faces, and put up with their exploring fingers. But tonight, she hesitated, afraid to run the gauntlet of what faced her in the clubroom. Afraid of facing up to the men who were waiting for her.

Angel raised her head from her knees and looked out over the heads of the men to the table at the rear of the room where Jimmy Matthews and his thugs were sitting. She shivered. Would she never escape them?

Sweat beaded her face and body and her hands slipped on the pole when she rose to her feet. But she couldn't remain on the stage. She would have to brave the grasping hands and the leers of the men in the audience before reaching the safety of her dressing room. But how safe would that be when Matthews was here?

Her legs shook when she climbed down from the stage. Tonight, the distance to the dressing rooms on the opposite side of the clubroom appeared longer than usual, and she hesitated for a moment before walking between the tables. Oblivious to the probing fingers of men pushing banknotes into her G-string, she stared straight ahead with her eyes fixed on her target and made sure her route avoided the table where Matthews sat.

The hand closed over her wrist just when she thought she was safe.

'The boss wants to see you.' Mad Dog thrust his face close to hers.

His breath was whisky laden and no matter how much she wriggled she couldn't escape the sour stench.

She tried to tug her hand free, but his grasp tightened.

'I don't want to see him.'

'Tough.' He dragged her to the table where Matthews sat watching her approach with a smile.

She grabbed the back of a chair and dug her heels into the carpet. 'You can't do anything here. It's too public.'

'But we don't have to stay here, do we? We could go outside.' His grip tightened even more. 'And if you're thinking of creating a fuss, I have a knife in my pocket with your name on it.'

Angel's heart thudded, and she wanted to scream, but she knew his promise wasn't an idle one. Mad Dog's reputation in Glasgow made sure of that.

The brute thrust Angel into a chair and stood behind her. She rubbed her wrist sure that by tomorrow there would be a large bruise. 'Well, I'm here,' she said. 'You didn't need to send that psycho to get me.'

Jimmy Matthews smiled at her across the table. 'Now, now, Lesley. I'm sure you wouldn't have come here of your own accord.'

'I've stopped using that name.'

'Ah, yes. I believe you are now called Angel. But you're no angel, are you, Lesley?'

'I'm more of an angel than you are.'

Jimmy's voice hardened. 'Enough of the chitchat. I have a job for you. And don't forget you owe me.'

'You mean, like the job you had me do in Edinburgh?' Angel closed her eyes as she fought the nausea building within her.

Jimmy Matthews nodded.

Angel glared at him. 'I did what you wanted. I planted the drugs in Georgio's nightclub and tipped off the police.'

'Good girl.' Matthews leaned over and patted her hand.

'But that wasn't enough for you, was it? You set Mad Dog on him and now he's in a wheelchair. That animal almost killed him.'

'That shows how lucky he was. It could have been worse.'

'You know, underneath that tailored suit, you're just a thug like all the rest of them. And speaking of thugs, where is Kevin tonight?'

'Ah, yes, Kevin. He sends you his regards and is waiting patiently for your return. So, once you complete this job you will return to Glasgow to perform your wifely duties again.'

'What you mean is I'll become Kevin's punchbag again. No chance.'

'Would you prefer Mad Dog?'

'Is that a threat?' She leaned forward and glared at Matthews, although her display of defiance cloaked the fear crawling up her spine.

'I never make threats, but I do make promises.' His tone held a hint of amusement. 'But first, I need you to pay back your debt by following my instructions.'

Angel sighed. It was like Edinburgh all over again, but Matthews might find that Tony might not be so easy a target as Georgio.

'What do you want me to do?'

'That's a good girl.' Matthews patted her hand again. 'I knew you would see sense.'

He leaned forward and whispered into her ear. 'I've left something for you in your flat. I want you to place half of it here in Tony's office and the other half in his home.'

'How the hell will I get the chance to do that?'

'I'm sure you'll find a way.' He gripped her wrist with fingers that felt like pincers. 'Just remember you owe me, and you know what I do to people who don't pay their debts.'

Angel shuddered. Matthews rarely did his dirty work himself, but the thugs in his employ were sadistic bastards.

7

Tony sensed something was wrong after Angel left the stage. Her steps faltered, and she looked afraid. She walked between the tables ignoring the pawing of various men. On other evenings she might smile at them and bat their hands away, but tonight she didn't do that.

His eyes narrowed when the man grabbed her wrist and she shrank away from him. He saw their lips moving, although he could hear nothing behind the one-way glass of his office wall. But when the man dragged her towards one of the tables he reached for his phone.

'Phil,' he said when the answering voice echoed in his ear, 'Jimmy Matthews and his thugs are in the club, and they've got hold of Angel. Find Gus and one of the others and I'll meet you at the cocktail bar.'

He straightened his tie, buttoned his jacket, and ran a hand over his hair before he left the office. Music filtered upwards magnifying in volume when he opened the door at the bottom of the stairwell. Closing it behind him he pulled the velvet curtain aside and emerged into the club.

Phil, Gus, and a bouncer, the one who was more muscle than brain, waited for him in front of the bar.

'What d'you want us to do, boss?' Phil kept his eyes on Angel who was now sitting in a chair at Jimmy Matthews' table.

'Follow me and when I give the nod, I want you two,' Tony gestured to Gus and the bouncer, 'to eject the big guy standing behind Angel. Phil, you can escort Angel back to the dressing room and stay with her until I get there.'

Tony threaded his way through the tables followed by the three men. He pulled a chair over and positioned it beside Angel.

'Take Angel to her dressing room so she can get ready for her next act,' he said to Phil. He smiled at Jimmy Matthews. 'We can't disappoint the punters. Angel is the one they come to see.'

Angel pushed her chair back and rose, but Mad Dog pushed her back down.

Tony's eyes narrowed. He stared at Mad Dog. 'We have a policy in this club that none of the girls should be manhandled, so I'm afraid I am going to ask you to leave.'

Mad Dog took a step forward, but Gus and the bouncer closed in on him from each side.

'We can do this peacefully or we can call the police.' Tony stared at Jimmy Matthews. 'It might be best if you advise your colleague to go quietly.' He resisted the impulse to call the man an ape.

'Wait for me outside,' Matthews said.

Tony waited until after his men escorted Mad Dog out before saying to Phil, 'You'd best take Angel to her dressing room now we've sorted that out.'

Music beat in their ears and the buzz of nearby voices echoed around them.

Tony placed his elbows on the table and leaned forward so they could hear his voice. 'What brings you to Dundee? I thought Glasgow was your stamping-ground.'

Matthews shrugged. 'Thought I'd take a holiday and tie up some unfinished business at the same time.'

Tony leaned back in his chair. Matthews was up to something. He knew Matthews' gang had been responsible for what happened to Georgio Modena, the Italian, when they took over his business in Edinburgh. Perhaps Matthews was planning something similar here.

'Unfinished business? I trust you're not thinking of trespassing on any of my properties or businesses.'

'I wouldn't dream of it.'

'In the same way you wouldn't dream of infiltrating establishments in Edinburgh? Georgio was my friend.'

'The Italian? Yes, I heard what happened to him. Such a shame. But nothing to do with me.'

Matthews pulled a cigar box from his pocket and offered one to Tony.

'I'm afraid we stick by the no smoking policy in this club.'

'Of course. It wouldn't do to break the law now, would it?'

'Something you have no problem with. But this is Dundee, not Glasgow, and we do things differently here.'

'Ah, yes. I'd heard that. But times change.'

Tony detected a hint of menace in the man's voice, but he was tired of the game playing. He stood and placed his hands flat on the table. 'I suggest you curtail your holiday and return to Glasgow. There is nothing for you here.'

He turned his back on Matthews and strode to the bar.

'A glass of my usual,' he said to Marlene. 'I need to get an unpleasant taste out of my mouth.'

8

Phil placed his hand on Angel's elbow and escorted her away from the table. At any other time, she would have pushed it aside. She didn't like him. But tonight, with Jimmy Matthews' eyes fixed on her, she was glad of Phil's presence.

She maintained her composure until she reached the dressing room, but once there she slumped into a chair and stared into the mirror with panic-stricken eyes.

'You all right now?' Phil hovered in the doorway.

'What do you think? Those men out there are dangerous. They'll be waiting for me when I leave.' Her shoulders slumped, and she clasped her arms around her middle to stop shivering.

'Tony instructed me to look after you, so I'll drive you home after the club closes. They won't try anything while I'm with you.'

Angel snorted. 'Would I be any safer with you, Phil?'

'Just trying to be helpful. But if you prefer to face them on your own...' he shrugged his shoulders.

'Tell Tony that if he wants to ensure my safety he needs to escort me home. He owes me that. Now get out and leave me to get dressed.'

He leaned over her. 'You sure you don't want me to give you a hand?'

His breath was hot on her neck. She didn't like the look in his eyes, but the chair prevented her from backing away from him. He was no better than Mad Dog underneath his polished exterior. There was no way she'd choose to be alone in his company.

'Close the door when you leave and make sure you give Tony my message.'

Phil hesitated in the doorway, a troubled look on his face.

'Tony said I was to stay with you.'

'And I'm saying I'd rather Tony looked after me himself. Now, get out, and leave me in peace.'

After he left the shivering started again. The memory of Mad Dog's hands on her arm and his whisky breath inches from her face combined with Jimmy Matthews' demands, filled her with despair.

'What am I to do?' she asked her reflection in the mirror.

'You need to get out of Dundee.'

Angel hadn't heard Candace enter the room.

Not taking her eyes off the mirror she said, 'It doesn't seem to matter where I go. They always track me down. I'll never be free unless I'm on the other side of the world.'

'If you want to be free we need to put our plan into action tonight. All you have to do is make sure Tony takes you home and you make sure he doesn't leave.'

Cars lined the street across from Teasers, and Luigi coasted to a stop behind the one nearest to the corner. This would ensure he wouldn't be seen while giving him a clear view of the entrance to the nightclub. He didn't have long to wait before he saw Mad Dog being pushed out the main doors by Gus and a bouncer. Jimmy, however, was nowhere in sight. Mad Dog was on his own. Three doormen, immaculate in evening suits which did nothing to hide their muscled bodies, stood inside the doors watching for trouble.

Instead of all hell breaking loose Mad Dog straightened his clothes, glared at them, and walked off along the street. Surprised, Luigi watched him go without causing havoc which was out of character for a man like him. Maybe something else was going down. Something more important.

Luigi twisted the throttle, and the powerful motorbike throbbed between his thighs as he prepared to follow Mad Dog. He throttled down again when the bruiser stopped at a car further along the street and got in. After several minutes when the car remained stationary Luigi realised the man was waiting for his boss to leave Teasers, and he switched the engine off.

Time dragged and Luigi's mind wandered. There was a guy in the car which was parked in front of his bike, and he watched him for a time but got wearied with that and fixed his gaze on the entrance to Teasers. The security men, their backs to the wall outside, watched the street with restless eyes. After a time, they retreated inside the building. More than likely they were bored watching the empty street.

The guy in the car opened his door, got out, and threw the butt of a cigarette onto the ground. He stretched and looked around him before crossing the road and vanishing up the alley leading to the rear of Teasers.

What was he up to? Luigi was tempted to follow him but didn't want to lose sight of his target, so he stayed where he was.

Ten minutes later, Tony's Beamer exited from the alleyway and turned right. It was still in sight when the guy ran out of the alleyway behind it, jumped in his car, and drove off after them.

Stranger and stranger. But he refused to be drawn away from his task of observing Jimmy Matthews and his gang. He had scores to settle there. And he trusted Fabio to cover for him if Tony arrived home early.

It was much later before Jimmy Matthews left the nightclub, and along with two others of his entourage got in the car beside Mad Dog.

Luigi powered up his motorbike ready to follow them, but the car remained motionless. It didn't leave until the dancers exited the club and walked along the street. Matthews must be checking them out.

But the car didn't follow the dancers, instead, it turned left at the next junction and sped off. Luigi followed close behind.

He was still on the car's tail when it stopped in the car park of the Apex City Quay Hotel. The men got out and sauntered towards the entrance laughing and joking as they went, oblivious to Luigi's watching eyes.

Luigi jotted the car number in his notebook and tucked it into his pocket before scanning the car park. More than likely there would be CCTV cover and he didn't want his motorbike to be identified, so he carried on along the street and tucked it out of sight in Chandlers Lane. Keeping his helmet on, he walked back to the hotel.

He sidled around the brick building at the entry to the car park taking care to stay out of the range of the camera trained on the barrier. A path bordering the building led to the entrance to the hotel. Keeping close to the edge of the wall and then the shrubbery bordering the path, he hurried towards the rear door. Another camera high on the edge of the building swung, monitoring the area. Waiting until it pointed away from him, he slid over the road and crouched low between the cars.

It didn't take him long to find the car he was looking for. He attached the tracker, retraced his footsteps to where he'd left his motorbike, and roared off homewards.

It was time to ask Fabio to make one of his special electronic gadgets and he was sure the boy could get everything he needed from the dark web.

9

The man who watched wriggled in his seat while regretting the lager he had drunk earlier. He should know better than anyone that you never drink before a stakeout. For one thing, it could make you sleepy and the other was the pressing need to relieve yourself. It was the latter causing his present discomfort.

He slipped out of the car, paused for a moment to ensure no one saw him, and then walked down the road away from Teasers. Once he was out of sight of the bouncers, he crossed the road and made his way back. Certain he hadn't been spotted he slipped into the narrow alley that led to the private parking area behind Teasers. The large refuse bins lined up in the corner provided the perfect cover for what he was about to do. It wasn't the first time he'd relieved himself behind them.

The back door to the club opened, spilling light into the parking area. He tucked himself further behind the bin and watched. Tony emerged with his minder. After a quick look around, he gestured to someone standing inside. By this time the minder had the engine of the car running, and Tony swiftly ushered the girl into the back seat of the car.

The watcher smiled. Something to report back at last. He waited until the car slid out of the yard behind the club and then ran to his own car and fired up its engine. Tony was taking Angel home. He mustn't lose them. He waited until the car ahead turned out of the street before following it.

When the car drew up in front of Angel's building he parked at the corner. Then, getting out, he positioned himself behind a bus shelter to snap Tony and Angel as they entered the building. He waited until her lighted windows went dark before getting back in the car to settle down for a long wait.

Tony's car drew up in front of the door to the tenement property which he owned. Angel, like most of the other dancers at the club, rented a flat in the building.

Brian stepped out of the driver's seat and held the car door open for her to alight, but she hesitated and stared up at the building. She needed to persuade Tony to accompany her to the flat. Once inside, she could set the plan in motion. If she was going to escape the clutches of Jimmy Matthews, this was the only way.

Whisky fumes mixed with the smell of cologne intensified as Tony leaned towards her. 'Brian will escort you to the door and check your flat to ensure you are safe.'

Angel clutched his hand. 'I would feel safer if you escorted me to my flat.'

'As long as you know I can't stay. I promised Madge I would come home tonight.'

Her lips twisted into a bitter smile. He hadn't always been so eager to get home.

'Please,' she said, 'check the flat for me and wait until I lock up before you go.'

'Wait for me,' Tony instructed Brian. 'I won't be long.'

Angel's pulse raced as he led the way upstairs to the second-floor flat. Once inside she poured whisky into two glasses while he checked the bedroom, kitchen, and bathroom.

'It's all clear,' Tony said when he emerged from the bedroom.

She thrust a glass into his hand. 'One drink before you go. You deserve it.'

Tony hesitated, and for a moment she thought he would refuse. 'It's your favourite tipple. It would be a shame if it went to waste.'

He swirled the liquid around in the glass, lifted it to his nose, and breathed in the smoky aroma. 'I don't suppose one more would hurt.' He took a large mouthful of the whisky rolling it around his mouth before swallowing. Moments later, the glass was empty.

'It's time I left.'

He stepped towards the door, but before he reached it, he swayed and grabbed the back of a chair.

Angel deposited her glass on the coffee table and reached out to steady him. 'I think you need to sit down for a moment.' She guided him into the armchair.

'Madge will be waiting for me.' His eyes closed and his head dropped forward.

Angel placed a hand on his shoulder and shook him, but he didn't wake. She waited another minute to be sure, then ran down the stairs to where Brian waited with the car.

'Tony has decided to stay the night after all and said for you to go home.'

'When will I come back for him?'

Angel detected a note of doubt in Brian's voice. Of course, the man would know Tony had intended to return home tonight.

'He said he'd phone you when he's ready.'

She watched him drive off before returning to her flat to wait for Candace and Linda to arrive.

After she dismissed Brian, Angel ran upstairs to her flat. Tony lay slumped in the armchair with one arm dangling over the side and a sliver of drool seeping from the side of his mouth. It only took a moment to open his jacket and remove his tie. She unbuttoned his shirt and removed the rest of his clothes. He wouldn't wake for hours.

Angel waited until she heard the girls returning from Teasers. A further wait until everything went quiet, then she stamped twice on the floor. It was the prearranged signal for their plan to begin.

'Help me get him into the bedroom,' Angel said when Candace pushed the door open and entered.

Angel knelt and draped one arm over his shoulder and waited until Candace did the same. 'On the count of three,' she said, 'one, two, three.'

Both girls heaved him out of the chair and, staggering under his weight, dragged him to the bedroom and threw him on the bed.

'Not a pretty sight.' Candace stood back and surveyed Tony.

A flicker of regret pulsed through Angel, but she suppressed it. She couldn't afford to get emotional now. It was far too late for that.

'Phone down and tell Linda we'll be ready for her in half an hour. It'll give me time to set the scene. We want to make it look good.' Angel unbuttoned her jeans. 'Best get it over with before he wakes up.'

'I'll pop into the kitchen until it's all over.' Candace picked up the glass Tony had used and replaced it with her own. 'I'll get rid of the evidence while I'm waiting.'

Half an hour later, a shadow flitted up the stairs and through the unlocked door to the flat. The figure crept through the darkness in the living room, and on reaching the bedroom pushed the door open. The gloom in this room was relieved by the faint glow of the streetlamp outside the window which cast a soft glow over the two bodies, one sleeping and the other feigning. Tony moved position but did not waken, not even when the camera flash split the darkness several times in succession. Satisfied the shots revealed the scene and that the faces of both would be easy to identify, the shadow slipped back out of the room.

As soon as she heard the door click shut Angel slid out of the bed and joined the two others in the kitchen.

Candace poured whisky into three glasses. 'Here's to the success of our plan.' The three of them clinked glasses before downing the contents.

10

Saturday

A massive weight nailed Tony's head to the pillow. This was the worst hangover ever, far worse than anything he'd previously experienced. He groaned, reluctant to open his eyes and make the pain worse. Madge didn't stir, but she lay closer to him than normal. Despite the pain in his head, he slung his arm around her. It took a moment for him to register the sticky substance his hand encountered and the metallic odour he'd smelled before. It was the smell of blood.

He drew his hand back and jerked his eyes open. Surely Madge hadn't done anything stupid?

Sleep tried to reclaim him, but he forced his eyes to stay open and peered at the grey shapes outlined by the early morning dawn. Where was he? This wasn't his bedroom. He tried to think, but his memory was lost in the sludge inside his brain.

Bile rose in his throat when he stared at the body lying beside him. She lay in a pool of congealing blood and looked like a lump of meat. He lurched away from her and landed with a thud on the floor. Pain throbbed through his temples, but he forced himself to stand and walk around the bed. He flicked on the bedside lamp. The girl's blonde hair covered her face, and the knife used to carve her body lay on the floor. He reached out and brushed the hair aside to find her face had also been mutilated. It was Angel.

A flicker of memory returned. Angel inviting him to stay and offering him a drink. He'd meant to go home. Why had he stayed? And how could someone murder her when they were lying in the same bed? An unbidden thought arose – maybe he had been the one to wield the knife. But why would he do that? What did he have to gain from killing this girl?

Unable to bear the sight of her mutilated body he heaved the duvet over it, letting out a ragged breath once he could no longer see her.

A car revved in the street outside arousing him from his reverie. He had to get out of here, otherwise, the police would lock him up and throw away the key. But blood covered his hands and body. He grabbed a tee shirt from the back of a chair, covered his hand with it, and opened the bedroom door after wiping the doorknob. He wiped the one on the other side as well.

Her shower was over the bath, so he stepped in and turned the water to hot. Once he satisfied himself no blood remained on his skin, he towelled himself dry and went on the hunt for his clothes. He found them in the living room, for which he was thankful because they were free of blood spatter.

Angel's phone lay on the coffee table, but he ignored it and searched his pockets for the disposable burner phone he used for the shadier parts of his business.

'I need you to come and get me,' he said when Brian answered. 'But don't use a car that can be traced, and when you get here drive up onto the pavement in front of the door so I can step into it without being seen.'

'Be there in ten, boss.'

Tony used the ten minutes to wipe all the doorknobs and anything he might have touched, although it was an effort to return to the bedroom where Angel's body lay. Last of all, he slipped the whisky bottle and glasses into his pockets and took the towel and tee shirt with him when Brian drove up outside the building.

Dawn was breaking before Tony left the building and, although he couldn't get a clear shot, the watcher aimed the camera at his target. Satisfied with a job well done he drove away, leaving with a camera full of incriminating shots.

Tonight, he had earned his money and payday was looming.

The Travel Lodge was quiet when he returned but he easily

found a space to park his car before returning to his room. He threw his camera equipment on the bed and debated with himself whether to phone his client now or wait until morning. What the hell, he'd been up all night, no reason why he shouldn't wake the bastard. If he complained he'd remind him he was the bearer of good news. His decision made he picked up the phone.

Kevin Matthews, his anger building within him, stood outside the tenement building looking up at the darkened windows. Denzil wasn't to know he was in Dundee when he took his call. Nor would he know what he intended to do to Angel. He bunched his fists in readiness. The whore was about to receive everything she deserved.

He crossed the street and slipped through the door. The stairwell was in darkness, and he felt his way up, treading carefully so he wouldn't make a noise. He checked the numbers and found the one he wanted two flights up. Inspecting the lock, he gave a grim smile. When would these tarts learn Chubb locks on their doors were no protection and could be opened in seconds? He fished in his wallet for a credit card and slipped it between the lock and the door frame. The door swung open.

Silence greeted him inside. The bitch must have gone back to sleep after she'd finished her dirty business with Tony fucking Palmer. He'd sort that bastard out once he'd given his wife what she deserved. He tiptoed across the carpet to a door set into the rear wall of the room. It led into a small kitchen. The next door he tried proved to be the bedroom, and he opened it wider.

Fists clenched, he strode to the bed and yanked the duvet off the sleeping form. Only it wasn't sleeping. He caught his breath as all thoughts of what he meant to do to her fled his mind. All he could see was the bloody form of his wife lying in the bed.

He dropped to his knees and covered his face with his hands. 'Lesley,' he moaned, 'what has that bastard done to you?'

After what seemed an eternity, he rose and brushed the tears from his face. Bloody Tony fucking Palmer was going to pay for this, he vowed, as he left the flat.

'Nice car,' Tony said. 'Be a pity to junk it when we're done.'

'No need for that, boss.' Brian kept his eyes on the road. 'I borrowed it from Ninewells Hospital. I'll have it back there before the night shift finishes. They'll never know it left the car park.'

Tony leaned back in the leather seat. He fished the burner phone out of his pocket and removed the sim card. 'We need to get rid of this as well as the other stuff.'

'Tide's in. We could chuck it in the river.' Brian hadn't asked what the other stuff was.

He drove the car over the Tay Bridge. 'Best to do it from the other side.'

Tayport was quiet at this time of the morning, and Brian found a suitable spot beside the river mouth. They used the towel to wrap around the glasses before smashing them and shaking the fragments into the water, then they weighted the towel and tee shirt with a stone and dropped them in as well. The whisky bottle didn't need weighing down and Tony watched it sink with a regretful eye. Waste of a good whisky.

Brian returned to the car and held the door open with his gloved hand. Tony stepped inside without touching anything even though he knew that when Brian returned it to Ninewells no one would think to check it for fingerprints. There was no CCTV coverage outside the Lochee building and no reason to connect the car with him.

'You drove me home last night after I saw Angel up to her door,' Tony said when he stepped out of the car at the side entrance to his home.

'Of course, boss.'

The house was silent and there was no sign of life when Tony crept up the path, unlocked the side door and slid inside. This part of the house was a restricted area. It held his office and a small meeting room. This was where he conducted most of his illegal business because the entry from outside was shielded and people could come and go unobserved. Sometimes he slept on the large sofa in the office, and if anyone noticed he hadn't been in the main part of the house he could claim to have spent the night there.

The reinforced connecting door opened silently, and he locked it behind him before he tiptoed up the stairs and into the bedroom where Madge lay comatose in a drug-induced sleep. She would never know he hadn't been beside her all night.

11

Luigi stood in the shadows at the rear of the hall. He'd been in the kitchen helping himself to a glass of milk when Tony sneaked into the house through the rear entry. Normally, when his boss arrived home, he would check whether he needed anything, but he didn't make his presence known when Tony emerged through the connecting door to the main part of the house. Instead, he watched from the shadows as Tony crept up the stairs. Tony's movements suggested he didn't want anyone to know he'd been observed returning, and it wasn't Luigi's place to question his boss. It didn't stop him from wondering where he had been all night, though. It wasn't like him to stay out.

Tony's bedroom door clicked shut and Luigi emerged from the shadows, but instead of returning to his own bedroom, he slipped into the control room where a bank of computers displayed images of the outer areas of the house. No one could approach unobserved. Backtracking the recording he deleted the images of Tony returning home.

He owed a lot to Tony, who provided a haven for him after his cousin, Georgio, had been beaten up by the Matthews' gang. Poor Georgio would be wheelchair-bound for the rest of his life.

Luigi hadn't wanted to leave Edinburgh, but Georgio had explained it would be for the best and, besides, there was Georgio's boy. 'Protect my son,' Georgio had whispered through his damaged vocal cords. 'I wouldn't put it past Jimmy Matthews to make good on his threat to bump Fabio off. That's the only reason I signed my clubs over to him.'

'What about you?' It didn't sit well with Luigi to leave Georgio behind.

'I'll be safe enough. They've taken over my businesses and

my workers and put me in a wheelchair. I'm no danger to them now. But they might see Fabio as a danger to their aspirations in Edinburgh. Get him away from here.' Georgio wheeled his chair to the window and looked out to the busy streets below. 'I've spoken with Tony Palmer, and he will protect Fabio. He expects you tomorrow.'

And so, Luigi and Fabio had come to Dundee, and true to his word Tony had taken them in, given them a home and arranged a place at Abertay University for Fabio. He would start his ethical hacking course in September. No doubt his studies would come in useful.

Satisfied there was no record of Tony's return on the surveillance equipment Luigi returned to his bedroom. Fabio stirred slightly in the adjacent single bed but did not wake. The boy had no trouble sleeping. Not like Luigi who hadn't slept well since the attack on Georgio. If he'd been with his cousin that night, he could have protected him, although Georgio had laughed this off and said it was more likely he would be six feet under. It was this failure that made him insist Fabio sleep in his room when he came to Tony's house. Sharing made it easier to keep his eye on the boy.

Candace woke to see dim light forcing its way through the window. Disorientated she stared at the grey shapes and shadowy corners of the bedroom while small puffing sounds came from the sleeping girl beside her. It would take an earthquake to wake her.

Footsteps whispered past her door. She slid out of bed and ran to the window expecting to see Tony leave the building. But the guy jumping into the red car parked at the kerb was too slim and wiry to be Tony.

She poked her partner in the ribs. 'I've just seen someone leave.'

The girl turned over and blinked the sleep out of her eyes. 'Was it Tony?'

'I don't think so, probably someone visiting one of the other girls, nothing to worry about.'

'D'you think Tony's still up there?'

'Doubtful. I heard the water pipes gurgling earlier so I reckon he's long gone.'

'What now?'

'I'm sure Angel won't want to be disturbed too early, so we carry on as normal and maybe pay her a visit later this afternoon.'

'Good idea.' The girl cuddled up closer to Candace. 'What will we do until then?'

'Sleep some more.' Candace reached for her. 'Then we could make use of that brown hair dye I bought when you weren't sure you wanted to remain a blonde. That should make you look more like the Linda I know rather than looking like Angel.'

Linda threw an arm around Candace and nuzzled into her neck. 'Sounds good.'

Kevin wasted no time in heading out of Dundee. No one knew he was here, and no one was going to know. He'd vowed vengeance on his wife so many times the police would be bound to jump on his back when they found her body and he could do without that hassle. Once he got back to Glasgow, he'd make sure Olivia would testify he'd been with her all night. Silly bitch was besotted with him and would do anything he told her.

His hands tightened on the steering wheel. The vision of Lesley's bloody body rose in his mind, and he could see nothing else. An angry blast of a car horn brought him back to his senses, and he realised his car had swerved into the outside lane. He jerked the wheel and the car behind him roared past.

Shaken, he pulled into the turnoff to Dunblane. The place was quiet this early in the morning and he stopped the car at the side of the road. His hands still gripped the steering wheel, and he rested his brow on them. Self-pity washed over him. He forgot all the times he'd threatened Lesley, intimidated her, and beaten her up. All he could remember was that he loved her.

After a time he fished his phone out of his pocket and stared at it before keying in the emergency number.

A disembodied voice asked, 'Emergency. Which service?'

Kevin hesitated a moment. 'Police.'

'Your name, sir?'

'I want to report a dead body. You'll find her at this address.' He provided the address, ended the call, and shoved the phone back into his pocket. The sooner the police found her, the better. It would give Tony less time to tie up any loose ends.

Any risk he'd taken making the phone call was minimal as the police wouldn't know Lesley's real name or his connection to her until long after he arrived home. Besides, it was better to have phoned from here because he didn't want the location of his phone call to show as Glasgow.

Tony was sure Madge wouldn't wake. The sleeping pill she always took ensured that, but it was prudent to take precautions. If he was beside Madge when she woke she would be convinced he'd been there since he finished work earlier this morning. Tiptoeing to the bed, he slipped out of his clothes, draped them over the back of a chair, and slipped under the sheets. He knew there was little prospect of sleep because his mind had been buzzing since he'd woken up next to Angel's dead body. But the softness of the bed and the warmth radiating from his wife soothed him. He wriggled into a comfortable position while he waited for her to waken. His eyes closed, and he descended into the darkness of sleep.

When he woke the bed was empty, and he was alone. His eyelids felt heavy, and he had to force them open. The curtains and blinds had been opened and sun streamed into the bedroom. He squinted and turned his eyes away from it. His head throbbed. He'd never had a headache this bad no matter how much whisky he drank, and last night's consumption was no greater than usual. He frowned. Had he been drugged? Was that why he was oblivious to Angel's murder while he was lying beside her? Or was he the one who attacked her while under the influence of something?

He pushed the last thought away. Although violence was part and parcel of his work he had never killed a woman. Why would he do it now? With a groan, he closed his eyes and dozed. It was better than trying to move his limbs to get out of bed.

The next time he opened his eyes Madge was standing beside the bed looking at him with a curious expression in her eyes. She was tidy, with brushed hair, although her face was bare of powder or lipstick. In the past, she would never have allowed herself to be seen without makeup, but everything changed after they lost Denise. He guessed the only reason she looked presentable was due to the aid of Liz, whose job was a mix of lady's maid, secretary, and personal assistant.

'You don't usually stay in bed this late, are you ill?' Her voice was flat, lacking interest or emotion.

'I'm never ill. It's a headache. Too much whisky last night, I suppose.' He couldn't admit to anything else, even to Madge. It wouldn't sit well with his vision of himself as a hard man.

'You came home late this morning.' Her eyes remained blank. 'Pressing business, I imagine.'

'I thought you were sleeping.'

'I always wake early but I keep my eyes closed hoping sleep will come again. It never does.'

'Did you check the time I came home?'

'Of course, it was half-past five.'

His mind whirled. Madge could demolish his alibi without even thinking about it.

He leaned out of the bed and grasped her wrist. 'If anyone asks, I was here all night.' He let go of her wrist. 'It's important, Madge.'

'If you say so.'

Nothing in her eyes changed, and she asked no questions. Tony just hoped if it came to the crunch she would remember.

12

After sleeping for a couple of hours Luigi showered and put on the black suit, white shirt, and black tie Tony liked him to wear.

'Now you look like a typical butler,' he'd said after Luigi took up residence.

Luigi wasn't sure what that meant and asked Tony what a butler was supposed to do. 'Just keep an eye on the house. Check out anyone who arrives here and ensure the safety of the household.'

It didn't seem much, and he often found himself at a loose end, but Tony didn't appear to mind.

He straightened his tie before he entered the kitchen. Big Bet, the cook, said he reminded her of James Bond. He didn't know whether that meant she was attracted to him, but he had a yen for her. Flour coated her arms and hands as she wrestled with a doughy mixture, and strands of hair flopped over her face. Luigi thought she'd never looked more beautiful. Glamour girls had never attracted him. He preferred a more mature woman, and he liked them big. And Bet met all the requirements of his perfect woman.

She looked up when he entered and brushed a strand of hair away from her face, leaving a smear of flour behind. 'You looking for some breakfast?'

'I can wait until you're ready.'

She lifted a lump of dough from the bowl and laid it on the floured worktop. Sprinkling the dough with more flour she grabbed a rolling pin and attacked it with vigour.

'What are you making?' Luigi crossed the room to watch.

'Pastry for a steak pie,' she said without looking up. She lifted the flattened pastry dough, curving it around the rolling pin and transferring it to a pie dish filled with diced steak.

Dusting the flour from her hands, she straightened, and smiled at him. 'Let's get you fed.'

Luigi's stomach churned, and it wasn't from the lack of food. Maybe she liked him a little.

In Edinburgh, Luigi would have made his move before now, but Tony's mantra was that you don't shit in your own nest. In other words, if you want to make a move on a woman you do it away from home. He wondered if it would make any difference if his intentions were honourable. The only thing was that he wasn't yet sure whether he could describe his intentions as honourable.

'You're quiet today.' Bet laid the plate in front of him. 'Anything worrying you?'

He shook his head. How could he tell her she was the one on his mind?

After he'd eaten, he inspected the footage from the security cameras before going around the house checking doors and windows. Tony's wife Madge was in the breakfast room staring vacantly out of a window to the garden beyond. She had an untouched bowl of cereal in front of her while she toyed with a piece of toast. Luigi remembered Madge, from previous visits, as a vibrant woman full of fun and with a devilish sense of humour, not this shell of a woman with no life in her eyes. The death of her daughter had done this to her.

'Can I get you anything?' Luigi stood awkwardly, wanting to reach out and hug her.

She shook her head. It was the only sign she gave that she'd seen or heard him.

He turned away from her with a heavy heart and continued to check the house. Satisfied everything was in order, he went outside to inspect the grounds.

Early in Tony's career he'd come to understand security was all-important. As a result, the front and side doors to his house were made from reinforced steel with a covering of wood, which gave them the appearance of ordinary oak doors. The ground to the rear was surrounded by a high wall and the only access was through the house. In the long distant past, many people topped their walls with broken glass to deter intruders, but that was no longer legal. Not that Tony had any compunction about breaking the law, but he preferred to keep the illegal parts of his business hidden. So, thorn bushes had been trained to grow up the walls, and they were now higher than the walls they covered. Anyone attempting to gain access that way would be torn to shreds. Over and above the physical deterrents, all areas were covered by CCTV, which gave ample warning of approaching visitors.

The weak spot was the back door which was sturdy and made of oak. Tony had intended to reinforce this door as well but had never got round to it. Luigi now stood there looking out. To his right was the patio with a garden table, chairs, and a swinging seat. This used to be a favourite place for Madge to relax in the sun, but now it looked forlorn and unused. Bees hummed around the flowers in the border to his left and fearing a sting he hurried to the lawn beyond.

Luigi stopped to breathe in the fresh air and the lingering scent of the flowers. He always felt at peace in this garden. It was an oasis in a busy city. Something he had been unaccustomed to when he lived in Edinburgh where people seemed to live on top of each other.

The angry buzz of an engine broke the silence. He listened for a moment before striding across the lawn to check the noise and ensure it wasn't intruders. You could never be too careful, and it was what Tony paid him for.

Two men were attacking the thorny growth at the far end of the garden, one of them wielded a dangerous-looking hedge trimmer while the other raked fallen leaves and branches into a heap. They took no notice of him and continued to work. Luigi wasn't even sure they knew he was there.

He stood for a moment watching, before announcing his presence. 'Hi, guys.' He raised his voice so they could hear him.

The two security men who doubled as gardeners looked around and nodded to him. Luigi nodded back. He didn't expect an answer. They were men of little words and a good deal of muscle. He had no doubt that should anyone be unwise enough to trespass into the garden, the hedge trimmer would be put to a different use.

Leaving them to it he continued his inspection.

It was another hour before Tony surfaced and came looking for him. His expression was grim, and the lines on his forehead seemed to have deepened.

'Can I get you anything, boss?'

Tony shook his head, and a frown gathered. 'I need you to be on your guard, Luigi. I saw Jimmy Matthews and some of his thugs at the club last night. There might be trouble brewing.'

Luigi clenched his fists, and his insides churned. He'd made a promise to himself he would make them pay for what they did to Georgio. He wouldn't rest until he'd wiped every one of them off the face of the earth. But he knew he was no match for their muscle, so he'd have to deal with them in a more devious way and the tracker he'd planted would allow him to do that.

'Would you like me to come to the club with you?'

'No, Luigi, I need you here to protect Madge.'

'Yes, boss.' Plans were already forming in Luigi's mind on how to deal with Matthews and his gang if they came calling.

13

Bill Murphy opened his eyes but lacked the energy to slide out of bed, so he lay on his back and contemplated the spider's web in the corner of the bedroom ceiling. The web seemed to increase in size every day, but he had yet to see the spider that made it. He wished he could be as invisible in the web which held him in its grip instead of having to dance to the tune of his new boss. She was determined to turn him into her idea of what a detective should be, smart, well turned out, and always on the ball. Something Bill had no wish to be. He reckoned he was a good detective in his own slovenly way and had no wish to be refashioned into something he was not.

The sound of a police siren wailed in his ear and jerked him out of his torpor. What on earth had possessed him to use that as a ringtone? He stretched out a hand and peered at the caller ID. For a moment he thought about ignoring the call. After all, it was his day off. He could say he was out of town, unavailable, drunk as a skunk, whatever. But if he made any of those excuses his life wouldn't be worth living. He pressed the accept button.

'Murphy!' Detective Inspector Rawlings' voice grated in his ear. 'Get yourself to this address, pronto.' She recited the address. 'We've got a murdered woman, and it's a nasty one by all accounts. I'm leaving Forfar now. I'll meet you there.'

'Yes, ma'am.'

A sigh echoed over the phone. 'I've told you before not to call me ma'am. Makes me sound as if I'm in my dotage.'

'Yes, boss.' He was speaking to a dead phone. She'd hung up.

He slid out of bed and rummaged for clean socks and a shirt. She'd give him laldy if he turned up in yesterday's clothes. Unable to find a clean pair of boxer shorts, he rescued the ones he'd discarded last night and, after a sniff, decided they would do. She'd never know the difference. His suit was slightly rumpled, but what the heck if she didn't like it, she could lump it.

Grabbing his car keys, he headed out the door. With a bit of luck, he'd get there first.

'Can't park there, sir.' The uniform standing guard at the door of the building gestured for him to move on.

Bill sighed and unbuttoned his jacket to show his warrant card dangling from the lanyard around his neck. He hated wearing it this way and would have preferred to carry it in his pocket, but the boss insisted they work according to the rules and regulations. She was a stickler for procedures.

'Sorry, sir. Can't be too careful, sir.'

'I haven't seen you around. New to Dundee, are you?' Probably straight out of Tulliallan police college, Bill thought. He had that fresh-faced, boyish look which gave the impression he wasn't old enough to shave.

'Yes, sir.'

'I thought so.' Bill looked along the street. He had expected a bigger police presence even though it was early.

'What's your name, Constable?'

'PC Douglas, sir.'

'You the only one here, Douglas?'

'No, sir. PC Hastie's upstairs and PCs Adams and Burns are out back checking if anyone is hiding there.'

'Having a sly puff, no doubt.' Bill knew Bruce Adams and had little time for him. The constable was an old-school dinosaur reluctant to move with the times. A slippery customer who stayed out of the firing line and dodged responsibility. The bosses should have plonked him behind a desk years ago.

'What have we here?'

'Dead body, sir. Female.' The constable looked down at his feet. 'She's been carved up good and proper, sir.'

Bill could swear the constable's face changed colour.

'You've seen the body?'

'Yes, sir. PC Hastie and myself. We got the call about forty minutes ago to investigate the report of a body at this address.' He swallowed hard and his face took on a greenish tinge. 'After we seen the body, we came straight out and called it in. They said they'd send the crime scene examiners, but they haven't got here yet.'

'Okay, walk me through it.' Bill fished his notebook out of his pocket.

The constable pulled out a matching notebook, consulted it, and in a dry factual voice recited. 'I was on car patrol with PC Hastie when we got the call at 7.40 am. The call handler said there had been a report of a body at this address and we needed to check it out, although he thought it might be a hoax call. We arrived at this address at 7.50 am, but it all seemed quiet. The street door was open as was the door of the flat on the second landing. There was no answer when we knocked and called out that we were the police, so PC Hastie entered first and I followed him in. The first room we entered appeared to be the main living room. It was empty. A door leading off this room was partially open and when we entered this room,' the constable's voice wobbled, 'we saw the body of a woman in the bed and there was blood everywhere.' He swallowed and took a deep breath. 'We passed the information to control and left the house. PC Hastie stood guard at the door, and he sent me down to stand guard at the entry to the building telling me no one was to enter or leave.' The constable's face was paler now than when he'd started to read.

'Your first body?' Bill closed his notebook and thrust it back into his pocket along with his pencil.

'Yes, sir.'

'First one's always the worst.'

He refrained from telling the constable that it wouldn't get any better.

'I'd better have a look.'

The building was one of the better Dundee tenements, with large windows overlooking the street and a long lobby inside the sturdy front door. He walked past the doors to the two downstairs flats before stopping at the bottom of the stairs to listen to the silence, thinking how unnatural it was considering what had happened here. It made his footsteps on the wooden stairs sound even louder. He would have expected curious faces gathering at doors, but nothing stirred. Two doors faced him on the first-floor landing, and he thought he detected the faint sounds of someone moving behind one of them, but it remained closed. He made a mental note to check it out after he'd visited the crime scene.

The officer on guard straightened up from his lounging position when Bill reached the second landing. Frank Hastie had been with Dundee Police for more years than Bill could remember, although he'd never risen beyond the rank of constable. He was a solid if uninspiring, police officer, who was marking time until his retirement.

'Thought it was the scene examiners. They're taking their time,' he said in a weary tone of voice.

'Sorry to disappoint you. Any chance of me having a peek at the scene?'

'More than my job's worth. You should know that.'

Bill leaned on the wall beside him. 'My boss isn't going to be pleased.'

'Can't help that. You know the drill. Nobody gets inside until the scene examiners say so. Can't have you contaminating the evidence.'

Bill knew it would serve no purpose to pull rank on him. Procedures were procedures and things had to be done by the book. He'd known a time when things hadn't always been like that, but forensics were all important in police work nowadays. As well as the pen pushers who insisted they abide by the rules.

'The constable on the front door said you were the first two on the scene.'

'That's right, but we managed to pull another couple of bodies from headquarters so we could check out the building and stand guard.' Hastie frowned. 'That bugger, Adams, should be standing guard with young Charlie. I'll have his guts for garters when I get away from here.'

'According to PC Douglas, Adams is out checking the

back green area.'

Hastie snorted. 'I've already checked that area. Burns and I did that first before we checked all the flats.'

'How did that go?'

'All clear, but the girls weren't pleased with being routed from their beds, and they didn't appreciate us having to look around to make sure no one was hiding inside any of the flats. One of them even threatened to put in a complaint because we didn't have search warrants.'

'How did you handle that?' Bill was curious.

'Simple, I just told her that if we couldn't get access it meant she had something to hide, and we'd escort her to the police station to be interviewed while we got the warrant.'

Bill grinned. Hastie didn't always do things by the book, but his methods were effective.

'Where are they all now?' He gestured towards a closed door further along the landing. 'This place is so quiet you'd think it was empty.'

'Gone back to their beds, I suppose. Most of them were bleary-eyed.'

'Strange, you'd think they'd be more concerned.'

'There's nowt stranger than folk. And this lot is stranger than most I've met.'

Bill surveyed the closed door in front of him. 'Any idea when the SOCOs will get here?'

'Should have been here by now. Probably too busy tarting themselves up before they come. Not like some folks.' His eyes raked over Bill's crumpled suit.

The words were hardly out of Hastie's mouth before a cheery voice shouted up the stairs. 'Is that someone taking my name in vain?' A white-clad man carrying a camera appeared at their side. 'Might have known. Bill Murphy, and Frank Hastie, Dundee's finest.'

'Boss wants me to have a look at the scene,' Bill said, 'but Frank here wouldn't let me in.'

'Quite right too. Can't have your size tens trampling all over the evidence.'

'You know me. I like to keep the boss happy.'

Colin snorted. 'Since when?'

'Come on, Colin. Help me out here. I need to have a shufti before she gets here.'

'Ah! Does that mean the delectable Kate Rawlings is on her way?'

'D'you fancy her or something?'

Colin laughed. 'I'll get started while you suit up. You'll find all the gear in the van parked at the door.'

14

The slamming of a car door, and the clump of feet on the stairs woke Candace. By the time she got to the spyhole in the door, she missed seeing the bobbies going upstairs, but was in time to see the baby-faced cop come down, and the arrival of another man half an hour later. She guessed he must be a detective because he wasn't in uniform. A mumble of voices drifted down the stairwell, and she strained to hear what they were saying without any success. She was tempted to leave her flat to ask what was going on, but a lifetime of avoiding the police won out and she stayed where she was.

'What you doing?'

The hand laid on her shoulder made her jump. She'd thought her partner was asleep.

Candace put a finger to her lips and shook her head. She didn't want the white garbed man, who looked like a spaceman, to hear them. After he vanished around the curve in the stairs, she whispered. 'The cops are upstairs, and I've just seen a forensics guy go up.'

'What will we do?'

'We stay schtum for now. It won't do us any good to become involved.'

'But the police will want to speak to us, won't they?'

'Probably, but we wait for them to come to us. We don't want them to think we have anything to do with it. And if they ask, you don't know any of the girls who live here because you don't work at Teasers. Got it?'

'If you think that's best.' Her face looked troubled.

Worry lines creased Tony's forehead. The arrival of Jimmy Matthews in Dundee meant trouble. The man was ambitious and didn't think twice about using violence to get what he wanted. He'd already made a dent in Edinburgh by taking over Georgio Modena's clubs, and Tony had no intention of letting him muscle in on his business. They'd find him a tougher proposition and there was no way he'd allow them to put him in a wheelchair as they'd done with Georgio.

But his wife was vulnerable, which was why he tasked Luigi, who had even less love for Jimmy Matthews than he did, with her protection. Liz was the next person he would have to warn. She mustn't let Madge out of her sight.

He left Luigi in the garden with instructions to brief the security staff and returned to the house. Wee Morag was clearing the breakfast table, although from what he could see the plates of food remained untouched. No wonder Madge was losing weight. A bird ate more than she did.

'Can I get you something, sir?' She moved the dirty plates to the edge of the table and plucked clean cutlery from the dresser drawer.

'No thanks, Morag. I was looking for your mistress.'

'She went upstairs after breakfast, sir.'

Tony nodded his thanks and turned to the stairs. He knew where she would be. The room where she spent most of her waking hours. Denise's room. Denise who was taken from them by a madman in January, six months ago. He should have her room cleared out but didn't have the heart.

She was sitting on the bed staring vacantly into space.

He stood for a moment in the doorway. As usual, he didn't know what to do. He wanted to reach out to her, gather her in his arms and soothe her, but his own grief was too raw.

Emotion deepened his voice. 'You shouldn't spend so much time in here. It's not healthy.'

'It's all I have left of her.'

'I miss her too, you know. But life must go on and sitting here won't bring her back.'

A deadweight settled around his heart. Not only had he lost his daughter, but he'd lost his wife as well. Anger welled up in him. Life wasn't fair.

He was on the point of reaching out to Madge when Liz

bustled into the room.

'Where were you?'

Apart from a fleeting spark in her eyes the woman did not react to the harshness of his tone. 'I was replacing Mrs Palmer's pills in the medicine cabinet, sir.'

Tony breathed deeply. Taking his anger out on Liz was pointless, and he needed her to keep an eye on Madge.

'I'm sorry. I'm under a lot of stress. There are people in Dundee who don't have my best interests at heart, and I think they might try to get at me through Madge. That's why I want you to be at her side every minute of the day, and if you feel she is in danger you must call for Luigi.'

'What kind of danger?'

'If anyone you don't know attempts to get near her, it's imperative you get Luigi. He'll know what to do.' Tony grasped her wrist. 'Nothing must happen to Madge. You understand?'

'Yes, sir.' She looked at him through eyes that reminded him of a cat. 'Now, if you'll let go of my wrist, sir, I'll be able to do what you ask.'

Despite his unease he left the room and trudged down the stairs where he found Luigi marking time in the hall.

'Phil and Gus are waiting for you at Teasers,' he said. 'And I've beefed up the security and alerted all the guys. Is there anything else?'

'Just make sure Madge is protected. I don't want anything to happen to her.'

'Sure, boss. Brian's waiting out front with the car. I thought you'd need him.'

Satisfied he'd done everything possible to secure the house and protect his wife, Tony joined Brian in the car.

Teasers dominated the street by its sheer size. But during the day it gave the impression of a vacant warehouse rather than the vibrant nightclub venue it was. The large wooden double doors, which had replaced the original glass ones, were closed. The windows were black and featureless. The neon lights switched off and dead. And no bouncers paraded the street outside maintaining order.

The car swung into the alley and purred to a halt in the parking area behind the club. Phil and Gus were already there. Both of them leaning on the bonnet of a battered Ford Focus and sharing a cigarette.

Phil approached the BMW and opened the door. 'You wanted us, boss?'

Tony hoisted himself out of the passenger seat. 'Yes, we've got a situation on our hands, and I think it's related to those Matthews' bastards who were in the club last night. Let's get inside where it's more private.'

Brian reversed the car into a narrow space between a dumpster and the wall before following them through the back door.

The corridor leading from the rear of the building led through a functional area of the club that members never saw. This was the lair of the cleaners, bouncers, and security staff. Not forgetting the door to the underground cellars. A place it was inadvisable to visit as some of Tony's enemies had found out to their cost. Faint sounds of music emanated from a room at the end of the corridor and a heavily built man with tattooed arms and neck peered out. Flickering monitors inside focused on all areas of the club, inside and out.

'Saw you coming, boss.' He pressed his thumb on a sensor to open the door.

The windowless foyer was dark and lifeless without partygoers to liven the place up. A door leading to the party area was closed, but the one on the other side of the foyer hung ajar and the smell of disinfectant and the clang of a bucket indicated the presence of a cleaner.

Tony didn't stop. He headed for the stairs leading to the nightclub and their feet echoed through the empty building as they climbed upwards. The clubroom looked shabbier in the daylight. The carpets and red velvet drapes lacked lustre without the light strobes of the glitter ball which hung lifeless from the ceiling. Tony rarely noticed, but today he stared at the empty club with dull eyes. The place was dead now, and it would remain dead without Angel to liven the place up.

'You okay, boss?' Phil came to a halt behind him.

'I was just thinking.'

He glared at Phil to mask the lethargy that swamped him. It wouldn't do to let him glimpse signs of weakness. Phil would be the first one to step into his shoes given half a chance.

He strode to the end of the room, lifted the red velvet curtain, and entered a number into the keypad of the door behind it. Phil, Gus, and Brian followed him upstairs to his office. It was time to turn the tables on Jimmy Matthews.

15

By the time Bill Murphy finished struggling with the forensic suit, he was out of breath and barely able to bend down to don the bootees needed to cover his shoes. Panting, he pulled the second one into place and straightened, hoping it was the suit that was contributing to his difficulties and not his out-of-condition body.

His eyes narrowed as he noticed the cop on duty at the door struggling to hide a smile. Cheeky bugger wouldn't find it so funny if it was him having to suit up. He scowled, pulled the hood up, and went back into the building.

'I'm knackered,' he said when he reached the door of the flat. 'Bugger it. How can the forensics guys work when they have to wear these all the time? I've only had this on for five minutes and I feel like a boiled chicken.'

Frank Hastie laughed. 'You look like one as well.'

Inside the flat, a video camera on a tripod stood at one side of the door, and stepping plates formed a pathway leading inside. Sounds of movement filtered out of a room which Bill guessed must be the bedroom and the scene of the crime.

Feeling like Dorothy following the yellow brick road, he stepped from one plate to the next until he reached the origin of the sounds.

Colin was kneeling on the floor of the bedroom, snapping photographs from that level. But it was the body and the smell that drew Bill's attention. The room reeked of a metallic smell similar to that of an abattoir. A woman lay sprawled on the bed. Her head rested on the pillow with her blonde hair coated with blood, spread out like a fan. Her face, if you could call it a face, was a mass of blood and pulp, reminding Bill of butcher's mince. His DI had been right when she described it as a nasty one.

He shuddered and left the room. He'd seen enough.

Colin rose to his feet and followed him out. 'Never thought I'd see the day you'd turn green at the sight of a body.' He handed the camera to Bill. 'Shove that in the box on the landing on your way out. I need everyone out of the way while I video the scene before anyone else arrives, and Karen will soon be here to dust for prints.'

'Video? You don't usually do that.'

'Ah! But we've talked your bosses into financing new software that enhances the video and can let you walk the crime scene without being present. Now, get your arse out of here and let me get on with it.'

Bill sighed. Gone were the days when he could just walk in and examine anything he wanted. Now he had to wait until forensics had finished in case he contaminated the scene. 'How long before I can do what I'm supposed to do?'

'And what would that be?'

Colin's eyes crinkled and Bill could swear he was smirking underneath his mask.

'Investigate. I'm supposed to be a detective and I need to examine the crime scene, you plonker.'

'All in good time. I'll bell you when we're finished here.'

Bill tore his face mask off and pulled the hood back from his head as soon as the door slammed shut. 'Bleeding suit is like a sauna. I wouldn't like to be in Colin's shoes having to wear it all the time.'

Frank shrugged. 'I suppose the forensic guys get used to it.'

'I'll be glad to get the damn thing off.' Bill stomped down the stairs his words echoing behind him.

The suit crackled, and the stairs creaked, but it didn't stop him from hearing the soft rustle coming from behind the door on the first landing. The same muffled sounds he'd heard on his way up. Someone was watching through the door's spyhole. He turned and stared at it, and he could have sworn he heard a sharp intake of breath. If it hadn't been for the forensic suit he would have rapped on the door.

He continued his descent, pulling at the fastenings before

he reached the bottom. The sooner he got this damn thing off, the better.

Emerging into the fresh air he shrugged his shoulders out of the suit and leaned on the van to avoid toppling over when he bent to take off the bootees. His breathing quickened as he tugged the suit's legs over his ankles. Damn it, you'd think they'd be easier to remove than this.

'You putting it on or taking it off?' Kate's voice interrupted his struggle.

He hadn't heard her approach. If she'd been anyone else, he would have glared at her and given her a rude retort. But she was his boss, and they were still getting used to each other.

'Trying to get it off.' Bill caught himself on the point of saying ma'am and changed it to boss.

'I take it you've inspected the scene?'

'As much as I could, but forensics are in there now and they've banished me until they're finished.'

'So, there's no point in me taking a look.'

'No, boss. They said they'd let us know when they're finished.'

'Do we know who she is?'

'Hadn't got that far, boss. I'm sure there'll be something in the flat to identify her. On the other hand, the neighbours might know.'

'What are you waiting for? Let's go door knocking. We need to get a handle on the victim and find out if anyone heard or saw anything.'

Bill scowled and shook his foot free from the confines of the white suit. He would have liked a few moments, sitting on the van tailboard, to catch his breath.

Neither of the downstairs flats answered Kate's knocks.

'The uniforms reckoned all the girls went back to bed after they checked the flats earlier,' Bill said.

'How can they sleep with all this going on?'

'I heard sounds from one of the first-floor flats. We'd likely have better luck there.'

He led the way up the gloomy staircase and hammered on the door of the flat. When no one answered he thumped on the door again. 'I know you're in there,' he shouted through the letter box. 'I heard you earlier.'

The door swung open. 'D'you have to make such a racket,' the girl facing him demanded, 'what with the cops stamping about upstairs and you thumping my door, when am I supposed to get any sleep?'

'After we've talked to you,' Kate said. 'I'm Detective Inspector Rawlings and this is Detective Sergeant Murphy.'

The girl stared back at them. 'And why should I talk to you?'

'You can do it here or we can interview you at the station. Whichever you prefer.'

Bill could see that Kate's official tone was riling the girl, so he stepped forward and smiled at her. 'You're not in any trouble. We only want to talk and I'm sure you must be curious about why we're here.'

The girl shrugged and stood back. 'You'd best come in then.' She glared at Kate, but when she turned her gaze to Bill there was something more welcoming in her eyes, and a smile tugged at the corner of her mouth.

Once inside, she perched on the edge of an armchair and gestured for them to sit on a sofa that had seen better days. 'What do you want to know?'

Bill brought out his notebook and rummaged in his pocket for the stub of a pencil, which always seemed to evade his fingers. He was starting to get the measure of Kate Rawlings. She wouldn't want him to take the lead.

Kate sat bolt upright on the sofa beside him. 'Last night. Did you hear any disturbance from upstairs?'

The girl shook her head. 'It was all quiet when I came home from work. I heard someone on the stairs early this morning, though. Bugger woke me up by slamming his car door.'

'What time would that have been?'

'Don't know. It was daylight, so maybe around about six. Couldn't swear to that, though.'

Kate looked thoughtful. 'Was it a resident?'

'Not likely. No one in this building would be out and about

that early in the morning. Whoever it was only stayed a few minutes before they clattered out again and drove off.'

'Did you look outside when they left?'

'I peeked out the window, but all I saw was the top of his head before he jumped in the car. I wouldn't be able to recognise him again.'

'What impression did you get? What kind of build did he have? Young or old? Anything that might help.'

'I didn't see him that well, but I reckon he might have been quite slim, definitely not fat, and I'd say younger rather than older because he ran towards the car door and jumped in. I'd say he was in a hurry.'

'What about the car?'

'Red with a white stripe along the top, sporty, something a young guy might drive.'

'You didn't get the make or model.'

The girl shook her head. 'I'm not really into cars.'

'Thank you for your help, but we'll want to speak to you again later in the day once we've determined what has happened.' Kate turned to face Bill. 'Is there anything you want to ask?'

'It would be helpful to have your name.' He addressed the girl in front of him.

A hint of red tinged Kate's cheeks at her oversight, but Bill ignored it. He wasn't interested in scoring points off his DI, but he was interested in the girl who was now studying him with curiosity. He couldn't decide whether her eyes were brown or green. They seemed to have specks of both, which gave them a magnetic quality.

'Candace Morgan,' she said. The green flecks in her eyes deepened.

Bill wrote the name in his notebook, determined not to be pulled in by her gaze.

'And how long have you lived here?'

'Not that long. A few months maybe. I came to Dundee at the back end of last year. I think it might have been November or maybe October.' She smoothed back a strand of magenta-red hair dangling over her face.

'You don't belong to Dundee.'

'I don't belong anywhere.' She put the emphasis on belong.

'Where were you before Dundee?' Bill heaved a sigh. It was like getting blood from a stone.

'Edinburgh.'

Kate leaned forward, her exasperation plain to see. 'The woman upstairs. Are you acquainted with her?'

'Acquainted? That's a funny way to describe it. I know everyone in this block. We all work together.'

'Can you provide us with her name?'

'Angel.' A smile tugged at the corner of her mouth. Bill sensed she was winding them up and knew what she was doing.

'What about her surname?'

'She didn't use one. Angel was her stage name, and that's all she used.'

Bill paused as he wrote the name down. His brow furrowed as he tried to remember where he'd heard the name before. 'You referred to Angel being her stage name.'

'Yes.' Amusement crinkled the corners of her eyes.

Bill resisted the urge to shake her. 'Where did she work?'

'Teasers. We all work there.'

'Everyone in this building works for Teasers? How come?'

'The flats come with the job. This building belongs to Teasers.'

'You mean it belongs to Tony Palmer.' Bill kept his voice flat to disguise his excitement. Maybe at long last he was going to get something on Tony. Something that would stick. Something he couldn't wriggle his way out of.

He closed his notebook. 'I'll need to speak with you again.'

'Does that come with the proverbial warning not to leave town?' She tilted her head to one side and smiled slyly.

'I wouldn't advise it,' Kate said, as she rose from the sofa.

After the door clattered shut behind them, Bill said, 'If all the residents work at Teasers, that explains why no one answered the other doors to our knocking. They'll either be

70

asleep or won't want to get out of their beds. I'll come back later if that's all right with you, boss.'

Kate nodded her assent. 'Time we had a briefing meeting. I'll see you back at the office.'

'Did you notice,' Bill said before they parted company, 'she never asked what happened to Angel?'

16

Candace stood at the window and watched the cops get in their cars and drive away.

The interview hadn't been as bad as she expected, although the woman was most definitely a bitch. The guy wasn't so bad. At least he seemed human. Funny, women never seemed to like her, but she could usually twist men around her little finger. She wondered if the guy, Sergeant Murphy, would be susceptible. No harm in trying. He was a man, and in her experience, men were gullible fools.

'Are they gone?' Linda crossed to the window and stood beside her. 'I thought I'd best stay out of the way.'

'Yes, but they're coming back. As far as they're concerned you don't live here, but you won't be able to stay out of the way forever.'

'I suppose not.'

'Remember, you didn't know Angel, so you can't give them any information about her.'

'Of course.' Linda pulled the tie belt tighter around her towelling robe. 'I found the brown hair dye in the bathroom cabinet. Want to give me a hand to apply it?'

Madge remained seated on Denise's bed long after Tony's footsteps receded downstairs, and the slam of the front door marked his departure.

The oddness of his behaviour wriggled its way through the fog in her brain. She'd sensed fear within him. It wasn't like him to be afraid of anything. Something must have happened, and she knew she should have tried to find out what worried him.

But the fog held her in its grip, twining tendrils of lethargy through her body and mind, making her limbs heavy and unresponsive and damping her curiosity. Energy was something she lacked, and she couldn't even respond to him.

'I thought I'd find you here.' Liz's voice sounded as if it came from a great distance, muffled and vague.

She hadn't heard the door open and didn't respond, nor did she look up. The woman crossed the room, her footsteps silent on the thick pile carpet. Madge fixed her eyes on the shoes that stopped in front of her. They were navy leather slip-ons, not the kind of shoes Madge had in her wardrobe. Not that she wore shoes nowadays. Shuffling about the house in slippers was as much as she could manage.

After Liz dispensed her pills and watched her swallow them, she knelt in front of Madge and took hold of her hands. 'Come and have breakfast. It's a lovely day.'

It was too much trouble to argue, so she allowed herself to be coaxed off the bed. Liz put an arm around her shoulders and propelled her out of the room and downstairs to the breakfast room.

She swallowed a few mouthfuls of cereal to keep Liz happy, then spent the rest of the time pushing scrambled eggs around her plate and playing with the toast.

'You don't eat enough,' Liz said.

'I'm not hungry and the tea has gone cold.'

'I'll get a fresh pot from the kitchen, but you must promise me to eat something when I return.'

Madge nodded her assent, although she had no intention of complying. Food tasted like ash in her mouth and even forcing the few spoonfuls she'd eaten made her want to gag.

Her fingers turned the piece of toast around and around on her plate and she stared out the window to the garden beyond. The sun-dappled bush, redolent with yellow flowers formed a perfect ball shape. There had been a time when she would have taken joy from it, but now her eyes stared unseeingly at the bush and beyond.

Footsteps in the corridor and the creak of the door opening heralded what she thought was the return of Liz. But the voice that spoke was masculine.

'Can I get you anything?' he said.

She shook her head and watched as he turned away from her with a look of pity on his face.

A flicker of regret surged through her. She hadn't meant to rebuff Luigi.

This grief of hers was affecting other people. She could see it in Tony's reaction to her and now Luigi. Maybe it was time for her to snap out of it. Time for her to start thinking about other people and start caring for those who mattered to her. But that was easier said than done and the weight of grief which sent her sobbing to her bed every night was a burden impossible to shift.

Jimmy Matthews was eating a late breakfast in the Apex Hotel when he got the call on his mobile. The screen lit up with the name of the caller and he toyed with the idea of ignoring it before deciding that might not be wise. He wiped his mouth with a napkin and lifted the phone.

A frown gathered on his face while he listened.

'Keep me informed of developments.'

He pushed the plate away, his appetite gone, and rose so quickly the chair rocked back, startling the waitress approaching the table with a toast rack.

His men, clustered at the far end of the dining area, raised questioning eyebrows when he reached them.

'Outside,' he said. He had no intention of telling them what was up while they were still in the hotel. Besides, he felt in need of fresh air.

They followed him out the doors leading to the car park. Once they were at a safe distance from the entrance Jimmy tapped a cigarette out of the pack he'd taken from his pocket and lit it.

'Plans have changed. The dancer's been topped.'

He inhaled smoke and held it for a moment in his lungs before exhaling.

'That other business we intended to take care of this weekend will have to wait.' He flicked ash off the end of his cigarette. 'Get the bags and clear the room. I'll wait in the car.'

After the men scuttled off to do his bidding, he ground the cigarette out under his heel and scowled as he thought of his unfinished business. Luigi and Fabio had thought they were safe under Tony's roof, but they weren't as safe as they thought.

He strode to the car. He would be back when things quietened.

17

Bill Murphy swallowed the last remnant of his bacon roll before he opened the team room door. Jenny Cartwright had the desk to the left of the door. The desk no one else wanted. She was hunched over her computer, engrossed in something technical, and didn't look up. Bill liked her, although he was damned if he understood what she was saying when she came over all techie. Blair Cameron was perched on the edge of Sid's desk, which was the next one along. He saw their heads bend together to whisper something before looking at him. Pair of plonkers. University graduates with their eyes fixed on the career ladder. He had as little time for them as they had for him and was glad his desk was on the other side of the room, as far away from them as possible.

Sue Rogers looked up from the file she was studying when he slumped into his chair.

'Early morning, was it?' She sniffed the air. 'You've had a bacon butty.'

'Didn't have time for breakfast. Boss called me out to meet her at a crime scene.' He rummaged in a drawer for a paper tissue to wipe the grease off his hands.

'I thought something was up when she came stamping in ten minutes ago without even a hello or good morning. What's up her hump?' Sue nodded towards Kate's office, a windowed cubicle at the end of the team room.

'Flea in her ear from forensics. They wouldn't let her into the crime scene.'

'Did you get a look?'

'I arrived just before Colin. He let me in while he was setting up his equipment, but by the time the boss arrived he'd started to video everything. Said he needed peace to do it.'

'That wouldn't have pleased her.'

Bill shrugged. 'She should know by this time that forensics needs to be in there first. Can't have us plods contaminating the scene.'

He stretched over the desk to switch on his computer. 'She's a stickler for getting everything documented. I'd better give the impression I'm writing a report.'

Sue snorted. 'Since when did you get so conscientious?'

'Who says I'm not?' He turned away from her and concentrated on the monitor, which was stuttering into life. The yellow Post-it note stuck to the edge caught his eye. Angel, of course, that's why the name seemed familiar. His in-tray was overflowing, but yesterday's piece of paper perched on top of the heap of stuff waiting for his attention. Grabbing it, he frowned as he read the scribbled details.

'Bugger it,' he said.

'What's wrong?'

'Yesterday's referral about a stalker. I was going to deal with it today.'

'And?'

'She's only ended up dead. Bloody hell.' He lowered his face into his hands. 'If I'd gone out yesterday, she might still be alive.'

'You can't be sure of that.'

'No, I can't. But,' he nodded towards Kate's office, 'she's going to have my guts for garters.'

Bill found Kate bent over a filing drawer. She didn't look up and gave no sign she'd heard him enter her office. He stood at the door and cleared his throat. This would not be easy. Best get it over with.

'You're back,' she said in her usual clipped manner, straightening up and placing several files on her desk.

Bill wasn't sure if it was a reprimand for his belated appearance at the office. If he hadn't stopped to get the bacon roll, he would have been here as fast as her. Maybe faster.

'We'd best get the team briefing started now you are here,' she continued.

'First, I need to tell you something.'

Kate shot him a questioning look.

'Angel apparently came to the office while we were having our meeting yesterday and the duty constable took the details. When I tried to follow it up, he'd finished his shift and his replacement couldn't find the referral because the computers were down, and it wasn't logged.' Bill hesitated, aware it sounded like an excuse. 'The gist of it is he found the information after a hunt, but it was too late for me to do anything about it. I was going to follow it up today.'

'You think if you'd attended to it last night, she would still be alive?'

Bill nodded and closed his eyes to get rid of the image of the girl sprawled across the bed. He was sure her face would haunt him for a long time. If only he'd followed up the referral last night instead of going home. What the fuck was so appealing about an empty flat anyway?

'And now you're angry with yourself.' Kate's voice had softened.

He stared at her. Why wasn't she angry with him? He'd expected a bollocking, and it hadn't happened. This was worse. The least she could do was tell him he'd fucked up.

'Yes, boss.'

The softness left her voice. 'Get over it. Your anger will not help us catch this killer. We have a briefing meeting to hold. Snap to it.'

18

Tony always referred to the rooms above the nightclub as his office, but it was more like a luxury apartment.

The oil paintings on three of the walls were originals by well-known artists, although Tony kept that information to himself. They were there for his pleasure, not something he wanted to share with his underlings.

Leather chairs and a matching sofa were arranged in front of and to the side of a large two-way glass window set into the wall overlooking the club area. On the side facing out, the glass appeared to be a mirror which, during the evening's entertainment, reflected the glitter ball's strobe lights. From inside, it gave a clear view of the whole club area. Many a night Tony would sit on the leather couch watching the activity below. The only give-away the room was an office was the mahogany desk with the executive chair behind it.

Tony settled himself in the chair and tapped his fingers on the desk.

'We all know there was a problem last night when Jimmy Matthews appeared in the club.'

'Yes, boss.' Phil's eyes narrowed. 'We made sure it didn't develop into a situation.'

Tony glanced over at Brian, but the man's face remained expressionless. Brian knew what had happened after they left the club, but Phil and Gus didn't.

'I'm afraid a situation did develop.'

Phil shuffled his feet and a look of unease flickered over his face.

'As you recall, the situation involved Angel.' Tony spoke in a quiet, measured tone but kept watching the men. He half rose from his chair and slammed his hands onto the desk. 'Angel is dead, and I want her killer caught.'

He straightened and walked to the mirrored wall. Staring out to the deserted clubroom, he continued to speak. 'Something was going on between Jimmy Matthews and Angel last night, and it wasn't pleasant. When I drove her home, she was terrified, and I reckon one of them is responsible for her death.' Tony turned to face Phil. 'I want to know where every single one of them went after they left here last night. Get all the lads on it. Trace their movements. I even want to know when they had a crap.'

'Will do, boss. Anything else?'

'Yes. I want to know why they targeted Angel last night, what's the connection, and why she was scared of them.' He turned back to stare sightlessly out of the window. 'And when you find out who topped her, you bring him to me.'

'Yes, boss.'

'What you waiting for? Get onto it.'

Tony leaned his forehead against the glass and stood for a long time staring into the club while the vision of Angel's bloody face played over and over in his mind.

Shadows lurked in the corners of the room and around the circular stages where the dancers performed every night. No sun ever permeated this area. The poles, stretching from the stages to the ceiling, had lost their silvery sheen and looked out of place. The red velvet curtains hanging limply in front of the larger stage at the far corner of the room where Angel had performed her magic no longer looked rich and sumptuous in the daytime gloom.

This nightclub was the epitome of everything he'd ever wanted and had turned him from a small-time businessman into what he was now. The early days hadn't been easy, but ambition spurred him on. Selling dodgy goods on a market stall when he'd been in his teens had soon generated enough capital to buy his first pub and then the next one and the next. He remembered the first time he'd seen this building, a dilapidated former cinema. The potential had been obvious. Madge had thought he was daft to buy it, but she didn't have his vision. The downstairs disco came first, attracting youngsters from Dundee and beyond, but it wasn't enough for

Tony. Shortly after came the private member facilities, the gaming room, and the tiny theatre where punters could watch movies you would never see at a legitimate cinema. Even that wasn't enough for him. He'd roofed over the downstairs area, separating the upstairs section of the cinema with its two floors of balconies from the premises below. The first floor refashioned into the nightclub area and Tony's quarters were situated above and overlooking it.

Earlier this year he'd spent a fortune refurbishing it with the glitter balls and the circular stages with central silver poles. The larger semicircular stage was reserved for the main act. The star. But his star act was lying in a bloody heap in her bed in a building owned by him. Not only that, but he'd been lying beside her oblivious to everything that had happened during the night.

How could he not have heard anything?

He turned his mind back to the events of last night. The run-in with Jimmy Matthews and Angel's obvious fear. Her insistence he take her home and his refusal when she asked him to stay. Not that he was immune to the charms of his dancers, but his affair with her in November and December of last year had long since burned out. Besides, he'd been behaving himself since his daughter's death at the start of the year. So why had he stayed?

It was the glass of whisky. His favourite brand, Angel had said, and she should know. He remembered drinking it but couldn't recall anything after that until he woke in the early hours beside Angel's mutilated body.

Angel must have set him up. But why? And if she was setting him up, why was she the one who was dead?

There was something here he was finding hard to understand, but the more he puzzled over it the more it came back to the same question. 'Why her? Why not him?'

19

Kate strode to the display boards and stood in front of them tapping her foot while the team gathered. Some of them pulled chairs over and others perched on desks. Voices quietened. The scrape of chair legs on the floor died away. Kate was fairly new to Dundee, but she was already aware of how the grapevine worked. There wouldn't be anyone who hadn't heard about the murder.

A whisper and a muffled laugh from someone at the rear broke the silence. Most of the team were settling themselves into chairs or perching on the ends of desks, but Blair and Sid, who were sitting at the back, had their heads close together and kept sneaking glances at her. She narrowed her eyes, her suspicions aroused. Some people seemed to take a delight in belittling others and Kate thought these two fitted the mould. Jenny Cartwright, the computer geek, was an easy target for them and it hadn't gone unnoticed the girl was often the butt of their snide comments. Kate pegged them as cops who would promote themselves at the expense of others. They probably wanted her to focus on them so they could treat her with the disdain she was sure they thought she deserved. The rest of the team seemed to be getting used to her. So far, none of them had treated her with the undisguised contempt that Blair and Sid had. Maybe they had an aversion to taking orders from a woman boss, or maybe they were simply boosting their fragile egos. Kate decided to ignore their interruption. She wasn't going to give anyone the chance to undermine her authority. Her gaze roamed around the people present and came to rest on Bill Murphy. At least he was genuine, and although he aggravated her with his lackadaisical attitude and sloppy appearance, she was sure he would never stand on anyone to get where he wanted to be.

She motioned to him to join her in front of the boards and turned to address the team.

'Uniformed officers were sent to investigate reports of a murder following a phone call at 7.30 am. They attended at 7.50 am and found the body of a young woman. This was reported to me, and I instructed DS Murphy to attend the scene. I'll turn it over to Murphy to do the briefing. Over to you, Bill.' She tossed him a marker pen and perched herself on the end of the nearest desk.

Bill caught the marker in mid-air and strode to the front. 'I arrived at the victim's flat at 8.25 am, shortly before one of the scene investigators showed up. The flat was two stairs up in a tenement block. It was similar to most flats of this type: living room, kitchen, bathroom, and one bedroom. The woman's body was in the bedroom sprawled on the bed, and it was obvious by her injuries she was dead. The attack appeared to be frenzied. She had been stabbed multiple times and her face had been mutilated.'

He swigged water from a bottle before continuing. 'A search of the flat will not be possible until the forensics team finishes. They will let us know when that is. We questioned one of the other tenants in the building and ascertained the woman's name was Angel.' He wrote the name at the top of the whiteboard. 'She worked at the nightclub, Teasers. I'm sure you all know it.' He drew a line under Angel's name and added, dancer, Teasers. 'The flat she lived in, as well as the entire building, is owned by Teasers and they use it to house their employees. This means it is owned by Tony Palmer.' He pointed to the adjacent whiteboard. 'It wouldn't surprise me if Palmer was involved in this, but he's not an easy man to pin down.'

Kate hoisted herself from the desk. 'Additional information is that Angel, who doesn't appear to have a surname, presented herself to the duty officers with a complaint that she was being stalked. This was scheduled to be followed up today. Unfortunately, events have overtaken us.' She avoided looking at Bill but was sure he must be squirming. 'This means we need to find out more about this stalker as well as Tony Palmer. It's not much, but it's a start.'

She nodded to Bill to add stalker to the board.

'Jenny, I want you to track down CCTV in the streets between Teasers and the crime scene. Find out if any of the houses or businesses in the area have cameras and get their footage for the relevant time period.'

'Won't Teasers have cameras outside?' Jenny looked up from her scribbled note.

'I'm sure they do, but I suspect Palmer will not sanction the release of any footage. We might need a warrant. That can be checked out when Bill and I track him down. We'll also visit the nightclub tonight.'

'Blair and Sid, you two are door knocking along the street. See if any of the neighbours heard or saw anything. Find out their impression of the occupants of the building and if any of them knew Angel. Take a note of anyone we might want to question further. Leave the inhabitants of the building for Bill and Sue to interview.' She hid a smile. That would take their egos down a bit. 'Bill and I have already interviewed Candace Morgan. We'll have another go at her after everyone else has been interviewed.'

'Bill and Sue, I want you to search the locus once forensics gives us the nod.'

Bill looked up from the board where he had been scribbling the tasks allocated. 'You don't want in on the interviews?'

'Ideally, yes. But I have a morning of meetings and it's best to get this moving fast rather than waiting for me to be free. After all, the first 24 hours are the most important in an investigation and we don't have a lot to go on so far.'

20

By the time Bill and Sue returned to the crime scene, the uniforms had got their act together and cordoned off the street. The solitary constable guarding the door had been replaced with a posse of officers intent on preventing anyone from infiltrating an area surrounded by blue police tape. Outside the tape, two men leaned against a nondescript van, one held a camera while the other had a box strapped to his chest and wielded a microphone. A cluster of other men and one woman congregated nearby and jostled each other for the best position to observe what was happening.

'Didn't take long for the hacks to get here.' Bill parked in the middle of the road. 'Buggers have clogged up all the parking spaces.' He glared at the reporters, knowing they were getting ready to pounce when he and Sue got out of the car.

The door of the building creaked open, and the group turned their attention to the white-clad figure who stepped out onto the pavement closely followed by two others. One carried what looked like a toolbox, while the other struggled with a camera and tripod.

'Best take our chance while they're otherwise engaged.' Bill peeled himself out of the boiling interior of his car. 'I'll be glad when we return to proper Scottish weather,' he grumbled.

'Isn't it time you got rid of this banger and got yourself a car with air conditioning?' Sue followed him onto the pavement.

'What? Get rid of my pride and joy? I'll have you know it's a vintage model.'

Sue snorted. 'Clapped out rust bucket more like.'

Bill conceded she had a point. The old girl was getting past her best, but a new car was a wee bit outside his budget. 'She runs fine, and she's never let me down so why would I want to change her?' But he was talking to thin air because Sue was already inside the blue tape and heading for the forensic van where the white-clad figures were divesting themselves of their boiler suits.

'Forensics is almost finished,' Sue said when Bill caught up with her. 'There's just Colin upstairs.'

'He's waiting for you lot as well as the meat wagon so he can bag the sheets and mattress underneath the body.' The girl who spoke shook her hair free from the net that held it. Karen or Carol, Bill thought her name was. She was the fingerprints girl.

Sue turned away from her and headed for the door.

'You'd better take these.' The girl waved a plastic overshoe.

'I'll take them.' Bill grabbed the bootees and latex gloves she shoved at him before following Sue inside the building.

His footsteps echoed up the stairwell and once again he experienced the feeling of eyes watching him when he passed a door on the first landing. Was it his imagination? Or was his paranoia resurfacing after all this time? Surely not. It had been a logical reaction after Evie left him for his mate, Craig. He'd convinced himself at the time it was natural to suspect he was the target of gossip, and that the quick aversion of curious gazes wasn't down to the workings of his tortured mind. But that was well in the past and Sue was the only one remaining in the team who knew what had happened and why Evie had left him. She had helped him work through the breakup, and she was the one person he trusted completely.

What he was experiencing now were gut feelings based on his instinct. They were nothing to do with paranoia because they were nothing to do with Evie.

He glared at the door. Nothing stirred, not even the slightest rustle. But someone was watching.

Sue's voice echoed down the stairwell. He couldn't make out what she was saying, but the answering rumble would be Colin briefing her on the crime scene.

'Ah, there you are,' she said when Bill reached the upper

landing. 'I thought you'd got lost.' She was leaning on the door frame. 'Bugger won't let me inside until I cover my feet.'

'Lucky I've brought you some bootees, then.' Bill handed her a pair of the overshoes. 'I've brought gloves as well.'

'I'll start in the kitchen and bathroom.' Sue snapped a double layer of latex gloves on her hands. 'You can do the living area. I don't suppose Colin will let us into the bedroom until he's finished bagging the bedding.'

'Too true.' Colin lounged against the bedroom door. 'Don't want to get any of your DNA mixed up with the specimens.'

'As if,' Bill said.

'Otherwise, the place is clear to be searched. Everything's been photographed and documented.'

Bill turned to survey the living room. This was part of the job he disliked, rummaging among the private stuff of some poor sod. Had to be done, though. Evidence was evidence.

An old-fashioned cocktail cabinet stood in the room's corner. It was as good a place to start as any. The top half contained bottles of gin and vodka, as well as bottles of the softer variety, including Coke, ginger ale, and orange juice on the lower shelf. No whisky, he noted. Our girl wasn't a whisky drinker then. The shelf above contained the glasses. He moved them around, his finger stopping when it reached two whisky glasses. Strange, why would she have whisky glasses but no whisky?

The lower half of the cabinet held a mixture of odds and ends. Cardboard shoeboxes with scissors, needles, and thread; makeup brushes, long past their best; pens and pencils; notebooks. He guessed she was in the habit of stuffing anything she didn't use daily into a box out of sight.

He rammed it all back inside and turned his attention to a sideboard that had seen better days. Inside were more cardboard boxes. She must have a thing for shoes, or was it just the shoeboxes? Most of the contents were junk, similar to what he'd found in the cocktail cabinet. But one box contained receipts and documents. He set it aside to be taken to the station for further scrutiny.

'Bill!' Sue popped her head out of the kitchen. 'You need to see this.'

Two polythene wrapped packages sat on the worktop.

'I found these stuffed behind water pipes at the back of the cupboard underneath the sink.'

Bill picked one up. The contents inside were a creamy beige colour and shifted between his fingers. He'd spent too many of his earlier years in the drug squad to leave him in no doubt about what the package contained.

'Shit, they must be worth thousands of pounds.'

'D'you think it's a drug deal gone wrong?'

'Could be. But why leave the drugs behind?'

Bill looked around the kitchen. Wall unit doors hung open, cups, plates, and cutlery were stacked on the table. A packet of corn flakes accompanied by a bowl of sugar and a jar of jam balanced on the top of the fridge. He guessed Sue had placed them there. If drug dealers had been searching for the victim's stash, the place would have been wrecked.

'Maybe they didn't know the drugs were here. Maybe they were trying to persuade her to tell them where they were and that's why she's so messed up.'

'It doesn't explain why they wouldn't have turned the place upside down to find them. Besides, most druggies would junk the place for the hell of it and take off with the telly to sell in the pub.' Bill gestured towards the flat-screen television in the front room. The only piece of modern equipment there.

'Pity. If it was a drug deal gone wrong, it would have meant more than one perpetrator and a quick closure to the case. Junkies can never keep their traps shut.'

'My money's on Tony Palmer,' Bill said. 'This was Tony's building, and she was one of his girls. Maybe this one rebuffed him and he got nasty.'

'That's speculation. Although you'd love it if it were true.'

'Will that be all, sir?' One of the uniforms dumped the box he'd been carrying on top of Bill's desk. The other two piled more boxes alongside them.

'Don't let me keep you.'

The three constables Bill had appropriated to hump the boxes of evidence back to the station didn't need telling twice, and they scuttled out the door without a backward glance.

Bill stared at the boxes with a lack of enthusiasm. 'Suppose we'd better make a start.'

'Oh, oh,' Sue said. 'The boss has just come in and she's heading this way.'

'That's all we need,' Bill muttered under his breath, hoping Kate didn't hear him. She was a bit too close for comfort.

'How much progress have you made?' Kate's eyes narrowed as she looked at them. She didn't appear to be in the best of humour.

'We've examined the flat and removed everything we considered might provide information about the victim, ma'am.'

Kate glared at him, and he quickly turned the 'ma'am' into 'boss'.

'Forensics. Have they finished?'

'The forensics officer in charge is still at the scene, boss. He's waiting for the body to be removed so he can bag the sheet and mattress.' Bill had almost slipped up and called her ma'am again but caught himself in time. 'He says there's an indication someone was in bed with her and he's hoping to get DNA from the sheet. Obviously, we couldn't access the bedroom in case we contaminated any evidence, but he examined the wardrobe and dressing table for us. He found her handbag, credit cards, and some other paperwork. That should give us a clearer picture of who she was and maybe throw light on why she was killed.'

Sue interrupted. 'We also found two packages of what looks like heroin in her kitchen. It could be a drug deal gone wrong.'

Damn! Kate was going to think he was a plonker for not telling her that right away. What the heck, she thought he was a plonker anyway so what did it matter? He would never be her golden boy. Not that he wanted to be, but it would make a change if she recognised him for the things he was good at instead of constantly deriding him for his appearance.

'What have you done with the drugs?'

'We've logged it in evidence, boss, and sent it off for testing.'

'Good.' Kate pursed her lips. 'Have you interviewed the residents yet?'

Damn fine she knows we won't have had time to do that. Was she trying to put him and Sue on the spot?

'We thought we'd go through some of the papers and stuff we brought back first. It might give us a better handle on the interviews. At the moment we're working in the dark.'

Kate nodded her approval, although her face was set in its usual grim lines. 'Blair and Sid. Are they still out door knocking?'

'They were still working their way down the street when we left to return here,' Bill said. 'I don't suppose we'll see them for some time yet.'

Kate tapped her fingers on the top of a box. 'I don't want to delay interviewing the inhabitants of the building, so I'll rustle up a couple of bodies to help you go through these.' She turned to face Sue. 'Bill and I will return to the locus and interview the girls who live there.'

The clipping sound of her footsteps echoed back to them as she marched out of the room.

'Sorry,' Bill said, 'leaving you with the grunt work. But I don't seem to have much choice.'

Sue shrugged. 'She likes to keep her finger in the pie.' She opened one of the boxes and groaned. 'You owe me for this, and I won't forget.'

21

The street was quieter when Bill and Kate arrived. The forensic vans gone as well as the reporters. Sid and Blair lounged against the wall at the top end of the street.

Bill stifled a grin at the look on their faces when Kate stepped out of the car. Cigarettes were quickly snuffed out, and they turned their attention to the nearest door.

'Busy, lads?' Kate said as she marched towards them.

'Waiting for someone to answer the door, ma'am.'

Kate stared at the cigarette butts in the gutter. 'And how many doors have you knocked on so far?'

Most of the street, ma'am.'

'Results?'

'Nothing of note, ma'am. The ones who were awake said the girls made the usual noise when they arrived at the building. One old biddy said it was a damn disgrace, but there was no point complaining because she rents her house from Tony Palmer and the girls are all his employees. Seems like Tony owns the entire street.'

'Well, don't let me keep you.'

Bill leaned against the bonnet of the car while he waited for Kate to finish with Blair and Sid. He was enjoying himself, and by the look on their faces, Bill reckoned Kate had put a rocket up their arses. Buggers deserved it, a pair of slimy toads, both of them.

'Right,' she said when she rejoined him. 'Best get started.'

Inside the lobby it was cooler than it was on the street. 'Where do you want to start? Top of the building or the bottom.'

She considered for a moment before climbing the stairs. 'Top and we'll work down.'

Breath wheezed out of Bill's lungs by the time he'd

climbed the last set of stairs and he bent over, hands on knees, to recover. He was seriously out of condition. A few days at the gym wouldn't go amiss.

Kate leaned on the bannister, trying to hide a smile but not succeeding. She was breathing easily as if the climb had been no more than a stroll along the pavement.

'Sorry, boss. I need to take more exercise.'

'Too many pies and fish suppers, more like.' The smile turned into a grin.

Bill could swear she sounded almost human.

After a moment, she said, 'Ready yet?'

Bill nodded.

There were two doors on the landing and Kate turned to the one on the right. 'You take the lead. I think these girls respond better to a man than a woman.'

'Yes, boss.' That was unexpected, he thought. She liked to be in charge. But Bill wasn't going to argue. He much preferred to take the lead.

He stepped forward and rapped on the door. A scurry of movement sounded from inside, but no one answered his knock.

'Police,' he said. 'We know you're in there. You'd best open the door.'

A few seconds passed, and he was getting ready to hammer on the door again when it swung open.

'Don't give a girl time to get herself decent.' Anger and insolence in equal measures flared from her eyes and she pulled the silk wrap tighter around her body. 'Well, don't just stand there ogling me like that. Come in so I don't have to give the whole world a peep show.'

Had he been ogling her? Bill didn't think so, although he'd never seen anyone quite like her before. A straight black fringe masked her eyebrows and her hair fell in bright orange and black waves to her shoulders. The anger reflected in her dark eyes had subsided to sullen resentment.

'This is harassment, you know.' Her eyes narrowed as she waved for them to sit on a sofa. 'Two cops were here earlier on. Pulled me out of my bed and demanded to inspect my flat.

Don't know what they expected to find but I'm sure they were disappointed.' She slid into a chair positioned side on to the sofa, so she wasn't looking directly at them.

He was on the point of telling this woman it would be in her interests to cooperate with the police when Kate laid a hand on his arm to restrain him.

'I'm sorry we have to trouble you in this way, but we would appreciate your help.' Her voice was low and sympathetic.

Her tone took Bill by surprise. No longer was Kate her officious self. Now she was expressing herself as a woman. It was something Bill could have sworn was alien to her nature, but it was having the desired effect on the young woman seated in the chair next to them. He took out his notebook and decided to let Kate get on with it. Her approach might get them results.

'The cops. They treat us all like whores, you know.' She leaned over to grasp a packet from a small table. Her hand shook as she lit a cigarette. 'I don't deserve to be treated like that. Dancers are not whores.'

'I'm in total agreement with you,' Kate said her voice like silk. 'But tell me a bit about yourself. I'm afraid I don't even have your name.'

'It's Flame, like my hair.' She shook the black and orange-streaked strands of hair and they cascaded around her face like flames in a fire.

'I was admiring your hair. But is Flame your professional name or your real name?'

A spark of mischief appeared in Flame's brown eyes. 'I wish it was my real name. Maybe I'll do a deed poll and change it because my real name, Wilma Stewart, doesn't really suit a dancer. Who wants to come and see someone called Wilma?'

Kate laughed. 'You've got a point. Where do you originally come from, Flame?'

Bill noticed Kate used the name the woman preferred. Who would have thought his boss could weasel information out of someone so resentful of the police? Even Sue, his partner, couldn't have done it better.

'Leeds, but I haven't been back there for years.'

'Does that mean you've been in Dundee quite a while?'

'About two years. I like it at Teasers. I've had worse bosses than Tony.'

'You've been dancing longer than two years then.'

'Yep. Started when I was eighteen in a club in Leeds. Danced there for a couple of years before moving to Manchester. Didn't like it there so I only stayed six months. Since then, I've had jobs in Edinburgh and Glasgow before landing up here.'

'Fascinating. But I suppose we'd better get down to the reason we're here.'

Flame's eyes grew wary, although Bill was sure she was unaware of how much information she'd already given them.

'You mean the murder downstairs?'

'Yes, I'm afraid we don't know very much about the victim apart from the fact her name was Angel. We were hoping for your help.'

'She wasn't much liked, and no one seemed to know much about her. She came here from Edinburgh at the end of last year. Her and that Candace turned up at the same time. Before that we didn't have a star dancer. We all got treated equal.' Flame inhaled until the end of her cigarette glowed red. 'Bloody Angel. Why should she get star treatment? She wasn't a better dancer than any of the rest of us, but she caught Tony's eye.'

Bill's interest quickened. His gut told him Tony was involved, and his gut was rarely wrong.

'You wouldn't happen to know her real name or where she came from before Edinburgh?'

'Nope, and none of the others know either except for maybe Candace. She was thick with her. Kept herself to herself, she did. Bit of a mystery woman if you ask me.'

'Last thing and then we'll get out of your hair.' Kate paused. 'Did you hear or see anything during the night?'

'Not a thing. I was knackered when we finished and slept like a log until those two cops hammered on my door this morning.'

'She doesn't like men,' Bill said after the door closed behind them.

'I latched onto that the minute I set eyes on her.'

'You did?'

'Yes, that's why I took over the questioning.'

'You want to do this next one as well?' Bill rapped on a door further along the landing.

'Let's play it by ear. If I decide to take the lead, I'll touch you on the arm.'

Bill didn't have a chance to answer because the door opened as soon as he knocked. She must have been standing behind it.

The girl facing them was as unlike Flame as it was possible to be. Slim, with pale reddish hair and a scattering of freckles over her nose, she looked like anyone's idea of the girl next door. Her face was free of powder and lipstick and her eyelashes were her own.

'I heard you coming.' She gestured for them to enter.

Half an hour later they were no further forward. They knew her name was Lucy Sampson. She originated from Nottingham and had worked at Teasers since January. She said she didn't know Angel all that well but didn't display any animosity towards her.

'Nice girl,' said Kate as they trudged downstairs.

Frank Hastie was leaning over the railings, staring down the stairwell, when they emerged onto the second landing. He straightened and resumed his post at the door of Angel's flat.

'Still here?' Bill raised an eyebrow.

'Yeah! The meat wagon's been, and the bedding's been removed, but we haven't been given the all-clear yet. Colin's arranged for someone to secure the door, so we don't get folks poking in for a look around.'

'I didn't notice you when we were on our way upstairs, PC Hastie.' Kate's voice had regained its officious tone.

'Sorry, ma'am. Had to ask one of the more amenable ladies if I could use her facilities. I wasn't gone for more than a few minutes.'

'Long enough for the scene to be contaminated. I'd better have a look around.'

'Yes, ma'am.' Hastie opened the door to the flat.

Bill followed Kate inside. The stepping plates had gone, and the living room looked reasonably tidy except for traces of powder on various surfaces. The bedroom seemed bare without the bed. A splotch of blood stained the carpet, but most of the blood had been contained in the bedding, which had now gone for examination.

'She was lying on the bed nearest this side of the room.' Bill pointed to the area beside the bloodstain. 'She was a bit of a mess and her face had been battered to a pulp. Whoever did this was angry. It wasn't a controlled attack.'

'Did she fight back, I wonder?'

'I suppose the post-mortem will tell us that, but the blood was contained to one area, the bed. It suggests she wasn't able to fight back.'

'D'you think the killer attacked her while she slept?'

'It's possible,' Bill said.

'I've seen enough, and we still have interviews to complete.'

Frank Hastie pulled the door closed as they left and watched as they marched along the landing to the next door.

'Good luck with that one. Her name's Ayisha Okeke and she almost had us for breakfast when we talked to her earlier.'

'By the looks of it, this one might respond better to your approach than mine.' Bill was still smarting over Flame's dismissive treatment of him.

Kate smiled. 'Afraid of women, are we?'

A flicker of resentment pulsed through him, and he repressed the retort that hovered on his lips. He'd best not forget she was his boss and although she was treating him better than usual today, it wouldn't last. By the time they'd interviewed everyone her heel would be back on his neck, grinding him into the dirt.

Ayisha Okeke loomed over them. A tall girl with a lithe muscular body that reminded him of Thumper, kicking the shit out of James Bond in one of the Bond movies. Her braided black hair was scraped from the right side of her head to hang in thin beaded plaits over her left shoulder.

He took a step back to look up at her and hoped she wasn't as lethal as Thumper.

'Bloody cops,' she said. 'Doesn't matter where you go in this bloody country the cops are always on our tails. I thought Scotland might be better, but I was wrong. I'm going to lodge a complaint about police harassment. Not that it'll do any good.'

Bill reckoned this woman had no intention of complying and that Kate's softly, softly approach would be useless.

He braced himself. 'You have a duty to answer any questions we ask in relation to the incident next door.'

'Incident?' Ayisha laughed. 'That's a good way to describe it. What you mean is the murder of the bitch next door.'

'However we describe it, you have a duty to answer questions.'

'I suppose you'll be trying to pin it on me because of the colour of my skin.'

Kate laid a hand on Bill's arm. 'No one is suggesting anything of the sort unless, of course, we find out otherwise.'

Ayisha snorted. 'D'you think I was born yesterday?'

'It might be better if we continue this conversation inside rather than letting everyone in the building listen in.'

'Don't suppose I can keep you out.'

Ayisha's beads rattled as she jerked her head for them to follow her inside. She made no offer for them to sit, but Kate sat on the sofa and gestured for Bill to sit beside her.

Ayisha perched on the arm of a chair and Bill wished they'd remained standing because it left her in a dominant position, looking down on them.

'We'll need some details first, like your name, where you come from and how long you've worked at Teasers.'

'I've already supplied all that to the plod outside.'

'I still need you to confirm the details.'

She snorted again and glared at them. 'Ayisha Okeke, Bristol, and three years at Teasers.'

Bill prised more information out of her before he asked if she had seen or heard anything during the night.

'Not a damn thing,' she said.

'You live next door to where the incident took place, and I'm sure there must have been some noise during the attack. Surely you would have heard something through the wall?'

'Have you looked at the layout of these flats? The shower rooms and bathrooms are against the party walls. That's two layers of rooms. I'm not likely to hear anything that takes place in the bedroom.'

'I didn't say the attack was in the bedroom.' Bill's voice was deceptively quiet.

'Where else would it be? There's only one bedroom and living room in these flats. I'm not going to hear anything unless it's in the kitchen or shower room.' Her voice halted, and a troubled look crossed her face. 'Mind you, I did hear water gurgle in the pipes in the early morning. No one's ever up at that time.'

'What time did you hear this?' Bill looked at her expectantly, hoping for a time frame for the killing.

She shrugged her shoulders. 'Early. It was still dark, although I could see shapes in the room.'

Kate leaned forward, breaking her silence. 'This gurgle in the water pipes does that mean someone was running a shower?'

Ayisha nodded.

'And that would be someone showering in Angel's flat?'

'Can't say for sure, the pipes gurgle when anyone in the building showers, although it's louder if it's upstairs or next door.'

'Thank you for your time,' Kate said. 'You've been helpful, although we may need to speak to you again.'

Ayisha glowered, and when they left, she slammed the door with a resounding thud.

22

Tony pushed all thoughts of what had happened to Angel to the back of his mind. He had a more pressing problem. Who was going to take her place? Which of the dancers should he promote to the top spot? Marlene would know.

'I'll be there in fifteen minutes,' she'd said when he phoned her and now, he could hear her feet clattering up the stairs followed by the door puffing shut behind her.

'Cops are all over the house and street where the girls live.'

Marlene lived two streets away in another of Tony's flats.

He tore his gaze away from the clubroom below. 'Someone killed Angel last night. We need to find a girl to fill her spot.'

He could see the questions in her eyes and face, but she didn't voice them. Marlene knew he would tell her when he was good and ready and not before. And he wasn't ready yet.

'I see. Had you anyone in mind?'

'I hadn't got around to thinking about it yet. I thought you might have some ideas.'

'There's Ayisha. That girl exudes sexuality, and she's different. The punters can't take their eyes off her.'

Tony conjured up the image of Ayisha with her beaded braids whipping around her head. Marlene had a point, but he'd also heard some racist comments when she performed. Not that the men uttering them would have thought they were being offensive. It was just the Dundee way.

He shook his head. 'Perhaps not. Don't want to encourage any unpleasantness.'

'What about Candace then? She's quite good.'

'I suppose. She has quite a sexual routine, but the punters liked the way Angel flicked her hair about when she was dancing, and Candace has short hair.'

'Yes, Angel used her hair to good effect. It was kind of like the dance of the seven veils. Now you see it, now you don't.'

'Lucy? She's a natural redhead, which makes her hair a shade darker than Angel's, but it's a similar length.'

Tony frowned, trying to remember which one was Lucy.

'She dances on the pole near the bar.'

'Ah, yes.' No wonder he couldn't remember her. He usually watched the dancers on the poles further out in the room. 'D'you think she's good enough?'

'She's as good as any of the other dancers, and I'm sure she could copy some of Angel's routine. Plus, she has an innocent quality that appeals to the punters.'

'That's it settled then. Let her know and we'll see how she does tonight.'

'If that's all?' Marlene turned towards the office door.

'What did you say her name was?'

'Lucy Sampson. I think you'll like her.'

The door closed with a click and the emptiness of the room overwhelmed him, echoing the emptiness in his soul.

Tony walked to his desk and slumped in the chair. He closed his eyes but could not erase the image of Angel's bloody face from his mind. What the hell had happened while he slept beside her, and why hadn't he heard anything? How long would it be before the police came knocking? They'd love to get something on him, but up to now, he'd been too clever for them. It would be ironic if they banged him up for something he didn't do.

Paperwork covered the top of his desk but work no longer appealed to him. Without thinking, he raised his arm and swept the lot onto the floor. The only thing that mattered was Madge. What would she do if they banged him up? How would she cope?

Blindly, he stumbled from his chair and headed for the door. He was going home.

The buzz of a saw and the murmur of voices drifted up the garden to where Madge sat on one of the patio chairs. Liz had insisted she come outside to enjoy the sun, and she hadn't had the energy to argue.

The smell of flowers and freshly mown grass sparked memories of happier days; the reason she had avoided the garden for so long. There were no happy days now, and it pained her to remember Denise who took her first steps in this garden. Denise playing on the grass. The swing and the chute that had graced the far end of the lawn along with the trampoline. Birthday parties and the marquee Tony had hired for these occasions. Denise, dancing under the stars with a succession of boyfriends whom Tony usually managed to scare off. None of them were good enough for his precious Denise.

A knife twisted in Madge's heart, and she fingered the pill screwed into the corner of her handkerchief. She'd told Liz she'd taken the pill and now she wished she had. It wasn't as if she needed medication. Not really. The doctor had been adamant they were only supposed to be a temporary relief because she wasn't clinically depressed. 'It's natural to be sad after the death of a loved one,' he'd said. But it didn't feel natural, and the pills gave her relief from pain and stopped her dwelling on Denise and the horrible way she'd been left to die.

She spread the handkerchief on the garden table and her fingers hovered over the pill. If she swallowed it the pain and the memories would vanish, but the fog would return. She couldn't decide which was worse, the fog or the pain.

The sound of approaching footsteps made the decision for her. She scrunched the handkerchief into a ball and tucked it into her pocket with the pill inside.

'Liz said you were sitting out here.' Tony laid a glass of her favourite fizzy water on the table and flopped into the chair next to her. 'It's good to see you outside enjoying the sun. It will put some colour in your cheeks.'

She stared at the glass of water. If it had been there a moment before she would have swallowed the pill without a second thought.

'Don't want you getting dehydrated,' Tony said.

'I thought you'd gone to the club.'

'I've done what I needed to do. I came back and did some work in the office but couldn't concentrate, so I came out to keep you company. Maybe we can talk. It's been a long time since we've done that.'

Despite the slowness of her reactions, she could sense something was wrong. His smile was more strained than usual and there was a tenseness in his face and body. But did she really want to know what was troubling him? She lifted the glass swirling the liquid inside until the last of the ice cubes melted, and when she sipped it, the water was tepid.

'Since we lost Denise, we've grown apart. I miss you, Madge.'

The pain in Tony's voice pricked at her lethargy making a small tear in the shield she'd erected. Could it be that his suffering was as great as hers? She'd always thought him tougher with an outer shell that was impervious to the pain of others. Why else could he do some of the things she knew he was responsible for? He thought she didn't know what he did to Denise's killer. But she did. To her shame she'd taken pleasure from the knowledge, even though she could never have exacted that level of revenge herself.

Her thoughts drifted, and she made no reply. After all, he didn't mean it. Their lives had been empty for months now and Tony's disinterest in her had been all too obvious. Her birthday had come and gone unnoticed. There had been no flowers this year, no nice bottle of wine or intimate meal. Not even a card.

Misery swamped her, and she felt inside her pocket for her handkerchief. With slow fingers, she unfolded it and removed the pill from its folds. She stared at it for a moment before popping it in her mouth and swallowing it with a gulp of the tepid water. At least the pill would banish the constant thoughts swirling in her mind and dampen her emotions to give herself a modicum of peace. She could vanish down the rabbit hole of oblivion where nothing mattered, and nothing could hurt her.

'What's that?'

Tony's voice floated into her consciousness.

'Only my medication. Liz said I should take it, but I forgot.'

For a moment she thought she detected concern in Tony's eyes, but as she settled back in her chair, she decided she must have imagined it.

She closed her eyes and her mind floated away into a place where there was no pain and no feeling.

23

Today had been a strange day, starting with Tony's furtive early morning arrival and subsequent warnings about Jimmy Matthews frequenting Teasers.

After Tony left for the club Luigi stayed on the alert, inspecting the house and gardens in a non-stop series of checks. He didn't need to be told how vicious that gang could be. He'd seen what they did to Georgio. Tony's last words echoed in his mind. 'I need you to protect Madge.' He'd die before he'd let any of them near her.

Luigi only relaxed after Tony joined Madge in the garden. That was another strange thing because his boss never came home in the middle of the day.

'Any problems?' Tony had asked when he surfaced from his office just after 4 o'clock.

'Nothing, boss. I kept my eyes open, but it's been quiet.'

'You're a good lad, Luigi. I'll be here for the next few hours. You can take a break.'

The kitchen was unnaturally quiet when he entered. Bet and Morag stood in front of the central island with a newspaper spread out on the worktop.

'Thought you'd be busy preparing tonight's dinner,' Luigi said.

'Didn't think anyone would have much appetite tonight after what's happened so I thought a salad would be in order. It doesn't need much preparation.'

Bet wet her finger and turned a page. Without looking up she answered the question he hadn't asked. 'I sent wee Morag for an *Evening Telegraph*. I heard an announcement on the radio this morning about the murdered dancer but didn't want to ask any of the men about it.'

Luigi joined them at the worktop.

'Look, they've even got a photo of her. She's called Angel, but I'd lay bets she's no angel, despite her name.'

He stared at the familiar face in the newspaper spread. There was no mistaking her. It was the girl he knew as Glenda, the girl who'd set Georgio up. The girl who'd been in cahoots with the Matthews' gang. His stomach knotted, and it took him all his time not to spit his bile out. As far as he was concerned, she'd deserved all she got.

The office was silent and dark. This was Tony's domain. A secure place where he could be alone with his dreams and thoughts. The problem was his thoughts at the moment were jumbled and unwelcome.

He thrust his hands in his pockets, frowned, and looked down into the shadowy clubroom lit only by a security light. Everything he'd done since leaving Madge sitting in the garden had merged into a blur and if anyone had asked, he wouldn't have been able to tell them what he'd done before coming here.

His mind churned as memories of Angel invaded his consciousness. Angel dancing, sinuous and sexy, winding herself around the pole on the centre stage. Angel's laugh. The way her mouth raised slightly more at one side than the other. Angel's face lying in a bloody mess on the pillow.

He blinked, trying to remove the images from his mind, but they persisted.

Why? That was what he couldn't understand. Why would anyone want to kill Angel? And why did someone want to pin it on him? Was he the reason Angel died?

A shaft of light split the darkness in the clubroom and a movement caught his eye. Marlene, closely followed by Kara, strode through the entry door. They would be heading for the bar which was directly below his mirror window. Marlene liked to have everything in order before the club opened.

Next to arrive was the guy in charge of the music, Daniel or Derek. Tony could never remember his name, not that it mattered. He'd been a DJ before he came to work for Tony and now spent his working life closeted in the tiny booth next to the bar.

The first of the dancers, the girl with the braids, was the next one to appear. Tony watched her until she disappeared through the door leading to the dressing rooms.

Soon the club would come alive. Music would fill the air and the punters would gather, drinking and ogling the girls as they danced, while he stood here in the dark, looking down.

Loneliness swamped him. The claustrophobic silence and darkness of his office were more than he could stand, but the willpower to move was lacking. He gritted his teeth. Surely he was stronger than this. There was no way he wanted to give in to this alien, helpless feeling threatening to swallow him. Where was his backbone?

He straightened, pulled his hands from his pockets, and strode for the door and the stairs leading down into the clubroom. Angel's killer was out there, and he intended to find him.

Marlene was busy setting up the margarita rimmers when Tony emerged from the office door.

'I didn't know you were here?' She finished pouring salt in the last rimmer before looking up. She replaced the salt container underneath the bar and walked over to him. 'You don't look good.'

It was an understatement. Tony looked haggard and drawn. Her hand reached for the bottle of Laphroaig and she poured a good measure into a glass.

'Get this down you.'

Tony leaned on the bar and gulped the whisky, but by the look on his face he barely tasted it.

Marlene had been with Tony ever since the beginning and she knew him as well as anyone did. She knew his weaknesses as well as his strengths. And she knew he had an eye for a pretty face.

Dancers came and went at Teasers, and Tony often had flings with them. Marlene was used to that. Then Angel arrived and caught Tony's eye. He had become obsessed with her, and Marlene remembered remonstrating with him one night after a tearful phone call from Madge.

'Go home, Tony. You're in danger of losing Madge.'

He had shrugged his shoulders and grinned at her, and she had known he wouldn't be taking her advice. That was when she'd feared he would leave his wife for this one. It had worried her, but she'd said enough. Although she was close to Tony, she knew better than to meddle too far into his affairs.

It had taken the death of his daughter earlier this year to make him realise what his family meant to him, and Angel had joined the ranks of dancers with whom he'd had flings. As far as Marlene knew, Tony and Angel became history.

But now Angel was dead, and Tony looked like shit. A worm of doubt wriggled into her mind, but she shook it away. There was no way Tony would ever harm any of his dancers.

Tony's finger traced the rim of the now empty glass.

'Did you sort out the dancers' rota for tonight?'

'It's all taken care of, although some of the girls weren't pleased with Lucy taking the top spot.'

'Angel will be a hard act to replace. Do you think Lucy is up to it?'

'We'll find out soon enough.'

Marlene wiped grains of sugar from the top of the bar. 'I was thinking about that after you left today.' She hesitated. 'How would it be if we rotated the dancers in the top spot? Maybe stick with Lucy tonight and then have a different girl tomorrow night and so on. That way, we curb any jealousy between the girls and the punters might like it and come back each time their favourite was performing. We could stick posters at the entrance to let them know which dancer will be on the main stage.'

'We can try that.' He held his glass out for a refill. 'I'll leave you to do the arranging.'

His face darkened and Marlene thought she detected a tear in his eye. 'But you know what? Every time I close my eyes when the performance is on, I'll still see Angel.' He gulped the whisky and set his glass on the bar. 'If I find out who did this to her, I'll make sure they regret it.'

'Angel told me she was worried about the stalker.'

Marlene turned to look at Kara. She hadn't realised the girl was standing behind her.

'What did she say?' Tony's voice was gentle.

Marlene reckoned he had a soft spot for the girl who was the daughter of one of his old flames.

'After they finished up each night a car followed them home. The other girls just laughed it off saying it was a weirdo getting his rocks off. But Angel was convinced he was following her.'

Marlene frowned. 'Had she a reason for thinking that?'

'I don't know, but she was worried about it. When I said she should report it to the police she didn't seem keen.'

'This stalker,' Tony's voice grew harsh, 'the girls might know more.'

'I'll question the girls, Tony. With the mood you're in you'll just scare them.'

Tony hesitated and for a moment Marlene thought he was going to insist on doing it himself.

'You know I'm right. And you don't want them to clam up. They'll tell me.'

'Okay,' he said, although it didn't sound as if he thought it was okay. 'Find out what they told the police while you're at it.'

Marlene nodded. 'You could check the CCTV. You never know, it might have captured an image of the car.'

'Why didn't I think of that?' Tony slapped his hand on the bar. He slid off the barstool and turned to leave. 'Let me know what you find out from the girls.'

A sense of foreboding hung over Marlene as she watched Tony weave his way through the tables on his way to the door. It was like watching a man well on the way to being drunk. And if there was one thing she knew, it was that Tony never gave the impression of being drunk even when he had a skinful. He wasn't himself, and it worried her.

24

The building always had sighs and echoes in the hours before Teasers opened for business, and tonight was no exception. Tony passed through the door to the back corridor leaving behind the ornate vestibule to enter the area only accessible to staff.

The corridor stretched before him, extending the length of the disco and clubrooms above. Bare electric bulbs lit the passageway and his footsteps clattered on the concrete floor.

A door on the left opened and a man, who looked as if he would be at home in a boxing ring, peered out. He was dressed in the customary white shirt, dark suit, and tie which, despite his bulk, fitted him perfectly.

If Tony's appearance surprised him he didn't show it.

'Can I help you, boss?'

'Anyone in the camera room?'

The bruiser shrugged. 'Not sure. But wee Danny usually starts before the club opens. If he's not there I can find him for you.'

Most of the space in the room was taken up with monitors. There were a couple of areas the surveillance cameras didn't cover for good reason, but he could see most of the activity inside the club as well as outside.

A slightly built man of indeterminate age sat in front of the monitors, his eyes large behind thick-lensed glasses.

'Danny?'

The man swivelled in his chair and peered at Tony.

'Sorry, boss. I didn't hear you come in.'

'Is all this saved on tape or something?' Tony waved a hand towards the screens. Technology wasn't one of his skills.

'It's saved to the cloud.'

Tony hadn't a clue what the man meant, but he guessed it

was some sort of backup system.

'Does that mean we can access recordings from a week or so back?'

'I can access recordings up to six months back. Was there something specific you were looking for?'

'The girls have been complaining that over the last week a car has followed them home after their shift.'

'No problem, boss. But it'll take a wee bit of time.'

'How long?'

'At a guess later tonight or tomorrow, depends on whether I can see anything. I take it you want details of the car and its registration.'

'As fast as you can,' Tony said.

'The car might not be too difficult, but the registration will be more complicated.'

Tony halted in the doorway. 'How come?'

'Depends on the angle and how clear the image is. But I know a guy who's good at enhancing images. I can punt it to him if you give the say-so.'

'Yes,' Tony said. 'I need to know who has been watching my girls.'

Flame was always the last showgirl to arrive at the club. When Marlene saw her slip through the door and head for the dressing rooms, she stopped polishing glasses and laid her cloth on the bar.

'You finish setting up,' she said to Kara. 'I'm going to talk to the dancers.'

The dressing rooms were to the left of the bar, beneath Tony's office, and an electronic entry system ensured the girls' safety when they weren't performing. Marlene keyed the number into the pad and pushed through the door to the corridor leading to the dressing room.

Several doors led off this corridor. This was where they stored everything needed to run the club. Catering equipment, additional tables and chairs, spare microphones and cables. Even Marlene wasn't sure what some rooms contained, although she had her suspicions. Tony didn't appreciate too much curiosity about his affairs, so Marlene knew better than to chance her luck.

Voices and laughter died away as the sound of Marlene's heels, clicking on the wooden floorboards, drew nearer. Ayisha, dressed in a tee shirt and jeans, appeared in the doorway to block her entry.

'Slumming it?' She flicked her braids over her shoulders, the beads clinking and reflecting the colour of the mirror spotlights.

Marlene stared into the girl's eyes. Ayisha liked to appear tough, but Marlene was sure it was an act to mask her vulnerability. Not that anyone would ever suspect Ayisha was vulnerable by looking at her.

'I don't think I need your permission, and you'd do well to mind your manners.'

'Manners, is it? I don't think that's what the wankers upstairs come to see. What do you think, girls?'

'I will not get into a pissing match with you, Ayisha.' Marlene kept her voice low and pleasant. 'But Tony sent me to find out about Angel's death and what you all knew about it. Unless you want to lock horns with Tony, I suggest you sit down and cooperate.'

At the mention of Angel, everyone in the room fell silent. A few of the girls shifted in their chairs. Roxy, who had started to remove her shirt, pulled it back on again. The girl next to her laid a makeup brush on the counter in front of her and turned to look at Marlene.

'What's there to tell?' Ayisha sat on the chair nearest to Marlene. She seemed to have appointed herself as the spokesperson. 'None of us saw or heard anything.'

'You said you heard water running in the pipes in the early morning.' Roxy reminded her.

'Yeah! So what? That could have been any of us. And even if it was him, I didn't see anything.'

'Candace saw something, though.'

Marlene pushed past the clothes rack which took up all the space at one side of the room. 'What did you see, Candace?'

The girl's eyes were like a cat's as they stared back at her and Marlene remembered she'd come to Teasers at the same time as Angel and they'd appeared to be friends.

'I looked out the window in the early morning and saw a guy leaving the building. He got in a fancy car and drove off.'

'Description?' Marlene snapped.

'I only saw the top of his head, but he moved like someone young, and he seemed quite slim. I wouldn't recognise him again.'

'What about the car?'

'It was a fancy one, red with a white stripe along the top and the bonnet. But I don't know much about cars so I can't tell you the make or model.'

'Okay.'

Marlene reckoned she'd got as much information as the girls were going to give her, but halfway to the door, she remembered she hadn't asked about the car following them home.

She turned back to Candace. 'Was it the same car that's been following you home all week?'

'No. That was a dark car. We thought it was some weirdo getting his kicks. He never did anything, just followed us.'

'You don't think it's connected?'

Candace shrugged. 'Your guess is as good as mine.'

Tony sat in the dark watching Angel's replacement on the main stage. Lucy had perfected the routine. She swayed in time to the music, caressed the silvery pole, and used her hair in the same way Angel did to create an erotic image guaranteed to rouse the customers and make them want more. But she wasn't Angel. No other dancer could ever match up to Angel.

He closed his eyes and tried to visualise Angel writhing around the silver pole; her golden hair swinging around her body in time with the beat of the music, the sensuality of her movements. But nothing came. The image in his mind of a bloody and battered body was the only way she now existed.

He shuddered and gulped a mouthful of whisky. It burned all the way down his throat to land in a fiery lump in his stomach. Even the pleasure of his favourite drink had been taken from him.

Tears stung his eyes. Self-pity welled up in him and he buried his head in his hands. For months he'd been suppressing these feelings, refusing to allow them to surface until now. Angel's death had brought everything back with a vengeance. When he thought of Angel's bloody body, it was Denise's face that invaded his mind, breached his defences, and brought the tsunami of grief he'd been denying to the surface.

It was just as well he hadn't remained in the clubroom after Marlene reported back to him. He wouldn't want anyone to see him like this. After all, he had a reputation to maintain, and he was under no illusions that if he showed weakness, someone would see an opportunity to take his place.

After he recovered and pulled himself together, he laid his glass on the arm of the sofa and forced himself to think about the information Marlene had prised out of the dancers. It wasn't much, the sound of water in the pipes. That was probably him when he showered, but at least he hadn't been seen. Then there were the two cars; the dark one that followed them home, and the red one early in the morning. Did the red car belong to the killer? Had the owner been in the room while he still slept his drugged sleep? If so, why hadn't he been killed as well?

Those two cars were the key to what happened to Angel, and he had to find them. At least, by tomorrow, he should have some feedback from the geek who monitored the CCTV.

25

Sunday

It was barely light when Kate drove to the office on Sunday morning. She wanted to pick through the evidence they'd accumulated before the team gathered for the briefing.

Two hours later, she had to admit what they had didn't amount to much. A preliminary report from forensics containing a description of the scene and a list of items they'd taken for forensic examination. It was anyone's guess how long they would have to wait before the test results came back.

The envelope attached to the report looked more promising. Kate slit it open and shook the photographs it contained onto her desk. She pushed the ones showing various views of the rooms to one side and concentrated on the images of the victim. Bill had been right when he described it as a frenzied attack. They were looking for someone with anger issues.

Her fingers toyed with the transcript she'd insisted Bill write last night before she allowed him to go home. The interviews hadn't revealed much, although there seemed to be a general dislike of Angel.

Was this a woman's crime? She didn't think so. To do as much damage to Angel as these photographs portrayed the perpetrator would have needed the strength to subdue her.

Her chair creaked as she leaned back to flex her shoulder muscles and relieve the tightness. She rubbed her eyes. They were gritty with lack of sleep. Why had she bothered to go home to Forfar last night? It wasn't as if anyone was there waiting for her, only an empty house and a cold bed. A sleepless night, with troubled thoughts whirling through her mind while she tossed and turned and wrestled with the duvet, had ensured a less than fresh start to the day.

Outside her office the team room was silent. Computers lifeless, keyboards quiet, and desks vacant, although a sense of expectancy hovered over the wall of whiteboards, plastered with notes and scraps of paper. She selected three photographs. The victim, the bedroom where her body was found, and her living room.

Her footsteps echoed in the empty room as she walked between the empty desks to the display boards. She attached Blu-Tack to the back of the photographs and stuck them at the top of the board beside Angel's name. On the side, she sketched a flow chart mapping out all the flats in the building with the names of the occupants.

Her brows gathered in a frown, and a sense of inadequacy swept through her. It wasn't enough. There were too many damned questions and not enough answers. She drew her fingers through her short, fair hair. Was it always going to be like this? Was she always going to lack confidence in her ability to do the job?

She stiffened and reclaimed her professional persona, although she knew it often rubbed her officers up the wrong way. But it would be a mistake to allow the team to see her indecision so that professional front was imperative.

A glance at her watch indicated Colin, the crime scene manager, would arrive at any moment to take part in the team briefing.

A quick dash to the washroom along the corridor to splash cold water on her face revived her, although her hair looked a mess. She ran a comb through it before striding back to the team room. Now she was ready for anything they had to throw at her.

26

Bill stuffed the last bit of the bacon roll into his mouth before pushing open the door into the team room. A finger prodded him in the ribs. He spluttered and choked to clear the lump of bacon from the back of his throat. 'What the heck?' he said when he got his voice back.

'Serves you right, you greedy pig.' Sue pushed past him. 'Next time you're having a bacon butty bring one for me as well.'

Jenny looked up from her computer screen and flashed him a nervous smile.

Blair sniggered and leaned towards the next desk to whisper something to Sid. No doubt it was something uncomplimentary. They never missed an opportunity to undermine him with their snide comments and air of superiority, despite the fact they were both constables while he was a sergeant. With their university education they would be fast-tracked, and they knew it.

Some of these days, Bill thought, I'm going to wipe the smirk off the faces of those two twats. He unclenched his fists and ambled towards his desk determined to deny them the satisfaction of seeing he cared about their crude comments.

Crumbs from the bacon roll tickled the back of his throat and he made a show of studying the papers he'd removed from his in-tray while he coughed to remove them. He suppressed a second cough and replaced his handkerchief in his pocket when Kate emerged from her office accompanied by Colin.

She surveyed the room and her eyes rested momentarily on Bill. Her nose twitched, and he was sure she could smell the aroma of his recently devoured bacon roll.

'Briefing meeting,' she said. 'Now everyone is here we can get on with things.'

She strode between their desks to the display boards at the end of the room.

Sue beckoned to Bill, and they both perched on the end of the desk nearest to the boards. Jenny joined them, and Bill got up to pull a chair out for her.

'Don't hang around.' Kate glared at Blair and Sid, who were ostensibly tidying the papers on their desk.

They looked at one another and shrugged before sauntering over.

'Thank you for joining us, although I'm sure you would rather spend your Sunday somewhere else.' Her voice dripped with sarcasm. 'We can get on with the briefing meeting now.'

Without warning, she tossed a marker pen at Bill. 'You can do the board.'

Caught unawares Bill lunged to catch it, knocking his elbow on the edge of the desk.

'That'll teach you to stay awake,' Sue whispered.

'Colin Watson has agreed to brief us on the forensics situation.' Kate nodded towards the crime scene examiner, who looked more human without his white suit.

'Not sure how much I can add,' Colin said. 'There are no results back from the samples we took from the scene. We've removed the bedding and mattress for forensic testing as well as various other objects. Going by the indentation in the second pillow it is possible the victim had company in the bed. If there is any DNA evidence, we should be able to find it. The post-mortem should indicate whether there was sexual activity prior to her murder.'

He turned to Kate. 'Has the post-mortem taken place?'

'Not yet. I'll arrange for someone to attend as soon as we're notified.'

Bill was sure she looked at him. 'Great,' he thought, 'I always get the good jobs.'

'We have new software which allowed us to video the crime scene and I've briefed Jenny on how to access and use it.' Colin nodded towards the young constable. 'Once she has it up and running you can walk around the scene in virtual mode and focus on the areas of interest.'

A pink tinge coloured Jenny's cheeks and her eyes looked large behind her oversized spectacles. Bill wondered whether she needed the specs or if they were something to hide behind.

'I've supplied the full set of crime scene photographs to Detective Inspector Rawlings.' He nodded at Kate. 'As you can see by the ones posted on the board this was a vicious attack, but that is the remit of the pathologist. I'm sure he will provide full details. In the meantime, I'll try to hurry the forensic tests along, but I'm sure you know as well as I do some tests can't be hurried and we are at the mercy of the lab scientists now.'

He gathered up his folder of notes. 'If that is all, I'll be off. You know where to find me, Kate.'

'What about the drugs found at the scene?'

'They've gone to the lab for testing, but I'd lay bets they'll come back positive for heroin.'

Kate waited until the door closed behind Colin before turning back to address Jenny. 'Any luck finding CCTV footage in the area?'

'There was nothing in the way of domestic CCTV. Most of the houses in that area are tenement type properties and they don't usually have cameras. But there were some small shops nearby and I've acquired their footage. I'm checking it out.'

'What about Teasers?'

'The only people there were some cleaners, and they didn't know anything about CCTV; they said we'd have to check with Tony Palmer.'

Bill turned from writing on the board and snorted. 'Tony Palmer's not going to play ball with us. He'll demand we get a warrant.'

'Then we'll get a warrant,' Kate said.

She turned to Blair and Sid, who were lounging in their chairs with a look of boredom on their faces. 'The door knocking. Any results there?'

Blair shrugged his shoulders. 'Some of them complained about the racket the girls made when they came home, but other than that no one saw or heard anything.'

'There was that one old biddy at the end of the street,' Sid said. 'She told us of a car that parks in front of her window every night when the girls return. She says it usually only stays half an hour, but last night it was still there when she got up to go to the loo at four o'clock in the morning. It was gone when she looked again at eight.'

'Any description of the car?'

'No! The old biddy said she doesn't know one car from another, but she thought it was a dark colour although it being night, she wasn't sure.'

'Jenny, see if you can spot a car on the route the girls took to walk home from Teasers. If it's there more than one night, we might have a lead.'

'Yes, ma'am.' Jenny scribbled a note on the pad of paper in front of her.

'Sue, any joy from those boxes you removed from the flat?'

'Nothing of note. Her bills are in the name of Angel Golding, so we now have a surname for her. Probably, that's not her real name, but there's no sign of any other name. I'll run a social security and tax check and a DVLA one, although she doesn't appear to possess a car. You never know, though, she might have a driving licence.'

'Good work,' Kate said. 'Stick with it.'

She turned around to look at Bill who was adding the information to the board. 'I'll let you brief the team on our interviews yesterday.'

Bill laid the marker in the groove in front of the board. 'We didn't get much information from the other occupants of the flats in the building. They are all dancers, they all work at Teasers for Tony Palmer, and apart from Candace Morgan, they all claim not to have seen or heard anything last night. What came across is that Angel was disliked and two of the dancers were particularly vindictive. The reason they gave was that Tony favoured Angel and, although she was a recent addition to the dancing team, he gave her the top spot. I think it throws a light on Tony Palmer and we need to look more closely at him.'

He turned back to the board and wrote three names on it. He pointed to the first one. 'Flame. Her real name is Wilma Stewart. Her hatred of the victim was obvious, and she didn't bother to hide it. She might reveal more during further questioning.' He pointed to the second name. 'Ayisha Okeke, which is her real name. Again, no love lost for the victim. However, she told us she heard water gurgling in the pipes early in the morning, although she was uncertain of the time. This last dancer is more interesting. Candace Morgan, she's the only one who seems to have been friendly with the victim, although she claims not to know her by any other name than her stage name, Angel. Candace claims to have heard someone on the stairs in the early morning. She was vague about the time but thought it might have been about six o'clock because it was daylight. He left in a red, sporty car with a white stripe along the top. She only saw the top of his head so she couldn't identify him.'

'What does that leave us with?' Kate studied the board. 'One, the victim was killed during the early hours of Saturday morning. Two, the scene has been examined by forensics and exhibits were taken for testing. Three, evidence has been acquired from the victim's flat and this includes two packages of drugs, thought to be heroin. Four, residents living in the street and the occupants of the building have been interviewed. Five, evidence from the interviews suggests the victim was disliked by her work colleagues. Six, evidence of a parked car in the vicinity, but nothing conclusive from CCTV footage.'

Bill, busy updating the information with her summary, was the only one to hear her sigh. He kept his eyes fixed on the board. His boss wouldn't appreciate seeing the flicker of sympathy he was sure flickered over his face.

'Most of what we've gathered comes from witnesses with a connection to Teasers. Considering that was where the victim worked a visit could come up with something new.'

Kate wound the meeting up by allotting tasks for everyone. Sue, with the help of Blair and Sid, was to continue examining the paperwork obtained from the victim's flat and try to identify Angel through all official agencies. Jenny was to continue examining the CCTV footage and look for details of the car parked in the street. Bill was to attend the post-mortem and he, along with Sue, was to accompany Kate to Teasers.

Bill paused with the marker in his hand after he finished adding the tasks to the board. 'What about Tony Palmer? I'm sure he's up to his neck in this.'

'There is no evidence of that.'

'Maybe so, but there's no way he has clean hands. He's behind most of the criminal activity in Dundee.'

'I remember you told me that before, but you also said there has never been any evidence to convict him of anything.'

Bill's shoulders sagged. Kate was right, but that didn't mean things couldn't change and if there was anything out there to connect Tony with Angel's death, he determined to find it.

'I still think we should interview him.'

'We will, but we'll do it after we've gathered more information from our visit to Teasers. We don't want to go in blind.'

'That will give him time to prepare, and he's a slippery bugger.'

Kate's eyes narrowed. 'Do you have a better suggestion?'

Damn, he'd annoyed her again. He seemed to do that all the time without even trying.

'I reckon if we interview him today, we'll catch him on the hop.' Bill studied Kate's face, but her expression gave nothing away. 'I could go out with Sue and do it this morning.'

'You have a point but hold fire until I run it past the super. He wants to be kept informed.'

Despite not having a clear answer Bill added Tony's interview to the tasks on the board. He'd get something on the man if it killed him in the attempt.

'Thank you, everyone. I'll expect full reports of your progress before tomorrow's meeting.' Kate gathered up the files scattered on the desk and walked to her office. Hesitating in the doorway she looked around the room and said, 'Blair and Sid. You'll take your orders from Detective Sergeant

Rogers today.'

Bill smothered a grin. They wouldn't like that. They made it plain they didn't like taking orders from a female detective inspector. Having to take orders from a female sergeant would not go down well.

27

Kate stood in front of Superintendent Stephen Jolly's desk. She'd finished updating him on the case, ending with the need to interview Tony Palmer as soon as possible.

'I realise you will wish to talk to Mr Palmer at some point, but is it necessary to do it today? It's not as if he's a suspect.' He continued to study the report and the photographs spread on the desk in front of him.

'It is always best to interview at an early stage before memories fade or become confused, sir.'

'Very well, but we've had trouble before when accusations made were found to be unsubstantiated. I would prefer not to have a repeat of that situation.'

'Yes, sir.'

He looked up from the photographs he'd been studying. 'Unpleasant business. I suggest you have an informal chat with Mr Palmer and assure him you are doing your best to find the culprit. I am sure he will want the matter cleared up as soon as possible so that it doesn't affect him when he puts himself forward for election to the council.'

'The council?' Kate couldn't keep the surprise out of her voice. 'I thought he was behind quite a bit of the crime in Dundee.'

'Nonsense. Mr Palmer is an upstanding member of the community. Now, if that is all.'

Kate left the room with her head spinning in confusion. She'd been led to believe Tony Palmer was a man with his fingers in a lot of criminal pies. It didn't quite gel with the super's description.

But she had the impression she'd been warned off. Maybe it was the outcome of the previous investigation which was making the super extra careful. Or maybe they were both members of the funny handshake club. Whatever the reason, she would have to tread carefully.

Bill sneaked a glance at Kate when they drew up in front of Tony Palmer's house. She was too quiet. He'd known there was something up when she returned from her session with the super. Her body had been rigid, and her voice brooked no argument when she told him she would accompany him to Tony Palmer's residence in the afternoon.

'Would it not be better to bring him in?' he'd said.

'No. We treat him with kid gloves,' she snapped before stalking off to her office.

He turned off the engine and stepped out of the car.

Kate joined him on the pavement. 'Remember,' she said, 'kid gloves.'

Bill nodded. It wasn't the way he wanted to conduct the interview, and he wondered if she'd been warned off. Well, he hadn't been warned off and he was determined to pin Tony to the wall if necessary.

The man who opened the door to them was tall with the type of dark good looks which reminded Bill of that Giovanni guy from *Strictly Come Dancing*. Bill never let on to any of his friends, well colleagues really because he didn't have friends outside of work, that he was a *Strictly* fan. In another life he would have loved to dance on the programme, but he had two left feet, so that was never going to happen.

'Detective Inspector Rawlings.' Kate waved her warrant card in front of the man's face. 'And Detective Sergeant Murphy. We are here to talk to Tony Palmer.'

His eyes flicked over the card. 'I will check if Mr Palmer is available.'

'Best if you invite us in.' Bill stepped forward. 'And if Mr Palmer isn't available, we'll be happy to talk to Mrs Palmer.'

The man had no option but to take a step back as Bill advanced.

'Very well, you can wait in the lounge.' He ushered them along the hallway and into an opulent room.

Bill's feet sank into the deep pile carpet. Tony apparently hadn't followed the modern trend of replacing carpets with wooden flooring. And even Bill could identify a genuine Lowry painting on the wall. He didn't doubt all the other paintings were genuine as well. Tony had come a long way since their early days at Greenfield High School.

Tony had been several years older than Bill and he'd been one of the bullies. Even then he ran the school rackets and many a time Bill, along with a lot of other kids, had responded to Tony's demands for their dinner money and handed it over rather than risk a beating.

'This place stinks of money,' Kate said after the man left them on their own.

'Yes, and it isn't honestly earned money.'

Both remained standing until Tony entered the room. Despite the heat he was immaculately dressed in a suit and white shirt, and he exuded confidence.

He adjusted the cuffs of his shirt before saying, 'How can I help you?'

Bill allowed a smile to cross his face. Tony wouldn't be so confident by the time he'd finished with him.

28

Tony looked at Bill and Kate with a confidence he didn't feel. But it was important to keep up appearances. 'I understand you are Inspector Rawlings.'

Kate nodded.

'You must be Sergeant Murphy. I think we have met before.' He knew perfectly well who Bill was and resisted the temptation to say, 'clashed swords.'

'Why don't we make ourselves comfortable while we talk?' He gestured towards a sofa. 'I hate standing when I'm in company.' He sat in an armchair opposite them. 'Luigi will bring us some refreshments.' He snapped his fingers at Luigi who stood in the doorway. 'A drink perhaps? Or some iced lemonade? It's important to stay hydrated in this heat.'

'Nothing for me.'

Bill's voice was harsh, and Tony noted there was no mention of a thank you.

'That won't be necessary.' The inspector sounded more pleasant. 'Perhaps we should just get on with why we've come.'

Tony waved Luigi away, and the man left closing the door behind him.

'I think I can guess. The sad business of one of my dancers.'

'I don't think sad quite covers it.'

'No, it doesn't.' Tony stared at the man sitting in front of him. He was an obnoxious twat. The woman inspector seemed much more amenable.

A thought struck him. Was this a case of bad cop, good cop? He settled back in his chair and waited to see.

'My dancers are like family to me. The loss of one of them under such tragic circumstances is like losing a daughter all over again.'

'I can understand that,' Kate said. 'I understand you lost your own daughter earlier this year in equally tragic circumstances.'

Something that sounded suspiciously like a snort sounded from the cop sitting beside her, but when Tony looked at him, he turned it into a cough. However, there was no mistaking the disbelief and antagonism in the man's eyes.

'We are trying to track the victim's last movements, but I need to clarify her details first. There seems to be some confusion about her identity.' Kate nodded to Bill to take notes.

'Her identity?' Tony frowned. What on earth did they mean?

'Yes. We are trying to build a picture of who the victim was. So far, we are in possession of her stage name, Angel Golding. But we are interested in identifying her real name. We thought your employee records might help with that.'

Tony shook his head. 'I'm afraid I only keep employee records for my permanent staff. The rest are self-employed and that includes the dancers. I keep a list of their names, of course, and supply them with accommodation should they need it.'

'What about Angel's National Insurance number? Surely you have that information?'

'Angel was self-employed. She handled her own taxes and insurance.'

The inspector's eyes hardened. 'You are telling us you have nothing on file that would enable us to trace her through official sources?'

'I only ever knew her as Angel Golding, and I would never presume to press for more details than the girls are willing to give.'

'Formal identification of the body will be required. This task is usually done by a relative.'

Tony met the inspector's stare. She wasn't such a soft mark as he'd thought.

'I'm afraid I can't help you there. All I know is that she

came to me from a similar post in Edinburgh.'

'If you can provide the details we can check with her previous employer.'

'I'm afraid I didn't press her for those details.'

'But surely her references would provide that information.'

Tony smothered a laugh. His dancers wouldn't appreciate him digging into their backgrounds, and he wasn't that interested. The main thing was being able to do the job. It didn't matter a damn what or where they'd been before they came to him.

'I'm afraid we don't request references for a dancing job. An audition is sufficient for our purposes.'

The inspector looked disappointed, although he suspected Murphy wasn't surprised.

'Tell me about Angel. What was she like?'

'I didn't know her all that well. She was a dancer, my star attraction, and a lovely girl. I provided her with accommodation as I do with all my girls and, as far as I knew, she was happy working for me.'

'When did you last see her?'

'That would be the Friday night show.' Heat built up under his collar. How much should he tell them? How much did they already know?

'What time did she leave the club?'

Tony resisted the temptation to rub his sweaty palms on his trouser legs. He had to maintain a cool demeanour. It would be fatal to allow his emotions to show.

'She left early, about midnight.'

'Was there a reason?'

'There was a bit of unpleasantness in the club. One of the customers accosted her, and I got the impression she was frightened of him. I made sure she got home safely so he couldn't bother her again.'

'I see. This customer. Can you give us a name?'

'Jimmy Matthews. He's a small-time businessman from Glasgow who just happened to drop into the club with some of his colleagues.' Tony stressed the last word so the two cops would get the gist of what he meant. 'He had his bodyguard with him, a thug who goes by the name of Mad Dog. I don't think anyone knows his real name. I had him ejected from the club because he was frightening Angel.'

'We'll need to access the club's CCTV to check this out. You can give your permission, or we can get a warrant.'

Tony nodded his consent.

Murphy looked up from his notebook. 'You say you made sure she got home safely? How, exactly, did you do that?'

'I escorted her home to ensure she wasn't molested on the way.'

'It seems you were the last one to see her alive.'

'Apart from the killer.' He glared at the sergeant. 'I accompanied her upstairs to her flat and checked the rooms to ensure no one else was there and then I left.'

'We only have your word for that.'

Tony calmed his breathing. 'I assure you, Sergeant Murphy, that you don't have to take my word for it. My driver, Brian Crowe, will be able to vouch for the fact that I left and returned home.'

'After you've briefed him, no doubt.'

'Not at all, Sergeant Murphy. He is here today. I will instruct him to answer any question you care to ask him.'

'Luigi,' he muttered into his smartphone, 'will you be so kind as to fetch Brian? I think he may be in the garage.'

Muffled voices seeped into the room and moments later Brian entered. The oily smudge on his cheek and the blue coveralls were evidence of what he'd been doing.

'Ah, there you are, Brian. Inspector Rawlings and Sergeant Murphy have some questions for you. Tell them the truth and hold nothing back. I wouldn't want them to think we're hiding anything.'

'Yes, boss.' He looked around the room. 'I'd best not sit down, boss. Don't want to get oil on anything.' He shuffled his sock-clad feet.

'Now, if that is all, I must get back to my wife.' Tony stood and headed for the door closing it quietly behind him as he left.

He'd kept his cool. That was the main thing. But now, anger surged. That bloody cop had it in for him. He could tell from his tone and expression. It had only been the woman inspector's presence that had prevented things from getting nasty.

'I'll be in my office if anyone's looking for me,' he said to Luigi as he passed him in the hall.

'Mrs Palmer was asking why the police were here.'

Tony stopped in front of the connecting door leading to the annexe. 'Tell her I'll explain after they've gone.' He hesitated. 'Don't let the cops near her. I don't want her upset.'

He passed through the door. It closed behind him with a thump, the only indication that it was more secure than an ordinary wooden door. This was his territory where no one came without his express permission. The place where he conducted his business away from prying eyes.

The annexe wasn't large. A small corridor flanked by a meeting room, a study, and a storage room. The steel enforced door leading out to the lane running down the side of the house was hidden behind shrubbery.

Sweat pooled in his armpits and his collar felt as if it was strangling him. He slumped in the leather executive chair behind his desk and loosened his tie.

What the fuck was wrong with him? He'd never lost control like this before, not even when his daughter was murdered.

29

'What did you find out?'

Madge turned from the window where she was watching the departure of the man and the woman. She was sure they were police. It was stamped all over them.

This morning she'd felt more sluggish than usual, and the day had not started well.

Tony's attempts to converse with her over the breakfast table had failed. She wasn't in the mood. Then, after playing with her breakfast and eating nothing, she'd resisted Liz's suggestion to sit in the garden.

'I'm going back upstairs,' she'd said.

The banging of car doors shortly after had drawn her to the window, and she'd watched the man and woman arrive. A flicker of curiosity invaded her lethargy.

'Liz,' she said without turning from the window. 'Find out what these people want.'

She remained, staring out the window long after Liz left the room, although there was nothing to see except for the car parked outside the house.

Nowadays, time had this habit of standing still for her and she was never sure how much of it had elapsed. It could be a minute, an hour, or a whole day. Her life was an endless loop of slow motion. So, she had no clue how long Liz had been away. But her return coincided with the departure of the strangers.

'They were the police, Madge. They came to see Tony.'

Liz always referred to her as Madge, and she wasn't sure whether she liked it. The woman was an employee and a recent one at that. But Madge didn't have the energy to correct her and insist on a more respectful title.

Police raids and visits were all part of the nightclub

business. Madge knew that. But it was rare for the police to come to the house.

'What did they want?'

'It's something to do with the death of a showgirl who worked at Teasers. She was murdered.'

With an effort, Madge turned away from the window. Why did her limbs always feel weighed down with lead?

She stared at Liz. She couldn't recall anyone mentioning this, although she recalled some whispered conversations.

'When did this happen?'

'She was found yesterday morning. She'd been killed during the night.'

'Where?'

'At her home. In one of the flats Tony rents to his workers.'

Dread sent a shiver up Madge's spine. Her legs weakened under her and the fog in her brain thickened. Surely Tony had nothing to do with this dancer's murder. He had his faults, and she knew he could be violent, but he'd never mistreated a woman in his life. At least, as far as she knew.

Tony turned the police interview over in his mind. What was it about this one that led to his scary loss of control? They'd interviewed him many times before without it having this effect.

Was it because of the vicious way Angel had been killed?

Even when he woke up beside her body with no recollection of how he got there, he'd managed to retain his control and extricate himself from the situation. So why did he feel his life was disintegrating now?

None of it made sense.

It wasn't as if he hadn't seen dead bodies before. And although he didn't like to get his own hands dirty he'd been responsible for at least one of them.

His daughter's death had dictated he have a personal involvement in the despatch of her killer, and he didn't regret it. The bastard deserved all he got.

Murphy had been involved with the investigation and he

was sure the cop knew he had a hand in what happened to Denise's killer. Not being able to pin that on Tony, despite subjecting him to some aggressive questioning at the time, had irked Murphy.

The cop seemed to have made it his mission to see him convicted in court and clapped in prison. Him, Tony, banged up in prison with the rest of the riffraff. How ironic that Murphy might succeed this time. The only time he was innocent of the crime the cop was trying to pin on him.

A flicker of movement from the monitor on his desk drew his eye. He enlarged the computer window to show the front of the house. The police were leaving. While he watched, they stood on the kerb discussing something before getting in the car and driving away.

He heaved himself out of the chair and headed for the door. It was time to explain things to Madge. He wasn't looking forward to it.

'What do you think?' Kate clambered into the passenger seat and buckled her seat belt.

'I still think Tony's up to his grubby neck in it.' Bill turned the key and the car's engine rumbled into life.

'His driver corroborated the story that he came home after seeing Angel up to her flat. If the times are accurate, he wouldn't have had time to kill her.'

'He's not likely to contradict Tony's story. Brian Crowe has been with him for years and he's the nearest thing to a pal Tony has.'

Bill felt Kate's eyes on him. 'What?'

'Let's keep an open mind. Once we close it to other possibilities we'll get nowhere.'

Bill said nothing. It was Tony. He felt it in his bones, and there was no way he was going to let him off the hook.

'I think we need to investigate the fracas in the club. Find out who Jimmy Matthews is and why Angel seemed frightened of him.'

'We only have Tony's word for that.'

Kate sighed. 'Yes, but we still have to check it out.'

Bill shrugged and kept his eyes on the road. He'd been a detective in Dundee a damned sight longer than Kate who had come to the team from the Forfar office earlier in the year. What did she know about Dundee criminals? And Tony was up there with the worst of them.

Tony found Madge lying on her bed while Liz applied a cold cloth to her forehead.

'Leave us.'

'She knows,' Liz said before she left the room.

Once they were alone, he sat on the edge of Madge's bed and clasped her hand. He willed her to sit up and look at him, but she kept her eyes closed and didn't move.

'Oh, Madge.' His voice broke. 'What has happened to us?'

Still, she didn't look at him and her rejection felt like a kick in the stomach.

'I want you to know I had nothing to do with Angel's death, although I'm sure the police are keen to pin it on me.'

He wanted to tell her he loved her, that she was the only woman he had ever wanted. But he couldn't find the words. Instead, he leaned over and kissed her forehead. He would try to speak to her again later.

Luigi was waiting for him when he descended the stairs. 'A guy called Danny was on the phone, but I didn't want to disturb you. Says he's spent all night checking out what you wanted, and he's got the car's registration and the owner's details including an address. He's emailed it to you.'

A fizz of excitement rushed through Tony's body. At last, something to work on. He'd find out why this guy had been tailing the girls. What he wanted from them and whether he had killed Angel.

Get hold of Phil and Gus. Tell them to round up two guys. The tougher the better. And tell Brian we'll need the car.

The email was specific. The car owner's name was Denzil Rafferty, a private investigator, with a Glasgow address.

Tony smiled grimly but with satisfaction. By the time his

guys finished with Rafferty, he'd be glad to spill his guts and tell Tony everything he wanted to know.

Tony's kiss reminded Madge of the love she'd always had for him, even though she'd been dead inside for the past few months. That was what losing a daughter did to you.

She raised a hand to her forehead and smoothed her fingers over the spot where she'd felt his lips. It was as if he'd left a token conveying his regret for their loss and how things were between them now. In her grief, she tended to forget that Tony had lost his daughter as well, although he didn't show the same sorrow she did. Men in his line of business couldn't afford to show weakness, and she wasn't sure if that made their suffering better, or worse.

Guilt welled up inside her in a big choking lump. He'd said he wasn't responsible for the girl's death, but even if he was, she didn't care. It was up to her to support him, and she hadn't done that.

She pushed herself up and swung her legs out of the bed, but she'd moved too quickly, and her head swam.

Gritting her teeth, she stood. She had to speak to Tony, tell him it was all right, and that she understood.

'What on earth are you doing?' Liz burst into the room and hurried to her side. 'You're swaying all over the place. Sit, before you fall.'

'I need to speak to Tony.'

Madge resisted the hands trying to push her onto the bed.

'I'm afraid he's gone. Took out of the house as if the devil were after him.'

Madge frowned. Had her refusal to acknowledge him been the reason for his departure?

'Where?' She gulped back a tear. 'Where has he gone?'

'He didn't say. I thought you might know; that's why I came to check on you.'

A question forced its way into Madge's consciousness. Why would Liz be asking her where Tony had gone? What was it to do with her? But before it took root, the fog closed in again and she sank onto the bed. It was too late to speak to Tony now.

'That's better,' Liz said. 'I'll make you a hot drink and you can have a nap. I'm sure you'll feel better later.'

It took all Madge's strength for her to nod her head.

30

It was late in the evening by the time Brian drove into a run-down cul-de-sac lined with tatty shops and dilapidated buildings. He pulled up in front of the address they'd been given.

'Not the most salubrious of offices.' Tony took in the shopfront with the painted-over window that said, *Private Investigator*, and underneath in smaller writing: *Missing Persons, Matrimonial, Surveillance. No job too small.*

The second car drew up behind them and Phil wound down the window. 'What now, boss?'

Tony nodded to Gus sitting in the passenger seat.

'Who else did you bring with you?' He pointed to the darkened rear windows.

'Ian and Ken. Ken has brought his chainsaw with him.'

Tony grinned. Ken was an enforcer who doubled as his gardener; while Ian, an ex-wrestler was a huge man who could have been a Bond villain if he'd had steel teeth.

'Good choice. It's time we paid Mr Rafferty a visit.'

'Place looks deserted.'

'Ah! But if you look up you can see a light at one of the windows, and I do believe our Mr Rafferty lives on the premises.'

'That lock looks pretty flimsy to me.' Phil nodded to Ian. 'I'm sure your shoulder will make short work of it.'

The door opened onto a small reception area with a desk and telephone and not much else.

The inner office contained more. A much larger desk, executive chair, computer, and a couple of filing cabinets. At the rear of this room was a door with stairs beyond. These obviously led to the investigator's living quarters.

'You and Gus go through the filing cabinets and see if you

can find anything that relates to Angel,' Tony said. 'While you're at it, see if there's anything referring to me or Teasers. Ken, you guard the door while Brian and I introduce ourselves to Mr Rafferty.'

'What about me, boss? What you want me to do?'

'Ah, yes, Ian. You can provide backup to me and Brian.'

'Will do, boss.'

Brian led the way up the staircase behind the door, followed by Tony and Ian, while Phil turned his attention to forcing open the filing cabinets.

Tony laid a restraining hand on Brian's arm when the squeak of a floorboard alerted him to someone behind the upper door. He put a finger to his lips and waited.

Denzil Rafferty stared gloomily at the bottle of Jack Daniel's sitting in front of him on the kitchen table. He didn't really like the stuff, but it made him feel like a detective in an American crime novel. The kind of tough guy who had a blonde draped over one arm, a cigarette drooping from the corner of his mouth, and a gun in the drawer of his desk within easy reach of his hand.

He lived in the flat above his office. A grubby shopfront that advertised his services as a private investigator. His clients were the desperate and the unsavoury, not like the clients of the upmarket investigation firms in the city centre, and he didn't have a beautiful blonde receptionist.

When Kevin Matthews hired him to find his wife and keep watch on her, he'd thought it was his chance to climb the ladder to better things because everyone knew who Kevin's father was. Maybe Jimmy Matthews wasn't the most notorious criminal in Glasgow, but he was going places.

But the whole thing had been a disaster and Kevin was refusing to pay up because his wife was dead, and he blamed Denzil for not protecting her. And there was not a damned thing he could do about it. There was no way he could face up to any of Jimmy Matthews' bruisers if Kevin took it into his head to complain to his father.

His hand stopped midway in its stretch for the bottle when the crash of a door being kicked in echoed up the stairs from his office.

'What the fuck!'

He reached for the baseball bat propped up beside the sink. Maybe it wasn't a gun, but it was the next best thing. The kitchen door creaked when he eased it open and he stood for a moment, holding his breath. Tightening his grip on the handle of the bat he crept along the corridor to another door behind which was the stair leading down to his office.

His breathing quickened, and he listened for sounds of movement behind it. When he heard nothing, he unlocked the door, grasped the handle, and turned it, to be faced with a guy who looked as if he'd done several rounds in a boxing ring.

The man's hand shot out and gripped his wrist, squeezing until he dropped the bat.

'You'll not be needing that, sunshine,' the man growled.

Denzil froze. Although he was a tall, well-built man, he was a coward at heart. The man in front of him might not be Mad Dog, but he looked every bit as dangerous.

The man who stepped out from behind the bruiser was well dressed and looked every inch a respectable businessman. But Denzil recognised him immediately. What the fuck did Tony Palmer want with him?

'Perhaps you can show me where we can talk in private.' Palmer adjusted his cuffs, although they didn't need adjusting. 'Along here, is it?' He walked towards the open kitchen door. 'Bring our friend with you, Brian. I wouldn't want him to think we were ignoring him.'

Sweat beaded Denzil's brow and he could hear noises downstairs in his office. How many of them were there? Too many for him to tackle that was for sure.

He didn't need a second nudge on his back to follow Tony to the kitchen.

Tony halted on the threshold. 'This will do nicely. We don't want to get too comfortable, and a little extra mess won't make much difference to this room.'

The bruiser behind Denzil pushed him into a chair and

Tony took the one opposite him.

'I expect you're wondering why we've come all this way to see you.' The soothing conversational tone of Tony's voice remained constant, but the menace behind it was unmistakable. 'You see, it has come to my attention that you have been following my girls home recently and I wondered why that was.'

Denzil squirmed. He wasn't brave enough to hold out on this man, but he knew there might be repercussions from either Kevin or Jimmy Matthews.

'Tut, tut. Cat got your tongue?' Tony leaned on the table and smiled at Denzil. 'Brian here is a pussy cat despite his size. Aren't you, Brian?'

'Yes, boss,' the big man said.

'But Ian, now. He's a different kettle of fish. I worry about him because once he becomes aroused there's no stopping him. Even I wouldn't attempt to interfere.' Tony examined his fingernails. 'Perhaps you'd like to ask Ian to come in, Brian. I'm sure he's becoming bored kicking his heels in the corridor.'

The man who entered the room was even larger than Brian. If this man went head-to-head with Mad Dog, he wouldn't like to bet which one would come out the winner.

'Ian is calm just now, but I'm sure you don't want to annoy him by not telling me what I want to know.'

Nausea twisted in Denzil's gut and acid forced its way upwards, burning his throat. The two thugs towered over him while Tony sat, waiting for him to respond. From what he could see, he was damned if he did, and he was damned if he didn't. But Tony and his goons were here, and Jimmy Matthews wasn't. The wise thing to do was tell Tony what he wanted even if it meant he had to vanish afterwards to escape Jimmy Matthews' wrath.

Denzil Rafferty stared at the two thugs, and Tony thought it was like watching a rabbit mesmerised by a snake.

Tony knew about snakes. He'd kept pythons during his

teens. It was a status thing with the young toughs in the neighbourhood and he'd always ensured his pythons were larger than anyone else's.

But that had been a long time ago, and he no longer needed to impress anyone. He'd made his mark. Few people were stupid enough to come up against him, although nowadays he rarely got his own hands dirty and considered himself a legitimate businessman.

The silence in the room hung heavy and the man sitting opposite him looked ready to shit his pants. Sooner or later, he would talk through persuasion alone. Tony hoped it would be sooner, although he would have no compunction in allowing Ian to dispense with a harsher form of persuasion should Rafferty prove to be stubborn or less open than he required.

Tony leaned across the table and pushed the whisky bottle in Denzil's direction. 'You look as if you need a drink.'

His words broke the spell. Denzil grabbed the bottle and gulped, gagging as the whisky hit his throat.

'What do you want to know?' His voice, roughened by the whisky, was no more than a croak.

'I want to know about your interest in my dancers and why you were following them home after they finished work?'

'It was a job, that's all.'

Tony leaned forward. 'Do not try my patience, Mr Rafferty. Spell it out for me. What was your interest?'

'I was hired to watch one of the dancers, but I was instructed not to approach her. Just keep watch to see if she entertained any gentlemen and report back.' He took another gulp of whisky. 'But there was nothing to report back. Not until Saturday, that is.'

'And why would that be?'

'That was the night she took someone home with her.'

Muffled sounds drifted up from downstairs breaking the silence gathering in the room.

'Which dancer are we talking about?' Tony didn't need to ask. He could guess the answer.

'The blondie called Angel.'

'Ah!' Tony's mind raced. This man was a witness. 'You saw the man?'

Rafferty closed his eyes and nodded. He looked as if was going to be sick.

'How long did you stay watching?'

'Until the man left.' The agony in his voice was painful to listen to.

Tony's eyes never left Rafferty's face. 'And you could identify this man?'

'It was dark. I couldn't be sure.' Rafferty stared at his hands.

He was lying, but Tony didn't blame him. In Rafferty's situation he would have done the same.

'But you have photographs.'

'Yes.'

'I will need them plus all the copies and the memory card you used.'

'Of course.'

Tony stared at him. This man had been there the night of the murder. If he was there when Tony left, he must have seen the killer enter the building during the night.

'Tell me. Who else entered the building after Angel arrived home and before the man left?'

Agony crossed Rafferty's face. 'No one.'

'You're sure about that?' Tony frowned. It wasn't possible. Someone must have come in because he, sure as hell, didn't kill Angel.

'I'm sure.'

The only sound in the silent room was Rafferty's ragged breathing. For a moment Tony felt sorry for the man, but he shrugged the feeling away. He couldn't afford to be soft. There was too much at stake. Besides, there was more information he needed from this man.

'Your client's name?' His voice was rougher than he meant it to be.

Rafferty's eyes darted anxiously around the room as if afraid he'd be overheard.

'Kevin Matthews,' he whispered.

Tony remained silent for a moment before saying, 'Matthews? Would that be any relation to Jimmy Matthews?'

'His son.' Rafferty's nervousness increased.

'Interesting.' Tony mulled the information over in his mind. Angel had never once mentioned any connection with the Matthews' family. She must have known about their reputation.

'And why would Kevin Matthews be interested in Angel?'

'How should I know? I just do the job. I never ask for any more information than I'm given.'

'I see. I'll need to have a little chat with Kevin Matthews, and I will require you to arrange for him to come here.'

Rafferty's eyes widened and his voice rose several octaves. 'Is that absolutely necessary?' Fear shone from his eyes.

'I'm very much afraid it is.' Tony didn't need to make threats or shout. Every soft-spoken word he uttered contained menace. 'Now make the phone call and get Kevin Matthews here.'

'He won't come just because I ask him.' Rafferty wriggled in his seat.

'Be creative. Tell him you've seen something on the photos you took that should interest him.'

31

'So much for the Sabbath,' Kate muttered as she got out of the car in front of the nightclub.

'Dundee folk will party any night of the week,' Bill said. 'Sunday is no exception.'

Sue and Jenny joined them on the pavement.

'So it seems.' Kate rummaged in her handbag for her warrant card. 'Let's get on with it.'

She marched up to one of the doormen. 'Point me in the nightclub's direction.'

'Membership card?' He peered at her through narrowed eyes.

'I don't need one.' Kate rammed her warrant card in front of his face.

He took a step back. 'Is this a raid?'

'No, just a friendly visit, but we could make it a raid if you don't let us in.'

'I'll have to check.' He stepped inside the doorway to talk into his headset.

After a moment, he returned.

'Top of the stairs. Someone will be waiting to meet you.'

Kate ignored the hostility in his eyes and strode inside. That had been easier than she expected. Considering Tony Palmer's reputation, she had expected more resistance.

'Hang on a minute.' The doorman stretched a hand in front of Jenny. 'She's too young. It's more than my job's worth to let her in.'

Kate turned back and fixed the man with a steely eye. 'If she's old enough to be a police officer she's old enough to accompany us inside.'

The man's arm dropped. 'Just doing my job.'

'Come on,' Kate said to the three officers, before

continuing on her way.

Music infiltrated the vestibule which was larger than she expected. A door on the right opened, the noise increased, and she glimpsed bodies gyrating in the dim interior before it swung shut.

'That's the disco,' Bill said. 'It's popular with the university students. The nightclub is upstairs.'

'What's behind that door?' She nodded towards her left.

'Members' private bar. But it wouldn't surprise me if more goes on behind that door than we're led to believe.'

'You've been here before?'

'We've raided it in the past but not recently. We got warned off. Tony is in cahoots with some powerful people in Dundee.'

Kate wondered if Bill was hinting that the powerful people included some high-ranking police officers.

A woman waited for them at the top of the stairs. 'Marlene French, I'm the manager. I understand this isn't a raid so how can I help you?'

After the hostile reception at the entrance, Kate hadn't expected such a warm welcome. But she wasn't fooled. She knew the woman standing in front of her would be just as obstructive but in a more subtle way.

'I'm Detective Inspector Rawlings, and these are my colleagues. Detective Sergeant Murphy, Detective Sergeant Rogers, and Detective Constable Cartwright.'

Kate could have sworn a flicker of recognition passed over her face when Marlene glanced at Bill and Sue.

'Perhaps I could have a word with your employer, Mr Palmer. I would be happy to explain the reason for our visit to him.'

'I'm afraid that won't be possible. He isn't on the premises at the moment.'

'That's unusual.' Bill's voice sounded from behind Kate. 'I thought he made a point of always being here.'

'He's out of town on business. I don't expect him back tonight.' Marlene's tone hardened. 'I'm afraid I will have to do.'

'I see,' Kate said. 'As the manager, I expect you will know a great deal about the business.'

Marlene nodded, but her expression was wary.

'I do most of the business side, although Mr Palmer has oversight of everything.'

'In that case, I would appreciate your cooperation. To begin with, Constable Cartwright will require access to the CCTV files.'

'Mr Palmer's consent would be required for that. Our customers expect anonymity when they visit our premises.'

'As you are the manager, I would expect you to have the authority to do that. But it's not a problem. Mr Palmer agreed to give us access to the CCTV footage when we interviewed him this afternoon.' Kate's voice hardened. 'We could, of course, apply for a warrant, but it seems a mite unnecessary in the circumstances.'

Colour rose into Marlene's face, and she snapped her fingers at one of the security men behind her. 'Take this officer to the CCTV monitoring room and instruct Danny to provide her with everything she needs.'

'Yes, boss.' The man beckoned for Jenny to follow him back downstairs. She looked like a doll beside his large frame.

Kate waited until Marlene regained her composure. The woman's colour and tense posture had shown her displeasure at the demand for CCTV access. And Kate wasn't sure it was as simple as a reluctance to breach customers' confidentiality.

'Shall we?' Kate nodded towards the clubroom. 'And perhaps you can explain your role as manager.'

Marlene smoothed a strand of hair from her forehead and gestured for them to follow her. 'I suppose I'm a jack of all trades. As well as running the bar I'm responsible for maintaining stocks and ensuring the smooth running of Teasers. I also do most of the hiring and firing unless there is an issue which requires Mr Palmer's attention.' She led them up to the bar at the far end of the room. 'Perhaps I can persuade you to have a drink while we talk.' She raised her voice to be heard over the sound of music.

'Not while we're on duty,' Kate said with a sideways

glance at Bill. No doubt he would have accepted if she hadn't been with him. But Bill didn't appear to have noticed. He was too busy watching the dancer nearest the bar.

Kate recognised her. She was the bolshy one with the beaded hairdo. Their eyes met and a malicious smile twitched the dancer's mouth as she twirled and caressed the silvery pole.

'Your dancers,' Kate said. 'Are you responsible for hiring them as well?'

She saw Marlene's eyes narrow before she answered. 'Yes.'

'How do you go about that? Do you advertise or use an employment agency?' Kate was thinking about what Tony had said earlier in the day.

'It's word of mouth. The dancers come to us looking for work and whether we take them on depends on whether we have jobs available.'

'What about references?'

Marlene laughed. 'What would be the point? They can either dance or they can't, and we make our decision based on an interview and how they perform. Now, the security and door staff, that's different. We look for references for them. We can't have just anyone providing security for our customers.'

'Does that mean you have information on record for your security staff but not the dancers?'

'That's right.' Marlene leaned over the bar. 'Was there some specific information you were looking for?'

'The victim's name for a start.'

'That's easy, it's Angel Golding.'

'Not her stage name, her real name.'

Marlene shrugged. 'It's the only name we have for her.'

'Are you sure about that? We do need to know her name in order to trace any relatives she might have. There is also the problem of who can identify her.'

'Sorry, I'd like to help but I can't.' Marlene paused for a moment. 'The only person who might be able to help is Candace Morgan. She was close to Angel. But whether she

147

knows more than I do is hard to say.'

Kate remembered Candace. She was the girl they interviewed on Saturday morning. The one with the startling magenta hair. The one who'd seen the red car with the white-striped roof.

Kate surveyed the clubroom. Dancers performed on small circular stages scattered between the tables. Curtains shrouded a larger stage on the other side of the room. Music filtered through speakers placed discreetly along the walls.

Bill and Sue had taken up position at the other end of the bar talking to a girl who reminded Kate of a young Jodie Foster. Kate had been so engrossed with Marlene she'd lost track of what they were doing.

'Sue,' she said leaning towards her, 'I want you to question Candace Morgan. She knows more about our victim than she admitted to when we interviewed her on Saturday.'

'Yes, boss.' Sue turned to the girl behind the bar and said, 'Duty calls. I'll leave you to Bill's tender mercies, Kara. Anything you can tell him will be helpful.'

Kara returned the smile. 'I like her,' she said to Bill. 'But she'll be lucky if she gets anything out of Candace.'

'I would prefer it if you questioned the dancers when they are off duty.' Marlene's tone was no longer as friendly. 'Our customers pay to see them perform.'

'We need to find out who Angel is. Until we do, we can't identify her or inform her relatives of her death.'

Kate moved down the bar and addressed Kara. 'If there is anything you know that would help us, we'd be grateful.'

The girl replaced the glass she'd been polishing on a shelf behind her. 'I'm afraid I can't help you with that. I only knew her as Angel. But I do know she was worried. That's why I suggested she talked to you.' Kara looked at Bill. 'Did she see you?'

Bill looked uncomfortable. 'She came to the police station, but I was unable to see her right away and she left. I was going to chase her up the next day, but circumstances intervened.'

'Do you know what she was worried about?' Kate leaned closer to the girl.

Kara hesitated before replying. 'Not really.' She picked up another glass to polish. 'But there was something odd happening last week.'

'Odd?' Kate narrowed her eyes. 'In what way?'

'I don't know if it's relevant.' Kara laid the glass on the bar. 'But some of the dancers were saying they were being followed home after they finished.'

'All information is relevant.' Kate nodded to Bill to take notes.

'But nothing happened. He just followed them in his car. They treated it as a big joke, although they made sure they stayed together.'

'How long had this been going on?'

'Probably five days over the last week.'

'Anything else you can tell me?'

Kara shook her head. 'It was just gossip. Maybe an admirer who fancied one of them.'

Kate pulled her mobile from her pocket and tapped on one of her contacts. 'Jenny,' she said when the call was answered, 'I've received information some of the dancers complained they were being followed home over the past week. Check for that as well as the incident inside the club. See if you can get a description of the car and a number plate.'

'Did you know about this?' Kate confronted Marlene.

'Can't say I was aware of it. But the girls always have admirers, so I don't pay too much attention.' She moved away from Kate to pour a drink for a man who had sidled up to the bar.

'Haven't seen you here before?'

His breath was hot on the back of Kate's neck, and she turned to glare at him. 'Back off unless you want to be arrested.'

Marlene cast her eyes upwards and sighed. 'You lot aren't good for business. D'you think you'll be here much longer?'

'There was something else I wanted to check out. Is there somewhere more private we can go?' The constant thump of music vibrating through Kate's head was making it ache.

'Through here.' Marlene gestured to a door behind the bar.

Kate followed, beckoning Bill to accompany her.

The room, obviously a storeroom for the bar, was small and filled with crates of bottles and cans.

Marlene perched on the top of a crate. 'What was it you wanted to know?'

'Mr Palmer informed us there was an incident that involved Angel in the clubroom on Friday night.'

Marlene shrugged, although her eyes had narrowed, and Kate reckoned she was trying to decide how much to tell them.

'There's no reason not to tell us,' Kate said. 'We'll be able to check out what happened on the CCTV, but I'd like your take on it.'

'It wasn't anything out of the usual. It was simply a customer requesting her to sit at his table.'

'I understand there were several men at the table and they forced Angel to sit with them. Is that something that often happens?'

Marlene squirmed. 'Admittedly one of them was heavy-handed, but we had security remove him.'

'But not the others.'

'No.'

'I will require to speak with the security men involved.'

'It was Phil and Gus, but I'm afraid they're not here tonight. They're with Mr Palmer.'

Bill, who had been lounging against a crate, spoke up. 'That's interesting. What is so important that Tony needs to take Phil and Gus with him?'

'How would I know?' Marlene glared at him.

'We will need to speak to them when they return. Back to the night in question. What happened after this man was removed?'

'Phil took Angel to the dressing room and then kept a watch on the men remaining at the table.'

'I see. And Angel, what happened to her after the incident?'

'I don't know because I was busy at the bar. She probably went home with the others.'

Marlene was lying. Kate was sure of it, but she left the

matter there. She'd get back to Marlene after they'd viewed the CCTV footage.

'Now, if that's all, I have work to do.' Without waiting for an answer Marlene flounced out the door.

Kate and Bill followed her to find Sue perched on a stool at the bar chatting to Kara.

'I got some more info from Candace, but she's still not telling us everything,' Sue said. 'It turns out she was closer to Angel than she previously admitted.'

'In the absence of anyone closer, we need to arrange for her to identify the body. We'll follow that up tomorrow.'

An hour later, Jenny joined them in the clubroom. 'Danny was helpful, and it didn't take as long as I thought it would. He seemed to know exactly what I wanted. He's downloaded the footage onto memory sticks.'

'Good work. I don't think there's much more we can do here. But we need to go over what each of us has gleaned from this visit before I hold the team meeting, and this is not the time or place to do it. So, I want you all in the office at eight o'clock tomorrow.' Kate looked at her watch. 'Or should I say today?'

32

'Kevin's at the casino and says he's on a winning streak. Says he'll come when he's good and ready.'

'You're sure he suspected nothing and that he'll come?'

'Yes, he said I wasn't to go anywhere until he got here.'

Tony smiled. The ploy had worked. Kevin would be anxious to see what the photos revealed although not anxious enough to come immediately.

'We'll wait for him in the office.'

Ian went first, and Brian followed pushing Rafferty in front of him, as they all encamped to the downstairs office. Tony sauntered down behind them. He didn't expect Kevin Matthews to talk as quickly as Rafferty had. But he would talk. Ian and Ken would make sure of that.

'It might be a long wait,' Tony said. 'We'd best tie Mr Rafferty to a chair in case he gets any ideas. After that,' he nodded at Ian, Ken, and Brian, 'I want you three to wait in the car outside and keep out of sight. Once Kevin Matthews arrives alert me and follow him in. If he brings anyone with him, you'll need to take care of them. Phil and Gus will stay here with me.'

'Yes, boss.'

Brian finished trussing Rafferty to the chair and the three of them left.

Phil fished a mirror out of his pocket, peered into it, and smoothed his hair. Satisfied with his appearance he sauntered to the open inner door and sat on the bottom step of the stairs. He gestured for Gus to join him.

The two of them were like matching shop dummies with their tailored suits and bottle-blond hair. But Tony knew their looks were deceiving and that it would be hard to find a more vicious pair.

'You didn't need to tie me up,' Rafferty complained. 'I was doing what you wanted.'

'I must admit you have been most obliging, but I really couldn't take the chance you might forewarn Kevin Matthews. Besides, if he sees you tied to that chair, he'll realise you were acting under duress.'

'Damned lot of difference that'll make with Kevin. He's a vicious bastard. He'll still take it out on me.'

'I can't wait to meet Kevin,' Tony said, 'and then we'll see just how much of a vicious bastard he is after my guys have finished with him.'

'I'm calling it a night.' Kevin pushed his chair back and stretched. He slid a chip over the table to the dealer and gathered up his winnings.

The dealer nodded his thanks while continuing to deal the next hand, and apart from a grunt from the man in the seat next to him no one else seemed to be interested. Not that Kevin cared. He never cared what people thought of him or what they got up to unless it affected him.

He sauntered to the cashier's cage to cash in his chips. Lady Luck had smiled on him tonight and he'd won most hands at the poker table. Once he started losing, he knew it was time to stop. He prided himself on not being one of the losers who kept playing until they lost everything they'd won.

As he pocketed his winnings, he wondered what Denzil had spotted in the photographs he hadn't noticed before. It must be something important or the man wouldn't have phoned him. He'd best check it out. But first, a spot of breakfast wouldn't go amiss. The casino served some of the best food in Glasgow.

After he finished eating and drained his second cup of coffee, he collected his car from the casino's multi-storey car park and drove out onto the street. Traffic was light, and he slammed his foot on the accelerator enjoying the roar as he gunned the engine. Cops were thin on the ground this early in the morning, although he would relish a car chase if any of them spotted him. It never seemed to happen in Glasgow, though.

If he crashed the car, so what, he'd just buy another one. He barrelled through several sets of red traffic lights, but his luck held, although he suspected the guy who'd skidded to a halt and mounted the pavement at the last set wasn't thinking the same.

His heart thumped as he raced to the corner of Denzil's street and screeched around it, wrenching the steering wheel back before he hit the building on the opposite side of the road. He whooped with delight convinced he was the best driver in the world. He should have taken up racing.

Braking sharply in front of Denzil's office he leapt out of the car and strode to the door. It was ajar. Denzil thought of everything. He'd left it open so Kevin could walk straight in.

The reception area was empty, but a light shone through the frosted glass of the top half of the inner door.

'What is it you've found?' Kevin said as he pushed the door open.

He stopped short. The man facing him, sitting in the chair behind the desk, wasn't Denzil. He narrowed his eyes. It was that bastard, Tony bloody Palmer, sitting there like he owned the place. Denzil was over in the room's corner tied to a chair with parcel tape stuck over his mouth. Another two men moved from the corner of the room to stand in front of the desk.

Denzil's eyes moved back and forth in a mute plea for Kevin to help him. But Kevin wasn't in the helping business, so he could whistle for any help from him.

'Bastard.' He reached into his pocket for the folding knife he always carried.

Before he could flick it open a gravelly voice behind him said, 'I wouldn't do that, sunshine. It wouldn't be good for your health.'

A hand gripped his wrist in an iron hold forcing him to drop the knife.

One of the men smiled and leaned towards him. 'Naughty, naughty. I wonder what else you have in your pockets?'

Kevin glared at him as exploring hands emptied his pocket contents onto the desktop, but he was helpless to do anything about it because whoever was behind him now had both his arms in a steely grip.

'D'you know who I am?' He risked a look behind him and wished he hadn't, for the man holding him was bigger than Mad Dog.

The man shrugged and ignored him.

'What you want me to do with him, boss?'

'I think we should go upstairs. I wouldn't want you to make a mess of Mr Rafferty's office. Use the kitchen. It will be easier for Mr Rafferty to clean up afterwards.'

'Move.' The man prodded Kevin in the back.

Kevin moved. His mind raced as they climbed the stairs. What the fuck did Tony Palmer want with him? They'd never crossed paths before, although Kevin knew who he was. He'd made it his business after the bastard killed his wife. The woman Tony knew as Angel.

Once they were in the kitchen the man who had continued to prod him until his ribs ached pushed him into a chair.

Another bruiser lounged in the doorway. Meanwhile, the smartly dressed one who had followed them smirked as he leaned against the sink.

'That's better.' Tony perched on the edge of the kitchen table and looked down at Kevin.

'What d'you want with me?'

'Just a friendly chat, that's all.'

'I don't know you and you don't know me. Why should we chat?'

'Why indeed?'

Tony fished in his pocket and brought out a pack of cigarettes. He shook two from the pack and tossed one of them to Kevin.

'You see, Kevin, I understand you have some information that would help me understand why one of my dancers was killed.'

'You killed her. What's to understand?'

'Why would you think that?'

'Because I've seen the photos which prove you were the only one with her that night.'

'Ah yes, Mr Rafferty's photos. They only prove what you want them to prove.'

'I saw her body. I saw what you did to her. You're a sadistic bastard, Tony Palmer.'

'You were there?'

A flicker of something crossed Tony's face, and Kevin didn't like what he saw.

'I was there after you left. That's why I know you killed her.'

Kevin glared his defiance at Tony. The man's calmness and self-control made him nervous. It was worse than being threatened.

'One thing I don't understand.' Tony's voice was silky. 'Why were you there at all? What was your interest in Angel?'

'I was there to take her home. Angel, as you call her, was my wife and her place was with me.'

'Ah, that explains some of it.' Tony tapped the ash from the end of his cigarette into a cup sitting on the table.

'And does your wife have a name apart from Angel?'

'She's Lesley. She's always been Lesley Matthews; despite the various names she's used since leaving me.'

The image of Lesley lying in that bed covered in blood arose in Kevin's mind. He could see her and smell the blood. And the bastard who killed her was sitting across the table from him as if nothing had happened. His anger increased, and he forgot the bruiser and the other men in the room watching everything with their beady eyes.

'I see. And is she the reason your father frequented my club on the night she was killed?'

Tony's question sparked his rage. 'That's your game, is it? Try to pin the blame on my father. You won't get off with that. He's going to wipe you out. Take your club and your fancy house. He's already got someone in there pandering to your slut of a wife. Just you wait. If he gives the word, your wife is toast, the same as mine.'

At the end of his tirade, he caught his breath aghast at what he'd revealed. He'd let anger get the better of him, and in striking out at Tony he'd betrayed his father. He should never have revealed there was a plant in Tony's house and that Jimmy Matthews meant to use Tony's wife to enable him to take over his business in Dundee.

Tony's expression changed and the pretty boy moved nearer to him.

'What do you mean? He's got someone in my house,' Tony roared. 'Who?' He stood and leaned over the table until he was nose to nose with Kevin. His eyes flared and his face tightened. Menace charged the air.

Kevin shrank back from him. 'Wouldn't you like to know?' The bravado of his words wasn't reflected in his voice.

'I'm sure Phil will manage to persuade you otherwise. You'll like him, even though he's a vicious bastard.'

Tony stalked to the door. 'Get the name out of him. I'll wait downstairs until he squeals.'

33

Tony's stomach churned and his head was so full of cotton wool he struggled to think straight. His feet clattered on the stairs, and he burst through the door to the downstairs office with an expression on his face capable of striking fear into the hardiest of men.

'What do you know about Jimmy Matthews planting someone at my house?' He glared at Denzil Rafferty.

The man wriggled in his chair uttering unintelligible noises and shaking his head.

Tony ripped the parcel tape gag from Rafferty's mouth eliciting a sharp scream from him.

'Well?'

'I know nothing about that.' He rubbed his face. 'I've told you everything I know.'

He turned anguished eyes towards Tony. 'Jimmy Matthews is going to kill me. At least untie me before you leave and give me a chance.'

Tony nodded to Gus. 'Cut the bugger free, but make sure he stays here. We don't want him alerting anyone.'

'Don't get any ideas,' Gus said as he sliced the ropes. He nodded towards the outer reception area. 'You'd never get past Ken and he's a dab hand with that chainsaw.' He raised his voice and shouted, 'Isn't that right, Ken?'

The grunted reply was indistinguishable, but it was enough to send a flash of terror across Rafferty's face.

Denzil rubbed his wrists. 'What are you doing to him?' He glanced nervously at the stairs.

'You don't want to know. But he'll talk sooner or later, and I'd prefer it to be sooner.'

Tony leaned his elbows on the desk while he inspected what they had extracted from Kevin's pockets.

'Bugger carries a lot of cash.'

'That'll be his winnings.' Denzil's eyes glittered as he looked at the wad of notes. 'Said he was at the casino when I phoned him. He's always been a lucky bastard.'

'Not so lucky now.'

Alongside the money, car keys, a wallet, a couple of tissues, some loose sweets, and several packets of white powder littered the desktop.

Stirring the packets with his finger, Tony said, 'Cocaine, you think? Or heroin?'

'If it's heroin it's the pure stuff. But I suppose he can afford the best and he has connections.'

Tony jabbed the car keys and beckoned Gus over. 'That stuff may come in handy. Check the bugger's car. If he has his works there we might give him a little trip as a reward when he squeals.'

Gus grabbed the keys and headed out the door.

'I've known Kevin a long time, and he's tougher than he looks,' Denzil said. 'You reckon he'll squeal?'

'I don't doubt it. The question is, how long will it take? But Phil has honed his skills over the years, and he can be quite persuasive.'

Tony smiled mirthlessly, but the wait was getting to him, and his mind was in turmoil.

He couldn't rid himself of his fears for Madge. Unable to settle he rose from the chair and paced, stopping frequently at the bottom of the stairs to listen.

His frown deepened. This was no time for his head to be filled with thoughts which spun and twisted, tormenting him. He needed to think. From what Kevin had blurted out he knew Madge was in danger, and he was here in Glasgow too far away to be of any help to her. If anything happened to Madge, he'd never forgive himself.

Denzil Rafferty studied Tony. The man was a conundrum. If it had been Jimmy Matthews here in his place Denzil knew he wouldn't have got off so lightly, and it was possible he'd have met a grisly end.

Sure, he'd been tied to a chair, but Tony hadn't been vicious about it. He wasn't too sure about the others, though. Tony claimed the one called Phil would soon make Kevin talk. Denzil blocked that from his mind. He didn't want to know.

A frown marred the dark good looks of Tony's face, and he seemed deep in thought staring into space. But he seemed more thoughtful than angry, so Denzil chanced his arm.

'If I'm going on the run, I'll need to collect a few things.' He hesitated. 'But everything I need is upstairs.'

Tony shifted his gaze to Denzil. After a moment, he said, 'Okay, but make it quick.' He turned to the other man in the room. 'Go with him, Gus. Keep an eye on him and don't let him near the kitchen.'

The kitchen was the last place Denzil wanted to go. He didn't want to see what Phil was doing to Kevin.

Denzil didn't even look at the kitchen door as he passed it but continued to the bedroom where he hefted a suitcase from under the bed. Conscious of Gus watching, he threw clothes into the case before reaching into the rear of the wardrobe and opening his safe. Grabbing documents, papers, money, and his passport, he threw the lot on top of the clothes. His laptop was sitting on top of the bedside table, and he thrust it into the case before closing the lid and snapping it shut.

He left his car keys where they were. Once he left, he didn't want to be traced.

'Got all you need?' Tony asked when he returned.

Denzil nodded. What he'd taken would have to do. It would be enough for him to start afresh.

Tony narrowed his eyes and contemplated the suitcase. After a moment, he looked up and said, 'Give the case to Ken and tell him to put it into the boot of the car. You'll need to help the boys with the clean up once the job's done.'

A chill ran down Denzil's spine, his stomach clenched, and bile rose into his throat. It wasn't over yet.

The thud of feet on the stairs heralded the return of Phil. He looked as immaculate as he always did without a blond hair out of place.

'Well,' Tony snapped.

'Didn't take much to make him squeal,' Phil said. 'The plant is Liz Stewart, that woman you employed to look out for Madge.'

'Bitch.' Anger suffused Tony's face. 'I took her on because Madge's doctor recommended her. I'll be having words with him.'

'What now, boss?'

'I'm leaving for Dundee. Gus and Brian can come with me. The rest of you can tidy up here and follow on when you're done.'

'What about him?' Phil nodded towards Denzil.

'Use him to help with the clean-up, but after it's done dump him at a railway station.' Tony turned to Denzil. 'If I were you, I'd get as far away from Glasgow as you can. Kevin's money will help you on your way.'

He turned back to Phil. 'I don't want any complications.'

Tony noticed the worried look on Denzil's face as he grabbed the wad of notes and stuffed them in his pocket.

'Just do what they say and, as long you don't return to Glasgow, you'll be all right.'

A few minutes later Tony's car joined the early morning traffic, but it wasn't travelling fast enough for him, and he was restless and couldn't settle.

Worry gnawed at him. His body tensed and his stomach churned. He was too far away. How much damage could Liz do before he got to Dundee? He considered phoning Madge, but there was no point in doing that. She wasn't strong enough to stand up to Liz. The other option was Luigi, but once the man was aware of Liz's connection to Jimmy Matthews, he might go ape shit. The last thing Tony needed was another body. But he had to do something.

He rummaged in his pocket for his mobile and tapped Marlene's number. Her voice was sleepy when she answered, and he knew he'd woken her. Quickly, he told her what had happened and stressed his concerns for Madge.

'Don't worry,' Marlene said. 'I'll go to the house and take care of it. I won't let Liz harm her.'

Tony leaned back in his seat and focused on the heads of Brian and Gus in the front seat of the car. 'Hurry,' he said, 'drive faster.'

Denzil Rafferty paused to regain his breath. It hadn't been an easy job strapping Kevin's body into the driver's seat, particularly when he was terrified the car would plunge into the quarry before he was ready. But it was done, and now all he had to do was press the accelerator, slam the door shut and stand back.

'It will be easy, and they'll never find the bugger in there,' Phil had said when he'd told Denzil how to do it. 'The water in that quarry is bottomless.'

But after it was done Denzil was in a cold sweat. He'd nearly gone over with the damned car.

The splash as it hit the water echoed in Denzil's head and added speed to his feet as he fled from the edge of the quarry and across the field. What the hell had he become involved in? He should have scarpered when he had the chance. But they would have found him, and he had no doubts he would be lying at the bottom of the quarry along with Kevin.

'Job done,' he wheezed when he reached the car waiting for him at the side of the road.

He slid into the back seat and sat for a moment regaining his breath. 'What now?'

The car lurched into life with a shudder making him reach for the seat belt. Ken wasn't the smoothest of drivers, and gear changes seemed to be beyond him. Driving at speed on the motorway was his forte, but these country lanes tested his driving ability.

Phil, sitting in the front passenger seat turned to look at Denzil, but before he could reply the car screeched around a bend on the wrong side of the road. Denzil, who was still buckling his seat belt was thrown forward, which was just as well because Ian sitting next to him was flung sideways, and he didn't fancy being squashed between the big guy and the car door.

Ian adjusted his position and Denzil straightened. He'd banged his nose on the back of Phil's seat and it hurt, but he wasn't going to complain.

Phil smoothed his blond hair and smiled at Denzil. It wasn't a pleasant smile.

'You did a good job,' he said. 'But you need to remember you're in just as deep as we are, so it would be a mistake to talk to anyone. And, of course, Jimmy Matthews will not be an option. Not when you've sent his son to a watery grave.'

Denzil tried to maintain a brave face. It wouldn't do to show these monsters he was afraid. But his insides were in meltdown, and he hoped Phil couldn't hear his stomach churning.

'We'll drop you at a station as Tony instructed and I suggest you board a long-distance train and hide where no one will find you.'

An hour later, when the car drew up at the entrance to Edinburgh Waverley Station, Denzil grabbed his suitcase and sped inside without a backward glance.

He had to get away. Away from Tony, Jimmy, the police, and anyone else who might come looking for him.

34

Monday later

Madge lay awake watching the room get brighter. For months now she'd woken early when dawn broke and night turned into day.

Months ago, her doctor had said it was an effect of the grief she felt over the loss of her daughter. 'It will pass,' he'd said. 'Time heals, you just have to be patient. I'll prescribe a short course of antidepressants until you get over the worst.'

But nothing changed, and when the pills stopped helping Liz had increased the dosage.

Worried Tony would disapprove of her growing dependency on the medication she'd tried to cut back hoping to stop altogether. But each time she'd suffered excruciating aches and pains, and Liz always came to the rescue telling her she needed to continue taking the pills.

This morning her mind was sluggish and her body a dead weight pinned to the mattress. The sound of the door opening pierced her consciousness and alerted her to someone else in the room. With an effort, she turned her head. Liz stood in the doorway. Something in the woman's eyes unsettled Madge, although her brain was too befuddled to let the momentary concern take root. The two women looked at each other for a moment before Liz smiled and the confusion in Madge's mind slid away.

'You're awake.'

Madge struggled to push herself up on her elbows. 'I always wake before it's light. I never seem to sleep longer.' It was an effort to push the words out. 'But you're up early. Or is it later than I think?'

'Doctor Davidson prescribed something new for you to try,' Liz said. 'But it needs to be an injection. I thought I'd do it before I brought your early morning tea and toast.'

Liz walked across the room, syringe at the ready.

Madge shrank back. 'But I hate needles. My doctor knows that.'

'It's for your own good.' She approached the bed. 'One quick jab. You won't feel it and then all your troubles will be over.'

The eight o'clock news had just started on the car radio when Marlene skidded to a halt in front of Tony's house. She was out of breath when she reached the front door and banged on it. Her hair was uncombed, and she'd thrown on the first clothes that came to hand. She looked a fright, and she knew it.

Luigi took one look at Marlene and tried to bar her from entering, but he was no match for her.

'Get out of my way.' She stamped inside and shouted, 'Madge, where are you?'

Bet, her hands white with flour, poked her head out of the kitchen door. 'Is that you Marlene? I hardly recognised you.'

Marlene tried not to let her irritation show. 'Of course, it's me. Who else would it be?'

'Oh well, if it's Madge you're looking for she'll be in her bedroom upstairs. She won't be up yet, but she always wakes early. That Liz will be with her.' Bet snorted. 'She'd be a damn sight better off without that interfering busybody. I don't know what possessed Tony to hire her.'

'Thanks,' Marlene said.

She took the stairs two at a time and burst into Madge's bedroom. One look was all she needed before she launched herself at the woman standing over Madge with a syringe in her hand. The syringe flew across the room bouncing off the wall and rolling into a corner.

'What the fuck do you think you're doing?' She grasped the woman's hair and forced her head back.

'My job,' Liz Stewart gasped. 'Giving Mrs Palmer her medication.'

'Does your job include supplying drugs and turning Mrs Palmer into a zombie? You do realise the supply of drugs is against the law, don't you?'

'That is a slanderous statement. Mr Palmer was concerned about his wife's mental health and employed me to help her recover.' She gasped as Marlene wrenched her head further back.

'That's a load of crap.' Marlene twisted the woman's hair between her fingers and tugged.

'You have no right to attack me. I'm the one responsible for Mrs Palmer's welfare, not you, and she is not to be upset.'

Marlene thrust her face closer to the woman until they were nose to nose. 'Is that a fact? Well, Liz Stewart or whatever you call yourself, I've talked to Tony, and he knows all about you and Jimmy Matthews. He knows why you're here and what you're up to. But you're not getting off with harming Madge any more than you've done already. I'll make sure of that.'

'You're mistaken. I have harmed no one. I've only been doing the job Mr Palmer hired me for.'

'Really?' Marlene thrust the woman in front of her and strode into the adjoining bathroom. She released her hold on the woman's hair and wrenched open the door of the medicine cupboard. 'And is this the way you do it?' She pulled boxes and bottles of pills from the shelves. 'By doping her to the eyeballs. No wonder she can't function.'

'I was only doing my job.'

'I don't see any indication that these are prescribed medications. Who is doing the prescribing? You?'

'Mr Palmer agreed his wife needed help.'

'I'm sure he did but knowing Tony's aversion to anything addictive, I'm equally sure he didn't realise how far you were taking it.' Marlene screwed the lids off various bottles and poured the contents down the toilet.

'You can't do that!' Liz made a grab for the bottles.

'Can't I? Just try to stop me.'

The woman's head struck the wall when Marlene pushed her away with a vicious slam to her midriff. She overbalanced and slid to the floor, clutching her stomach. 'You'll pay for this,' she gasped, forcing the words out between bared teeth.

Marlene ignored her while she finished flushing the pills.

Returning to the bedroom she found Luigi kneeling in front of Madge holding her hands.

He looked up. 'Mrs Palmer said I wasn't to interfere.'

'It's that damned Liz. She's been feeding Madge with all sorts of pills. I'd lay bets Tony didn't know what she's been doing.'

'Why would she do that?' Luigi frowned.

'Because she's a spy for Jimmy Matthews. Tony's on his way and this isn't finished yet.'

Luigi's face contorted into a scowl, and he strode to the bathroom door.

Liz grabbed his arm. 'Leave her to me. Don't touch her. She's quite capable of screaming rape.'

For a moment Marlene thought Luigi was going to ignore her, but he unclenched his fists and returned to Madge's side.

Liz, who had eased herself into a sitting position with her back pressed between the toilet bowl and the bidet, relaxed. The expression of fear left her face to be replaced with a contemptuous look directed at Marlene.

'You think you're clever, but once Jimmy finds out how you've treated me it'll be payback time.'

'What makes you think you're going to be in a position to tell him?'

Marlene watched with amusement as Liz attempted to stand. 'I wouldn't do that if I were you, not unless you want me to hit you again. On the other hand, I could let Luigi loose on you. I'm sure he has a very good reason to hate Jimmy Matthews.'

The two women glared at each other, but Liz remained seated on the floor.

'Don't you move a muscle, or you'll regret it.' Marlene strode to the phone on the bedside table.

'This is the Palmer residence. I wish to speak to Dr Davidson.' The answering voice sent her blood pressure soaring. 'I don't give a damn that the surgery isn't open yet.

This is an emergency and I need to speak to him now.'

'Damned woman told me to dial 999 and hung up on me,' she said to Luigi.

She redialled the number. 'Do not hang up on me again. My call concerns your husband's reputation. This situation has arisen because of his negligence.'

There was silence at the other end of the phone.

'Dr Davidson recommended a woman to care for my employer's wife, and this woman has been feeding her drugs and trying to poison her. She needs urgent care, and I'm sure your husband would prefer to treat her rather than having to explain why one of his patients died because of his actions.' Marlene's voice was terse and brooked no argument.

'Yes, I'll wait.' Marlene drummed her fingers on the bedside table while she continued to listen.

A few moments later the phone crackled in her ear. 'It's Madge Palmer, doctor. She's in a bad way due to all the drugs you've been supplying.' She paused to listen. 'If you're not prescribing the drugs then who is? That damn nurse you recommended Tony hire has been feeding her pills like sweeties. I suggest you get here pronto for Madge's sake. We need to get this sorted out.' She slammed the phone down. 'The doctor's on his way.'

She returned to the bathroom door and eyed the woman sitting on the floor with contemptuous eyes. 'I don't fancy being in your shoes when Tony finds out what you've been doing.'

35

Tony collided with wee Morag, the maid, as he barged into the house.

'They're all upstairs,' she gasped as she recovered her balance.

He ran upstairs, taking them two at a time, and was out of breath by the time he pushed into the bedroom.

His eyes took in the scene in front of him. Madge, lying on the bed. Dr Davidson examining her. Luigi standing guard at the open bathroom door. Marlene, hovering behind the doctor with an anxious look on her face.

Marlene looked up and crossed the room to meet him.

'Liz is in the bathroom, and I've got Luigi making sure she doesn't leave. I was tempted to throw her out bag and baggage, but I was sure you'd want to speak to her.'

Tony nodded. 'Has she harmed Madge?'

'Depends on what you call harm.' Dr Davidson straightened up and replaced his stethoscope in the bag at his feet. 'I would say she's become dependent on her medication and within an hour or two she'll go into withdrawals.'

Tony's mind whirled. He knew Madge hadn't been herself and that she'd been subdued and lacked energy. But drug addiction? How on earth had he not seen that? Maybe if he'd spent more time at home instead of burying himself in the business to cope with his own grief, he might have noticed. All those days and nights at the club instead of being here where Madge needed him. How could he have been so blind?

'You prescribed the pills.' Tony rounded on the doctor.

Davidson held up his hands. 'I prescribed a short course of antidepressants to help Madge deal with her grief. They were never intended to continue this length of time and no further prescriptions were issued when the course was completed.'

169

'Who then?'

'I can answer that,' Marlene said. 'It was that woman in there, Liz Stewart,' she nodded in the bathroom's direction. 'She's been feeding Madge a mixture of pills. I've flushed them all down the toilet, but the containers are over there.' She pointed to the dressing table.

The doctor shot a disgusted look at the woman crouched in the bathroom before saying, 'I've had a look at the labels, Madge has been taking quite a combination of pills and stopping them suddenly could have a disastrous effect. I think it would be safest to wean her off them under medical supervision.'

'Not hospital,' Tony said. 'That's too public.'

He paced the room. Once Jimmy Matthews found out about Kevin, he'd be out for revenge. Nobody was safe here, least of all Madge. Tony was confident he'd be able to take care of himself, but he couldn't risk any more harm being done to his wife. Madge needed somewhere safe to go where Matthews wouldn't find her and where she would get the help she needed.

'Find somewhere private. I don't care what it costs.'

He knelt beside the bed and grasped Madge's hand. 'I'm sorry. I should have noticed what was happening, but we're going to get it sorted.'

He bit his lip. Her face was pale without makeup, her hair lank and uncombed, and her blouse buttoned up wrongly. It saddened him to see her like this.

Tears filled Madge's eyes. 'I'm a disappointment to you.'

'Never.' Tony gripped her hand tighter, but when she winced, he loosened his grasp. 'Once your medication is sorted out, you'll be fine again, and we can get our lives back to what we were before.' He didn't continue, but both knew he meant before Denise died.

A smile trembled at the corner of Madge's mouth, and he could have sworn there was a flicker of relief in her eyes.

'I've arranged a bed for her in a private clinic not too far away.'

Anger surged in Tony again when he heard the doctor's

voice.

'We hired Liz Stewart on your recommendation.' Tony stood and glared at him with accusing eyes.

'I certainly recommended Liz Stewart to you. A very dependable woman,' Davidson said. 'But that woman in there is not Liz Stewart. I don't know who she is. But I'll be contacting the real Liz Stewart to find out what happened.'

As quickly as it had arisen Tony's anger with the doctor subsided. It wasn't Davidson's fault. He'd been taken in the same way Tony had. It was that damned woman, Liz, or whatever her name was. A spy in his house, planted by Jimmy Matthews.

Something would have to be done about her, but he'd never harmed a woman in his life, and spy or not he had no intention of starting now. But neither could he let her get off with the harm she'd done to Madge.

He strode to the bathroom door and considered her for a moment.

'Jimmy will make you pay for this.' Her voice and eyes were defiant daring him to hurt her.

The smile that twitched the corner of his mouth held no humour. 'Matthews made a big mistake when he planted you in my house with the intention of harming my wife. He would be well advised to remain in his own territory. There is nothing for him here.' He turned his back on her.

It went against everything he believed in, but he lifted the phone and dialled. It was time to call in a favour.

36

Kate was five minutes late. She arrived at the team room to find Bill, Sue, and Jenny already there. Sue was examining her in-tray, while Bill lolled in his chair with his feet on an adjacent one. He looked as if he was on the point of going to sleep. Jenny was the only one who seemed to have an excess of energy. She had her computer fired up and her eyes gleamed behind her large-framed glasses.

'You're on the teas and coffees,' Kate said to Bill before she dumped her bag and belongings in her office.

She could have sworn she heard him moan. But that might have been tiredness rather than resentment at having to be the tea person.

'Okay, what do we have?' She drew a chair up to Jenny's desk and beckoned Sue and Bill to join her.

Jenny adjusted her spectacles and consulted her notes. 'I've obtained copies of the relevant footage. The episode where our victim was accosted by some customers gives a clear view of all those concerned. I've also managed to get a reasonable image of the car stalking the dancers. The number plate is unclear, but I might be able to enhance the images.'

'Good work, Jenny. Once you get a number plate pass the information to Blair and Sid. Get them to track it down.'

'What about you, Sue? I think you said last night that Candace had been a bit more forthcoming.'

Sue consulted her notebook. 'After some coaxing Candace told me she and Angel had come to Dundee at the same time. They'd both worked in Edinburgh for a club owner called Georgio Modena but they left.' Sue looked up. 'I got the impression it was in a hurry. She was evasive about this, but I gathered there had been some violence during a takeover bid and their boss was hurt. I pressed her on how well she knew

Angel and whether she ever worked under another name, but she claimed they'd only met in Edinburgh, and she didn't know anything else.' Sue closed her notebook. 'I think she knows more than she's telling us, though.'

'I think you may be right. Bring her in to identify the body. She'll probably resist but lean on her if necessary. If she is a lot closer to our victim than she wants us to think that may be a way to get under her skin. Then we can see where we go from there.'

A waft of air from behind her made Kate turn around. In the doorway, resplendent in full uniform, stood Superintendent Jolly. Kate wondered if he knew it made him look like an officious prick.

He beckoned to her and strode towards her office at the end of the room.

'Sorry, folks,' Kate said with an apologetic lift of her eyebrows. 'It seems that duty calls.'

Bill didn't need to ask. Kate was in a foul mood.

'We'll take your car,' Kate said as they walked towards the parking area behind police headquarters.

'Where to?' He inserted the key into the car's ignition. But he couldn't help wondering why she preferred his clapped-out Ford gas guzzler to her own brand-new Toyota hybrid model. Maybe she mistrusted her reactions behind the wheel, given her state of mind.

'Tony Palmer's residence.' She stared straight ahead. 'Apparently, he has a problem that needs to be fixed. And we're the fixers.'

It was clear to Bill this job left a bitter taste in her mouth.

He drove in silence for a time, but curiosity got the better of him.

'What have we been tasked with?'

She sighed. 'According to the super, we must drop everything we're doing to investigate an attempt on Mrs Palmer's life. Uniforms are waiting for us at the house to facilitate the arrest.'

Bill's hands tightened on the steering wheel. Madge Palmer had been in his class at school, although she'd been Madge Wilson then and he'd had a crush on her. She'd never given him two looks, though. Her tastes were for older teenage boys, and it was no surprise when she hooked up with Tony Palmer.

'Tony's tried to kill his wife?' Bill had trouble speaking. His insides were doing strange things and his breath seemed stuck in his chest. He forced himself to exhale.

'No, not Tony. He called it in. Said it was one of his staff, some sort of nursing assistant or companion to his wife. He's claiming it's linked to a takeover bid of his business by a Glasgow gang.'

'I suppose the super has a point. But it would have made more sense if the attempt had been on Tony's life, not Madge's. Did he give you any details?' Bill's forehead creased with a frown. Why Madge? Why not Tony?

'No! That's the point. All he said was that Palmer phoned and demanded something be done. I did try to say we would interview the woman concerned after the uniforms brought her in, but he wasn't having that. He got quite stroppy and ordered us to attend to it right away.' She remained silent for a moment before continuing. 'Seems to me that Palmer just needs to snap his fingers, and he gets special attention.'

Bill could tell by the look on her face she was seething.

When they drew up behind the police van sitting outside Tony's house, she jabbed the seat belt button and the belt pinged back with a clatter. 'Better get it over and done with,' she muttered through her teeth as she rammed the car door open and stepped outside.

One of the uniforms leaning against the van straightened. 'We were told to do nothing until you arrived and to wait for your instructions, ma'am.'

Tony paced the room. He was losing control. His mind whirled with the effort to sort his thoughts out and make sense of everything that was going on.

He had no regrets over the tactics he'd used to make Kevin Matthews talk. If he hadn't found out what Jimmy Matthews was up to, he could have lost Madge. And all because of this bloody feud that Jimmy had instigated. It was a damned good job he'd found out in time. But it wasn't over yet, and he didn't know what was in the syringe Marlene had wrestled from Liz Stewart. Thank goodness he had rescued Madge in the nick of time. He could only hope that lasting damage hadn't been done and she would recover and be her old self again.

Afraid his anger at Liz would upset his wife he nodded to Marlene to attend to her. He'd never felt so lost before, nor so helpless. All he felt able to do was watch and hope for the best. Tears pricked the back of his eyelids and he blinked hard to stop them from rolling down his face.

Madge lay on top of the covers staring out the window with blank eyes, oblivious to everyone in the room. She roused when Marlene grasped her hand, and the ghost of a smile hovered on her lips when she turned to look at her friend. She propped herself up and swung her legs over the edge of the bed. 'Long time, no see, stranger,' she murmured in a voice lacking energy. 'What brings you here?'

'Tony was worried about you and asked me to come.'

'He worries too much.'

Marlene undid the buttons on Madge's blouse and refastened them. 'That's better. Can't have you going to the clinic without looking your best.'

Tony clenched and unclenched his hands as he recommenced his pacing. He'd expected the police before now. What was keeping them?

He strode to the window and glared out. A police van was parked at the kerb, but the cops inside didn't seem to be in a hurry to get out. As he watched, a car drew up behind it, and the inspector, the attractive one, got out followed by Bill Murphy. His eyes narrowed. He could handle the woman cop, but he wasn't so sure about Murphy. That bugger was just itching to bang him up, and he didn't need much of an excuse. This time, though, Murphy wasn't here to put the screws on him. He was here at Tony's own request, and Tony would make sure he knew it.

'The police are here.' He glared down at the figures standing in the driveway. Were they going to stand there rabbiting to each other forever?

Marlene stopped brushing Madge's hair. 'Not before time. Will I pop downstairs and let them in?'

Tony pushed his annoyance aside and nodded his assent. It wouldn't do Madge any good if he lost his temper.

37

The door to the house opened before Kate stopped speaking to the two officers.

Marlene strode down the steps towards them. 'Tony is waiting for you upstairs.'

Kate sensed an underlying impatience in the woman's voice. It struck a different chord from how she'd presented last night when she was business-like and in control. Did this reflect Palmer's state of mind?

'I believe Mr Palmer lodged a complaint this morning.' Kate suppressed her earlier annoyance at being summoned and kept her voice even and professional.

'That is correct. If you follow me, Mr Palmer will explain everything.'

Marlene was waiting for them at the top of the wide staircase. She led the way along the landing until she reached a door behind which they could hear movement.

'Tony is waiting for you inside.'

Kate stepped forward, but a movement at her rear alerted her to one of the uniformed officers pushing forward to enter the room. She held out an arm to block his way.

'Stay here until I call you.'

The taller of the two looked down at her. 'With respect, ma'am, we were ordered to bring the suspect in for questioning.' His resentment at having to take orders from a woman was obvious as he towered over her. She suspected that was a deliberate action meant to intimidate.

She stiffened. 'I suggest unless you want to be on the sharp end of a false arrest charge you would be advised to wait until I question the witnesses.'

His eyes flickered, and he looked away from her steely gaze. 'Yes, ma'am.'

Satisfied she had put him in his place, Kate turned away. But underneath her calm exterior, she seethed. Bloody Jolly. He might have ordered her to investigate Palmer's complaint, but she was damned if she would charge someone without investigating first. After all, she was the one on the firing line if it all went wrong, not him.

Marlene stood in front of her holding a door open.

Aware of the dynamic between Bill and Palmer, Kate said, 'I'll do the questioning and you take the notes.' This was not the time for these two men to spark off each other.

Her first impression when she entered the bedroom was one of chaos.

Tony paced back and forth with a frown on his face. A bedraggled looking woman sat on a chair beside the unmade bed, while a man, well past middle age, leaned over her with his fingers on her wrist. Kate guessed he must be the doctor.

Marlene joined a dark-haired man, standing with arms folded in front of a door through which she glimpsed a bath and shower cubicle.

Palmer stopped pacing, but his frown remained. Kate sensed he wanted to upbraid her but was holding himself back.

'I believe you wish to file a complaint against an employee?'

'That's putting it mildly.' Tony's scowl deepened. 'She put my wife's life in danger. I want her arrested. You'll find her in there.' He pointed to the door where Luigi and Marlene stood guard.

'On what grounds?'

'I told you. She endangered my wife's life by administering her drugs.'

'You have evidence of this?'

'All the evidence I need.' Tony looked ready to explode.

'The evidence you need may not be sufficient for a court. Perhaps you'd better start at the beginning and explain what has been happening so I can decide.'

Tony slumped onto the end of the bed, although the rigidity of his body betrayed the tenseness within him.

'I suppose it must have started when we employed that

woman in there.' He nodded towards the bathroom door. 'My wife was grief-stricken after the death of our daughter, and Dr Davidson suggested we employed Liz Stewart who had previously been his practice nurse. I agreed because it seemed the best thing to do at the time and the woman arrived two days later.' He looked up. 'How was I to know she was an imposter? I don't know how she managed to take the real Liz Stewart's place, but she did.'

Tony continued to talk, explaining his wife's gradual slide into depression, which he realised now was due to the drugs Liz had been administering to her. He paused often while he related events, although he did not go into details about how he discovered Jimmy Matthews had planted her in his house.

'Now, are you going to arrest her?' His eyes narrowed and his expression became threatening.

Kate could see how he'd acquired his reputation as a hard man, but if he thought he could intimidate her, he was mistaken.

'It could be argued that Mrs Palmer took the medication voluntarily. I need a lot more evidence than that.'

An angry red blush rose from Tony's neck into his face as he struggled to compose himself.

Marlene grabbed his arm before turning to face Kate. 'When I entered the room this morning Liz was attempting to inject something into Madge's arm and from what I could see, she was resisting.'

'And the syringe. Where is it?'

Marlene pointed to a corner of the bedroom on the other side of the bed. 'I knocked it out of her hand, and it landed up there. I thought it best not to touch it.'

'Good thinking.' Kate turned to Bill. 'D'you have gloves and an evidence bag?'

'Yes, but it's a needle and I don't have one of those tubes to put it in.'

'I'm sure we could rustle up a plastic container,' Marlene said.

Kate nodded her acceptance of the suggestion.

'But first, I want to check with Mrs Palmer whether she

was consenting to the injection.'

Madge hadn't moved from the chair since they'd entered the room.

Kate knelt beside her, noticing the drooping shoulders and the listlessness of her body. 'How are you feeling?' she asked, wondering how responsive the woman would be to her questions.

Madge turned to look at her with expressionless eyes.

'I wanted to ask you about your medication. How do you take it and who gives it to you?'

'Liz sees to all that.'

'What kind of medication is it?'

'Pills. The doctor prescribed antidepressants after Denise,' her voice faltered, 'died.'

'Did he say how long you would need to take the pills?'

'Only for a short time until I felt better.'

'And do you know how long you've been taking them?'

Madge paused and Kate could see she was struggling to think.

'I'm not sure. Time seems to stand still, and I have difficulty knowing what day it is.'

'What about injections? Have you ever needed those?'

'My doctor knows I don't like injections.'

'But have you ever had an injection to help you cope?'

Madge shook her head, although it seemed to be an effort for her.

'This morning when Marlene arrived. Liz was preparing to give you an injection. Did you say she could do it?'

'I told her I didn't want it, but she said it would be for my own good.'

'Thank you, Madge. You've been very helpful.' She stood and turned to face Tony. 'I'll need to take the rest of her medication for analysis. We may not have sufficient evidence for an assault charge, but we might be able to detain her for supplying drugs to Madge.'

'I'm afraid I flushed most of the pills down the toilet.' Marlene looked uncomfortable. 'There are some boxes left with blister packs in them.'

Kate narrowed her eyes and glared at Marlene. 'That was clever.'

'I didn't think. I was furious and didn't want her doping Madge any more than she'd already done.' Marlene's shoulders drooped. Her hard professional image slipped, and she looked more vulnerable.

'It's more than likely she'll have a stash in her own room of whatever it is she's been feeding Madge.' Bill's voice broke the tension between the two women.

A look of relief passed over Marlene's face. 'I'll pop downstairs for that container.'

Kate watched the woman go, then turned to answer Bill.

'Of course,' she said. Pity she hadn't thought of that first, but she'd never admit that to Bill, although she supposed he guessed. 'It will be up to the fiscal to decide whether there's enough evidence to charge the suspect, but we can detain her for questioning and see where we go from there.'

'Not before time,' Tony said. 'There is also the question of her taking the job under false pretences and that could only have been with the intention of harming Madge.'

'And the evidence for that?'

'Dr Davidson confirmed to me that the woman I employed to care for Madge was not Liz Stewart.'

Kate turned to the doctor. 'You can confirm this?'

Davidson bristled, and his expression showed his annoyance. 'That woman in there,' he pointed to the bathroom, 'is not Liz Stewart. I have never seen her before. The person I recommended is a motherly person who is completely reliable. Liz worked for me before she took early retirement and would have been an ideal companion for Mrs Palmer.' His voice broke. 'I don't know how this could have happened, but I will be contacting Liz to find out how that woman managed to impersonate her.'

'What about the medication you prescribed?'

The man stiffened even more. 'I prescribed a short course of Prozac which I did not visualise continuing after six weeks. It was the reason I recommended Tony employ Liz to monitor the medication to ensure it did not become problematic.

Prozac is not considered to be addictive and would not have left Madge in the state she is in now. Goodness only knows what that woman has been feeding her.'

'Have you ever prescribed intravenous medication?'

'Certainly not.'

'Make sure you provide your full name and contact details to my sergeant. I'll need you to make a statement to that effect.'

'Is this necessary? I've already told you everything.'

'As far as the court is concerned, without an official statement, what you've told me would come under the heading of hearsay.' Kate adopted her most official voice. In her experience, doctors were a problem when it came to court evidence. It wasn't the first time she'd had to fend off objections to attendances at police stations to provide statements and subsequent court appearances.

Davidson grunted but supplied Bill with the details.

'If you're finished with me now, I'll need to check with the clinic and make the final arrangements for Madge's admission. She's waited long enough, and it's not beneficial for her health.'

Kate nodded her assent.

'You can phone from downstairs,' Tony said. 'It's less cramped.' He opened the door and led the way out of the bedroom.

Following Tony to the door, Kate said, 'I will need to search the suspect's room and maintain access to this room until my investigation is complete. Please make sure your staff are aware.'

After the others left, the room was less crowded. Kate felt more able to breathe and think without Tony standing over her and demanding she must arrest Liz Stewart. It felt as though a lot of the tension had gone out of the room with his departure.

Madge, in the meantime, seemed to have shrunk back into her chair as she stared into space, which made Kate wonder about the woman's relationship with her husband. Was she always this docile? Tony evidently cared about her, otherwise he wouldn't be so angry about her treatment. But was it a domineering relationship? Was Madge a woman who needed to escape from an overbearing husband?

These were all questions to which she didn't have answers.

Apart from all that, she wasn't even sure what to charge Liz Stewart with or whether she had sufficient grounds to detain her. Damn, what a bleeding mess. Was she losing her grip?

She should have insisted on doing the investigation in a controlled setting like the police station. But Superintendent Jolly had insisted she conduct it here. What was it about him and Tony Palmer?

She pushed the thoughts out of her mind and braced herself to question the suspect. It couldn't be any more chaotic than what had already gone before.

Bill shuffled his feet, and she sensed his impatience.

'Right,' she said. 'Let's talk to the suspect and see what she's got to say for herself.'

Did she imagine it? Or did Bill just let out a puff of air that showed he was thinking, at last?

Inside the bathroom, the woman sat between the toilet bowl and the bidet with her arms hugging her knees. Defiance was written all over her face and her eyes gleamed darkly through a strand of hair that had flopped over it.

'I'm Inspector Rawlings,' Kate said. 'I have some questions to ask you.'

The woman pushed the strand of hair away from her face revealing the beginnings of a bruise on her cheek.

'I want that woman charged with assault.' Liz glared at Marlene, who was now standing in the doorway.

Kate hadn't heard her return.

'And I want the rest of them charged with false imprisonment.' Liz waved her arm in the direction of the other room. 'What right do they have to keep me here against my will?'

Kate ignored her outburst. 'You can start by giving me your name and your home address.'

'Liz Stewart. And I live here on the premises.' She swayed slightly as she pulled herself up to a standing position.

'I mean your real name and where you come from.'

'I've given you my name.'

'According to the doctor who recommended Liz Stewart for this job you are not that person.'

Liz glared at Kate but did not answer.

'The pills you've been supplying to Mrs Palmer. What can you tell me about them?'

'All I ever did was provide her with the medication prescribed by her doctor.'

'According to the doctor that medication should have ceased several months ago.'

'You've only got his word for that.'

'Are you saying the doctor lied to me? Why would he do that?'

'You tell me. I only ever gave Mrs Palmer the medication she wanted. I never forced her to take the pills.'

'And the injection you attempted to give her? What about that?'

'I'm saying no more without my lawyer present.'

The woman's attitude was getting up Kate's nose, and she knew nothing was to be gained by continuing.

'In that case, we'll continue the questioning at the station. Ask the officers to come in, Bill?'

'Are you charging me?' The woman's eyes narrowed.

'Not at the moment, but I am arresting you in order to continue our enquiries.'

'On what grounds?'

'Common Assault.'

'I assaulted no one. I was the one assaulted.'

'You attempted to assault Mrs Palmer by administering drugs with a syringe. Under Scots Law, that is sufficient justification to arrest you. I could also add the possession and supply of drugs, and I am sure we can think of several other reasons as well.'

'You can't do that.'

In response, Kate read the woman her rights and cautioned her before nodding to the two officers to take her away.

'I'll be contacting my solicitor.' Liz's voice was strident, but she left with the two constables, although Kate heard her protesting all the way down the stairs.

Kate leaned against the bathroom wall and inhaled deeply. This blasted investigation was a mess, and she wanted to compose herself before going back into the bedroom. Bill glanced at her with curiosity in his eyes, but she avoided his gaze. She had no intention of letting him know how out of control she was, although he probably guessed. Damned man was too astute for his own good.

'Let's get this tied up. I'll check out the bathroom cabinets. You can bag the pill bottles and packets and anything else you can find.'

'Yes, boss,' Bill said.

'After that, we need to search the suspect's room once we find someone to show us where it is.'

The sooner they finished up here, the better. She couldn't wait to get back to the station. This house was stifling her.

38

Guilt consumed Tony as he helped Madge down the stairs. She seemed frail.

He knew he'd turned in on himself after Denise's death. He'd concentrated on work as the solution and buried himself in it to the extent he'd ignored what was happening at home.

'I'm sorry, Madge,' he said when they reached the bottom of the stairs. 'I'll try to do better in the future, but I need to stay here to keep my eye on things until the police leave.'

He drew her into an embrace. 'It's all right. Marlene will go with you, and I'll come as soon as the police leave.'

Dr Davidson was waiting for them at the front door. 'I noticed Madge shaking. We need to get her to the clinic so they can monitor her condition.'

Marlene joined them in the vestibule. 'D'you want me to accompany Madge?'

'If you would. And stay with her until I get there.'

Tony clenched his fists, digging his fingernails into his palms to prevent himself from crying out as Marlene helped Madge into the car. It should have been him. He was the one who should be accompanying her. And in another life, he would have. But he was Tony Palmer and there was too much to lose if he took his eye off the ball. He couldn't risk having the police snooping when he wasn't there. So, he stood on the doorstep until the car was out of sight and then turned back into the house and up the stairs.

Luigi met him on the landing. 'The police have questioned Liz, but she isn't talking. They are taking her to the police station to question her further.'

Tony nodded and stepped forward to enter the bedroom, but the door opened before his hand reached the doorknob.

'Please stand aside, sirs.' The uniformed officer's voice

was polite but firm.

Liz Stewart raised her head and glared at Tony as they ushered her out.

'Jimmy won't take kindly to this and as soon as he sends his lawyers, I'll be out. The charge won't stick. They've got nothing.' Her voice faded as they hustled her down the stairs.

He frowned, knowing only too well what a good lawyer could do, and he supposed Jimmy Matthews could afford the best. But she didn't deserve to get off with the harm she'd done to Madge. Still frowning, he pushed through the door into the bedroom.

Bill Murphy looked up from where he was bagging the empty pill bottles and packets. 'Thought you'd gone.' He thrust some more packets into evidence bags.

'Sorry to disappoint you, but I thought you might need my help.'

Bill snorted.

Kate emerged from the bathroom.

'Well?' Tony said.

'I'm afraid we got nothing out of the suspect, although we've detained her for further questioning.'

'Have you got enough to charge her with?' Tony's voice was gruff as he tried to keep his anxiety at bay.

'That's not up to me to decide.'

'If not you, then who?'

'The procurator fiscal, of course. She decides whether there is enough evidence for court. But at the moment, I'm not sure we have.'

'If you find drugs in her room will that be sufficient?'

'It will help. But it depends on what drugs we find. If they're illegal drugs, we could be home and dry. Not so sure if it's the kind of medication that's legal.'

'Better get on with the search, then. Her room is just along the corridor.'

'Do you know where to go?' Marlene asked, raising her voice so the driver would hear her.

Brian glanced at her in the rear-view mirror. 'Yes. The doctor gave me instructions. Says he'll meet us there.'

'Why do I have to go to the hospital?' Madge struggled to think her way out of the sludge in her brain. She wanted to protest, to argue, to say she refused to go, but the effort was too much.

Marlene reached for Madge's hand. 'It's not a hospital,' she said. 'It's a private clinic. Tony is worried you've become dependent on your medication which is why he's booked you in. He says Dr Davidson has assured him the treatment there is the best money can buy. The clinic staff will be there to monitor your treatment and to make sure you don't come to harm.' Marlene drew a breath. 'Tony just wants the best for you. Surely you can see that?'

There was silence for a time while Madge struggled to make sense of what Marlene was saying. Was she dependent on the pills she'd been taking? Did that mean she was an addict? The one thing Tony detested was addicts and their addictions.

There had been so much going on today she found it difficult to think. It wasn't like Tony to allow the police into his house. And why had everyone gathered in her bedroom? The number of people had been so overwhelming she'd shut off. Perhaps she should have paid more attention. Was this all a ploy to get rid of her? No, Tony wouldn't do that. Or would he?

She shook her head to clear her mind of the thoughts and doubts creeping in. 'I could get treatment at home. Tony could get someone in to help me.'

'He doesn't want to risk someone else trying to harm you. That's the reason he wants you to get your treatment in the clinic.' Marlene paused and seemed to think. 'There is another reason.' She tightened her grip on Madge's hand. 'Tony is in trouble. A lot of trouble. Do you remember what happened to Luigi's uncle Georgio?'

Madge struggled to remember. Of course, Luigi. She'd forgotten he came to live with them.

'I think so.'

188

'The gang responsible for putting Georgio in a wheelchair is now trying to take over Tony's club. There might be a lot of violence and Tony wanted you in a safe place where they can't get at you.'

'Why would they want to do that?'

'Don't you see? They've already tried. They planted Liz in your house so she could harm you.'

Madge stared at her with disbelief shining in her eyes. She didn't believe a word of it. Marlene always stuck up for Tony and would lie through her teeth for him if necessary.

They had left the town behind, and she stared out of the car window at the passing scenery. She'd been conscious for a long time that things were no longer the same between her and Tony. They'd grown apart. After Denise died, Tony spent more and more of his time out of the house. And she'd withdrawn into the haze of her medication. But had he always been at his club like he claimed, or was he spending time with one of his tarts?

A surge of anger chased the apathy from her brain. 'He wants to be rid of me!' She gasped for breath. 'He's going to bring one of his fancy women to the house to take my place. I'm not having it, and you can tell him from me he needn't bother visiting. I'll go to his bloody clinic, and I'll get clean, but that's as far as it goes.'

She clamped her lips shut and turned her face away from Marlene.

'You've got it wrong. Tony just wants to keep you safe while you recover.'

Marlene's voice faded into the background as her words washed over Madge. She continued to stare out at the countryside while all her doubts about Tony's motive for sending her away niggled in her mind.

'I'm glad that's over.' Kate subsided in the passenger seat while Bill put the car into gear and drove off.

Bill held his tongue. Kate had been in a foul mood all morning. Probably something to do with the super's instructions to follow up on Tony's complaint.

'Bugger wasn't keen on coming to headquarters to make his statement, though.'

Kate rummaged in her bag and brought out a pack of mints. She popped one into her mouth and held the pack out to Bill. 'Want one? It might help get the bad taste out of your mouth after this morning's session.'

'I'm driving.'

How on earth did she think he could wrestle with a sweet at the same time?

She unwrapped it and held it in front of his mouth. At his nod, she popped it between his lips.

That was a first, he supposed. The mint was so strong it nipped his tongue. It also reminded him it had been a long time since breakfast and set him craving for a burger or a bacon butty. On the other hand, a Dundee pie would slide down quite nicely, particularly if it was topped by baked beans. He stared at the road in front of him to suppress the cravings. Kate would never contemplate stopping for anything so mundane as food.

When they reached headquarters the car park was full.

'I'll carry on while you find a parking space,' Kate said, her hand on the door handle.

Bill drew up in front of the rear entrance to let her out. What a bit of luck. There was a snack shop not far from here. He could always say he had trouble parking.

The house was quiet once the police left. Madge was on her way to the clinic while Luigi had retreated to the kitchen to consult the cook about lunch, although that was the last thing Tony was thinking about.

A large brown envelope lying under a couple of flyers on the hall table drew his eye. The post must have come while they were busy upstairs. He picked it up and turned it over in his hands. Strange, it had no stamp and along the top, it said 'Private and Confidential'.

Intrigued, he took it through to his office, making sure to

lock the door behind him so he could open it in privacy. Once inside and seated at his desk, he sliced the top of the envelope with a paper knife and shook the contents out.

The photographs made him draw in his breath. They were photographs of him, asleep in bed with Angel lying beside him. The attached note said, 'I know what you did'.

39

'Superintendent Jolly was looking for you,' Sue said when Kate walked into the team room.

'Considering he was the one who sent me out to investigate a complaint, you'd think he would have known I wasn't here.' Kate bit her lip, realising her comment had been more of a moan than anything else. It was all right for the team to let off steam to each other, but it was unprofessional of her to do the same.

Despite pushing the events of the morning to the back of her mind her resentment remained. The decision on how to conduct the investigation of Palmer's complaint had been taken out of her hands when the super insisted she investigate it herself. If she'd had her way, she would have sent Blair and Sid. That kind of investigation would have been right up their street. As it was, the two of them were huddled over their desks trying to look busy.

Kate strode over and stood in front of them until they were forced to look up.

'Have you traced that number plate yet?'

'Number plate, ma'am?' Blair stared at her with an insolent gaze he didn't bother to conceal.

Sid leaned back in his chair and smirked.

Their attitude wasn't enough for her to take them to task but just enough to get under her skin. If ever she felt the urge to punch someone it was now, and it took an effort to stay calm.

'Yes.' Kate kept her voice stiff and formal. 'The one I instructed Jenny to pass to you after she enhanced the CCTV image. Are you telling me she didn't do that?' She glanced towards Jenny, but the girl kept her head down.

'I assumed that was Jenny's job.' Blair's voice sounded

less certain, although the insolence was still evident.

'If you had bothered to get here earlier this morning you would have known I left instructions for you to trace the number once Jenny identified it.' Kate paused to draw a breath. 'What have you been doing all morning?'

'Checking through the evidence boxes of items removed from the victim's flat.'

'And have you found anything?' She made a point of staring at Blair's desk and then Sid's. Both looked suspiciously tidy apart from the coffee cups, some crumbs, and a couple of screwed up paper bags.

'There's a lot of stuff to get through.'

'I can see.' Kate turned her back on them. Prats. It wasn't worth wasting breath on them.

Jenny looked up when Kate moved away from Blair and Sid.

'I've managed to trace the number. It belongs to a private detective in Glasgow.' She checked a sheet of paper in front of her. 'Name of Denzil Rafferty.'

'Why would he be interested in Angel?' Kate thought for a moment. 'Get on to Glasgow and see what they know about him.'

She crossed the room to Sue's desk. 'What about you, Sue? Any progress?'

'I've contacted Candace Morgan and arranged for her to identify the body this afternoon. Thought I'd collect her and take her home again. It will give me a chance to talk to her.'

'Any joy finding out Angel's real name yet?'

Sue shook her head. 'Nothing so far. Everything we took from her flat is in the name of Angel Golding, and there's no trace of her under that name with any of the government agencies.'

Kate marched back to Blair and Sid. 'You two. I have a job for you. Bill and I brought in a suspect from our investigation this morning. I want the pair of you to follow it up. She's been working at Palmer's house under a false name. I specifically want to know who she is and whether we have enough to charge her with an offence. Bill will brief you on the details when he gets back from parking the car. In the meantime, run her prints to see if we can come up with a name.'

She hid a smile when she turned away. She'd had enough of Tony Palmer this morning. Blair and Sid could take the investigation over from here. It would allow the rest of them to concentrate on the murder case.

The door to the team room swung open and Superintendent Jolly strode in. He beckoned to Kate and marched towards her office.

'Looks like he means business,' Sue said.

Business I can do without, thought Kate, but didn't say out loud.

'I expected you to report the result of your investigation into Mr Palmer's complaint to me,' Jolly said as soon as she followed him into her office.

'I had intended to do that, but I have only just returned.' She continued to speak without giving him the chance to respond. 'We have brought the female suspect in for questioning and I have allocated follow up of the case to Detective Constables Cameron and Low. We are just waiting for the suspect's solicitor to arrive before the interview can start.'

'Good,' he said somewhat grudgingly. 'Cameron and Low are excellent officers. I'm sure they'll get results. I anticipate those two will go far.'

'Yes, sir.' Kate wasn't so sure that Blair and Sid would get results. Not if the suspect remained uncooperative.

She waited until Jolly left before she slammed her fist onto the top of her desk. Blair and Sid's brown-nosing was yielding results with the hierarchy, but she would be damned if she would agree with Jolly that they were excellent officers.

'You took your time. Where have you been?' Sue looked up when Bill entered the team room.

Bill shrugged his jacket off and placed it on the back of his chair. 'Had to park the damned car on the top storey of Bell Street car park. All the other spaces were full. And, to top it all the bloody lift wasn't working, and I had to tramp down all those stairs. You ever walked down those stairs? Damned smell is something you don't forget in a hurry.'

'Oh, stop moaning. At least you haven't been stuck inside like us plebs.'

'Sure, I've had a great morning. Kowtowing to bloody Tony Palmer. How come we have to jump when he snaps his fingers?'

'You've had a bee in your bonnet about Tony Palmer for as long as I've known you. Truth to tell it makes you a wee bit irrational.'

'Bugger's got off with far too much in the past. It's time the law caught up with him.'

'You mean it's time Bill Murphy caught up with him?'

'Whatever.' Bill slumped in his chair and prodded his computer's on switch.

His eye was caught by Superintendent Jolly emerging from Kate's office.

'I see the big boss is back again. Most I've seen of him for the past month.' A thought crossed Bill's mind. Did Tony have the super in his pocket? Surely not. And yet the niggle of suspicion wouldn't go away.

It was several moments before Kate showed her face and not before they heard a thump coming from her office.

'I think she's kicked something,' Sue whispered.

'I bet she wishes it was the super. Wouldn't mind a kick at him myself.'

'Oops, here she comes. Better look busy.'

Bill opened a Word document on his computer and fished his notebook out of his pocket while watching Kate advance out of the corner of his eye. She looked grim and purposeful. He wasn't scared of her, but he had built a degree of respect for his new boss. All the same, he hoped her mood wasn't due to something he'd done.

Kate stopped in front of his desk.

'Reports,' she said. 'A full report of Palmer's interview for me and a summary of all the relevant details for Blair and Sid. I've allocated the Liz Stewart investigation to them for follow up. They'll need the information before her solicitor arrives so they can make the most of questioning her.' She turned to Sue. 'What time are you collecting Candace Morgan?'

'Two o'clock.'

'Take Bill with you. He was present when we interviewed her.' She turned back to Bill. 'That means you need to get Blair and Sid briefed, and those reports finished before you leave.'

'Bugger it,' Bill said after she was out of earshot. 'Does she think I'm superman?'

40

Candace watched yet another car drive along the street without stopping, but it wasn't quite two o'clock yet. The tightness in her chest increased, a lump rose into her throat, and her fingers beat a tattoo on the windowsill. Why had she agreed to identify Angel's body? But she knew why, and it hadn't taken much persuasion by the policewoman to get her to agree. It was something she had to do even though she would rather not.

She wrenched her gaze away from the street and turned to look at Linda, sprawled on the sofa as if she hadn't a care in the world. Her eyes softened and her face relaxed into a smile. Everything she'd ever done had been for this woman, the love of her life. She would be nothing without her. And if that meant identifying the body, then so be it.

Linda looked up with a smile when Candace perched herself on the edge of the sofa and stroked her hair.

'You sure you want to go ahead with the identification? It won't be nice to have to look at the body. You could tell them you'd changed your mind.'

'It's best I do it.' Candace dreaded the task. She still saw the body in her nightmares, all bloody and broken. Maybe that mutilated face would haunt her dreams for years to come.

'Better you than me. I never want to see anything like that again.'

Candace pulled Linda into her arms and hugged her. 'Don't worry about me. If I keep my cool, I'll be all right. They'll expect a bit of emotion. If I shed a few tears or break down, it won't matter.'

A sharp knock at the door startled them.

'They're early,' Linda said, a note of panic in her voice.

Candace released her. 'Make yourself scarce.' She leapt

197

off the sofa and darted across the room to open the door to the bedroom before pushing Linda inside. 'Stay quiet. I don't want them questioning you.'

Pulling the door shut, she stood for a moment to compose herself and steady her breathing.

The second knock was even louder, and she ran a hand over her hair before answering it.

'Oh!' She caught her breath when she saw there were two of them. 'I thought it would just be you and me. I didn't expect Sergeant Murphy as well.'

Sue smiled at her. 'We thought you might like the extra support, and as you've met him before he volunteered to come along.'

Candace shrugged, but her eyes lingered on Bill Murphy. She could have sworn he'd been interested in her when the tight-arsed woman cop had questioned her on Saturday. But he hadn't been able to get much of a word in. She'd wondered at the time how the questioning would have gone if he'd been on his own. It wouldn't do any harm to cultivate him.

'We heard voices when we arrived. Is there someone else here?' Sue gazed around the living room.

Damn, they must have been lurking outside the door when she and Linda had been talking. Candace's mind whirled. 'I had the telly on. I switched it off when you knocked.' She grabbed her handbag from the table and checked its contents to avoid looking at them.

'You sure you're ready to do this?'

Candace noted the concern in Sue's voice.

'I'm as ready as I'll ever be,' she said. 'Let's get it over and done with.'

'That's the formal identification out of the way. One more task to strike off the list.'

'She was calmer than I expected.' Sue's voice was thoughtful. 'Considering we've been told they were close friends.'

Bill turned to lead the way down the stairs. He never liked

having to be present at identifications. Too much emotion made them difficult to handle.

A movement on the stairs above and a low hissing sound made him stop and turn around. A few steps above them a girl crouched in the shadows.

He moved towards her. 'Did you want something?'

The girl peered anxiously at Candace's closed door, put a finger to her lips, and beckoned. After exchanging glances with Sue, they followed her upstairs.

'I was watching for you,' she said as soon as they were inside her top-floor flat.

'Why?' Bill recognised her. Lucy something or other.

She gestured for them to sit on a sofa but didn't answer.

'Tea, coffee?' she asked as soon as they were seated.

Bill recognised delaying tactics when he heard them. He also knew witnesses offered more information if interviews were conducted at their own pace.

Working with Sue, their thoughts were often in tandem, and she confirmed this when she said, 'Tea would be fine.'

Bill knew Sue thought he was a human dustbin because of his liking for fast food. But he had developed a taste for good coffee and no longer appreciated the instant stuff, which he was sure Lucy was offering. So, he said, 'I'll have tea as well.'

After clattering about in the adjacent kitchen, she reappeared with three mugs balanced on a tray, a bottle of milk, a bag of sugar, and an open packet of digestive biscuits.

'Sorry, I don't have plates and things.'

'That's all right. We don't have any back at the station, we're used to it.' Bill took the tray from her and placed it on a side table. 'I'm sorry, but I've forgotten your name.'

'It's Lucy Sampson.' She sank into a chair facing them. 'I'm not sure whether you know.' Her voice trembled and a pink flush tinged her cheeks. 'And I don't know whether it's important.' The rest of the words came out in a rush and the flush deepened. 'Candace has a girlfriend. She keeps her away from the rest of us and the only person who ever talked to her was Angel.'

'You're right. We didn't know.' Sue pulled out her

notebook. 'This girlfriend. Is she with Candace now?'

'I think so, but I haven't seen her since...' her voice trailed off.

'Since Angel was murdered.' Bill kept his voice soft, not wanting to alarm her.

Lucy nodded and turned her eyes away from him to stare at a spot on the wall just beyond his shoulder.

'Does this girlfriend have a name?'

She shook her head. 'She keeps out of sight. I bumped into her once on the stairs. That's how I know.'

Bill sipped his tea and considered Lucy's answer. If she'd only seen her once, how did she know she was living with Candace? Maybe she'd been doing a bit of spying on them, which led him to wonder why she would do that. He decided not to push it.

'Is there anything else you can tell us about this girl?'

'Not really. But when she first came to live with Candace she had brown hair, and then she dyed it blonde and wore it the same way as Angel. I got the impression she might be copying her. I think she's gone back to being a brunette.' Lucy traced her fingers around the rim of her mug before looking up. 'That's all I know. But I thought I'd better tell you.'

Bill wondered again about Lucy's motivation in sharing this information with them but realised that was all he was going to get out of her.

He placed the mug of tea on the side table. 'Thank you for the information, Lucy. You've been very helpful.' He rose from the sofa, gesturing for Sue to join him. 'We'll be on our way and leave you in peace now.'

'You won't tell Candace it was me who told you, will you?'

Her voice echoed behind them as they stepped out to the landing.

'I see no reason we should,' Bill said, and the door clicked shut behind them.

'It looks like we'll have to interview Candace again.'

'What did you make of Lucy?'

Bill was still wondering why the girl had lain in wait for

them to make sure they knew about Candace and her girlfriend. Did she have an ulterior motive? Or did she just dislike Candace? When they had interviewed the other occupants of the building their dislike of Angel seemed to be unanimous, although he couldn't remember Lucy expressing an opinion.

'She seemed pretty straightforward, although I'd say there seemed to be no love lost between her and Candace.' Sue stopped on the stairs and looked at Bill with raised eyebrows. 'What's going on in that head of yours? You seeing conspiracies?'

Bill shrugged. 'I just wondered. But come on, if we're going to question Candace again, we'd better get on with it.'

They clattered down the remaining steps and knocked on Candace's door.

'You again,' she said when she opened it. 'I thought we'd finished for the afternoon.'

'Sorry for that,' Bill said. 'But we haven't interviewed your roommate.'

'Roommate?' She looked startled.

'Yes. The other girl who lives here.' Bill stared into her eyes until she looked away. 'When we interviewed you before, you omitted to tell us she lives with you. You either ask her to show herself or we charge you with police obstruction.'

'She's not involved with Teasers and doesn't know any of the other dancers. I don't see how it concerns her.'

The creak of the bedroom door opening made them both turn. The girl standing there was taller than Candace. Her eyes were masked by large, black-framed spectacles, and her hair was scraped back in a ponytail. She wore creased jeans and a baggy shirt.

'It's all right, Candace. I don't mind.' She crossed the room and stood beside her.

Bill wasn't sure what he'd expected but given Candace's flamboyant appearance it hadn't been someone as nondescript as this girl. Still, he supposed, opposites do attract.

'What do you want to know?' She looked at Bill and

ignored Sue.

'We'll start with your name.'

'Linda Taylor.'

'And your date of birth?'

She rattled off her date of birth, and Bill did a quick calculation in his head. That would make her nineteen. He'd thought her older than that, maybe mid-twenties. But judging someone's age had never been his strong point.

'Angel, the murder victim. How well did you know her?'

'I wouldn't say I knew her. I met her a couple of times, but I don't think she liked me, so I stayed out of her way. Besides, I don't mix with the other residents in the building. We have nothing in common. They all work at Teasers, and I don't.'

Sue had been scribbling Linda's replies in her notebook, but she looked up to ask, 'Where were you on the night of the murder?'

'I was here. We both were. But before you ask, I didn't hear anything. I'm a sound sleeper.'

'I told you she didn't know anything.'

Candace grabbed the girl's hand and glowered at Bill and Sue. 'I'll not have you upsetting Linda, so if that's all, I'd like you to leave.'

Bill caught his breath, surprised by the anger in Candace's voice and her fierce expression. He'd never been good at handling angry females, although he never had a problem facing up to a man.

He glanced at Sue and raised an eyebrow in a silent query about whether to draw the questioning to a close.

She nodded her assent and tucked her notebook into a pocket. 'We may have to come back. But we'll leave it for the time being.'

Outside, after the door slammed behind them, Bill stared at Sue in puzzlement. 'What was that all about? It wasn't as if we were being heavy-handed.'

'A bit too overprotective if you ask me,' Sue said. 'It makes me wonder if they've got something to hide.'

41

Kate's head throbbed. She'd seen enough of Superintendent Jolly this afternoon to last her a lifetime. In the normal run of things, Jolly was a will-o'-the-wisp, difficult to pin down and practically invisible. What was it about this complaint by Tony Palmer that had him breathing down her neck? She glared at the phone, defying it to ring again.

To top it all, Bill and Sue hadn't returned. How bloody long did it take to make an identification, for heaven's sake?

She stomped out of her office and marched down the room to stand glaring at the whiteboards. They were getting nowhere fast. The victim, Angel Golding, didn't seem to exist apart from being a body in the mortuary. Her fingerprints weren't on record. She had no National Insurance number, no tax records, no driving licence, and no passport. She was a ghost.

The clatter of the office door opening and closing heralded the return of Blair and Sid from interviewing Liz Stewart. They'd better have something for her to keep Jolly off her back.

The two constables didn't seem in any hurry to report to her as they sauntered to their desks. Kate's hackles rose. What did they think she was? An ornament?

Her heels clacked a staccato rhythm on the floor as she headed towards them.

'Well,' she snapped. 'What did you find out?'

'Couldn't get anything out of her. It was a no comment interview.' Blair shifted uneasily on his seat and Sid cast her a sidelong look.

'Nothing at all. Not even her real name?'

'It was her solicitor, Andrew Masterson. He's that hotshot one from Glasgow, with the reputation for getting everyone off. He wouldn't let her say anything and told us we have to charge her or let her go.'

'We'll hold her for the full twenty-four hours; that will give us time to have another go at her in the morning. A night in the cells might make her more talkative, but if she doesn't, I'll have no problem persuading Superintendent Jolly to grant an extension.' The only problem was, Kate wasn't convinced it would make any difference. The woman was stubborn.

Blair stood and buttoned his jacket. 'If that's all, ma'am.'

'Don't be hasty. What about her fingerprints? Have you checked them against the database?' Kate wasn't in the mood to let him off the hook.

'The guys downstairs are doing that.'

'And the results?' Kate could lay bets Blair hadn't bothered to check.

He shrugged. 'I'm not a fingerprint expert.'

'But you do know how to use a phone, I presume. What, may I ask, is stopping you from checking?'

'Yes, ma'am. Right away, ma'am.'

Kate detected resentment in his voice.

'Get on with it and report the findings to me.' She turned on her heel and marched to her office.

Once inside, she resisted the urge to kick something. Those two prats, who considered themselves God's gift to Police Scotland, always irritated her with their barely disguised insolence. But she vowed she'd lick them into shape, whatever it took. If they didn't like having to take orders from a woman, that was tough.

The ringing of the phone interrupted her thoughts. Still seething, she lifted the handset.

'My office, Inspector Rawlings. Now.' Superintendent Jolly's voice was clipped.

Kate felt as if she were being summoned to the naughty stool. What had got his hump up this time? She couldn't help wondering if Tony Palmer was pulling the strings.

'Yes, sir.'

'Sit,' he said when she entered his office.

She would have preferred to stand but did as she was told.

He leaned forward and regarded her through narrowed eyes. 'From what I can see you have made no progress on this investigation of,' he consulted a paper on his desk, 'Liz Stewart. It's not good enough.'

'My team has been working on this case all day, sir.' She tried not to let anger seep into her voice.

He ignored her while he studied the sheet of paper. 'There is nothing here that tells me who this woman is or what she was up to.'

'The suspect has been uncooperative, sir.' She resisted adding, apart from applying thumb screws, there's not much more we can do.

Not a flicker of emotion passed over the superintendent's face. Kate had no clue what he was thinking. She had no doubt he blamed the lack of progress on her, and she braced herself for whatever he was about to dish out.

Instead, he replaced the paper on his desk and heaved a sigh. 'Talk me through the investigation, from the beginning.'

Some considerable time later, after Kate had described everything down to the last detail, he leaned back in his chair. 'So, the main stumbling block is her identity. She's using an alias and you haven't been able to find out her real name.'

'That is correct, sir. We've done all the usual checks, but until we can identify her, we're stuck and she's giving nothing.'

'What is your current plan?'

'A night in the cells to soften her up and we interview her again in the morning before the twenty-four hours are up. Then, unless we get an extension, we'll have to let her go.'

'I see.' He tapped his teeth with the end of his pen. 'I could consider granting an extension dependent on the outcome of the next interview and the procurator fiscal's opinion on whether we have a case. Report to me tomorrow and I'll consider it.' He stood, and for the first time since she'd entered the room, he smiled at her. 'Good work, Kate.' There was a warmth in his voice that hadn't been there before.

Despite that, Kate left his office with an uneasy feeling in the pit of her stomach. Just how much checking had Blair and

Sid done before interviewing Liz Stewart? It was never a good idea to interview a suspect without gleaning as much information about them beforehand.

Bugger it. She should never have entrusted them with this even though she didn't rate it as a high priority compared to the murder case.

Her irritation mounting, she entered the team room prepared to take the two of them to task, but it was empty. She'd spent longer with the superintendent than she'd realised, and with no orders issued for overtime work, everyone had pounced on the chance to finish at a reasonable time.

Tony's day had been one shock after another. He had barely recovered from the events of the morning and the police investigation inside his house when the incriminating photographs had arrived. Even though he'd stuffed them back into the envelope and locked them in his safe they still preyed on his mind. Then, to top it all, Madge had refused to take his phone calls.

'I'm afraid your wife does not wish to speak to you.' The smooth voice of the nurse at the other end of the phone echoed in his mind. 'She has asked you not to visit.'

When he had objected, he had been told politely but firmly his entrance to the clinic would not be allowed.

The rest of the day passed in a blur. He'd tried to busy himself with things to do but the house was unwelcoming, and he was glad to escape to Teasers. At least he would have amenable company there. But when he arrived, he'd stomped to his office overlooking the clubroom without a glance at anyone else.

Now he stood, with his forehead pressed against the glass of the window, looking down at the dancers. Monday was always a quiet night and their motions as they twined themselves around the dance poles seemed desultory, lacking the vitality that a busier night brought.

But Tony was past caring. His head was focused on those

photographs and trying to work out who sent them and what they wanted. And that message. What did it mean? He shuddered. He was sure he hadn't killed Angel, but whoever sent the photographs seemed to think otherwise. Or maybe they just saw it as a chance to make money. No doubt a demand would come. It was just a matter of time.

Pressure built up behind his eyes and his head ached with the effort of trying to solve the puzzle. Was it someone connected to the club? It had to be someone who had access to Angel's room. Did that mean it was one of the dancers? He vowed to find out.

He gulped another mouthful of whisky. Then he turned and threw the glass across the room. Damn it. He wasn't going to let anyone get the better of him, and drinking was a fool's game when there was so much at stake. He vowed another drop wouldn't pass his lips until he'd solved the mystery of who sent the photographs, found out what they knew and found out who killed Angel. His hand reached for the bottle. Who was he kidding?

42

Kate left home early to beat the early morning traffic. Besides, it ensured she arrived in the team room before everyone else. But she hardly had time to pour herself a coffee from the machine before Jenny Cartwright arrived, closely followed by Sue Rogers.

The young constable padded over to her desk, slung her duffle bag on the floor beneath it, and switched on her computer. Meanwhile, Sue joined Kate at the coffee machine.

'I'll need this before the team meeting starts.'

'It's wet and hot,' Kate said, 'but not much else can be said in its favour.'

Sue laughed. 'You've never said a truer word.'

The pair of them walked back along the room. Sue slipped behind her desk and Kate carried on to her office. She liked Sue. The woman was everything she admired in an officer. She was smart, competent, and could be trusted to do the job. Not like some of them. She scowled as her thoughts turned to Blair and Sid. The only thing they were concerned with was how fast they could climb the ladder. They were pen pushers in the making.

Kate turned her attention to the folders she'd taken out of the filing cabinet. Opening them, she frowned at the contents. This murder case was going nowhere fast, and the investigation of Tony Palmer's complaint was getting in the way. Once again, she wondered why Superintendent Jolly was interested in it. As if she'd jinxed herself, she looked up to see him standing in the doorway.

'Sir?'

'I thought I'd join you for the team meeting. See where we were at.'

'Yes, sir.'

Just what I need. She suppressed the moan that rose to her lips. It wouldn't do to aggravate him. She glanced at her watch. 'We should be ready to start in a few minutes.'

Kate stared out at the team room and was relieved to see Bill Murphy walk in with his usual bacon roll. He was always last to arrive.

'I think we can get started now, sir.' She sidled past him in the doorway and strode to the display boards at the end of the room.

The team members joined her with no prompting. Even Blair and Sid, who usually loitered, were quick off their marks. Probably because Superintendent Jolly was present. However, Jolly remained at the rear, for which she was thankful. His presence was distracting enough without him making himself more obvious than he was.

'Where have we got to with the investigation?' She tossed the marker to Bill and nodded to him to start the briefing and update the whiteboards.

'We have a murder victim, Angel Golding, although we don't think that is her real name. We have crime scene photographs. Various exhibits have been submitted for forensic testing. This includes two packets of drugs removed from the victim's flat. Tony Palmer, as well as the other occupants living in the victim's building, have been interviewed. And there is evidence the victim was being stalked.'

Bill grabbed his cup and gulped a mouthful of coffee. 'We know that Tony Palmer escorted her home from Teasers and inspected her flat for intruders at approximately midnight, although he claims to have left and returned to his home. There is only his word he left, but his driver confirms Palmer's statement.' The tone of Bill's voice indicated his disbelief. 'The witness statements didn't reveal much. One of the victim's neighbours, Ayisha Okeke, a dancer employed at Teasers, heard water running in the pipes in the middle of the night. Another neighbour witnessed a car arriving and leaving in the early morning. We have a description of the car, but she could only see the top of the driver's head and thought he was young and slim. That car has not yet been traced. A witness statement from Tony Palmer refers to a disagreement between the victim and a group of men in Teasers who were apparently in the company of a man named Jimmy Matthews, who is believed to be a gangster from Glasgow.'

'That's very comprehensive, Bill.' Kate turned to Jenny Cartwright. 'You were following up the CCTV of the car reported as following the victim. What have you found out?'

Jenny adjusted her spectacles and stood up. 'I was able to get the car's number plate and traced it to a private detective in Glasgow by the name of Denzil Rafferty. Police officers in Glasgow checked it out, but apparently his premises were burned out early on Monday morning. An investigation is ongoing and there is a suspicion it was arson. Denzil Rafferty has not been located.'

'Have we made any progress in identifying the victim?'

Sue leaned forward. 'Bill and I accompanied Candace Morgan to the mortuary to identify the body. She identified it as Angel Golding. Said she was sure because Angel had a strawberry birthmark on her left shoulder which she usually covered up with cosmetics. She has never known her to use any other name. I've done various checks, but Angel Golding is not registered anywhere. No National Insurance number, no tax records, no health records, no passport. It's as if she was invisible and never existed. We can only assume she was using a false name.'

'What about this altercation Angel had with Jimmy Matthews? Is anyone following that up?'

An awkward silence filled the room until it was broken by Jenny. 'I'm not sure if it's related, but Blair asked me to check the fingerprints of Liz Stewart and they came up as belonging to a Liz Matthews.'

Kate glared at Blair. She'd asked him to do it and he'd offloaded it to Jenny.

'Interesting how the name Matthews keeps popping up.' She reflected on the alleged altercation between Angel and Jimmy Matthews in Teasers. Was that a coincidence? Or was there a connection to Angel's murder?

'We need to follow that up which means we need an extension to carry on interviewing Liz Stewart or Matthews for a little longer.' She looked over to Superintendent Jolly.

'Granted. We need to get to the bottom of this.'

'Right,' Kate said. 'Tasks. Sue, keep on digging and try to find out more about Angel Golding. Bill, chase up forensics. Jenny, you've already spoken to someone in the Glasgow force, see what they can dig up on Jimmy Matthews and his gang, including any connection to Liz Matthews. We'll continue to interview her, and I'll join Blair in the next one. Now we know who she is she might be more forthcoming, although I doubt it. And after that, I'll talk to the procurator fiscal to see if we have enough evidence to charge her.'

Kate could already guess the fiscal's response and reckoned that by tomorrow, they would have to release Liz Stewart. Superintendent Jolly was not going to be happy about that.

43

Kate picked up the file and strode out of her office. She beckoned to Blair to accompany her to the interview room.

Liz, flanked by her solicitor Andrew Masterson, appeared composed. Anyone looking at her would never guess she'd spent a night in the cells. Her eyes flicked over Kate and rested on Blair when they sat opposite her.

This wasn't going to be easy. Kate laid the file on the table and switched on the recorder. She did the preliminaries; date, time, and people present before addressing Liz.

'Can you give your name and permanent address for the tape?'

'No comment.' A smile twitched at the corner of Liz's mouth.

'You have been working for Mr and Mrs Palmer since February of this year as nurse-companion to Mrs Palmer. Can you confirm this?'

'No comment.'

'You have been using an assumed name, Liz Stewart, while you were in their employ. Is that correct?'

'No comment.'

'We have reason to believe that you have been supplying Mrs Palmer with medication during that time. Can you confirm this?'

'No comment.'

'We have reason to believe that your name is Liz Matthews and not Liz Stewart, as you claim. Can you confirm this?'

Kate watched Liz closely and saw the flicker in her eyes at the mention of her real name. She thought for a minute that the woman was going to respond, but Masterson placed a hand on hers and the moment passed.

'No comment,' she said.

Several fruitless questions later Kate was forced to admit defeat. She ended the session and clicked off the recorder. 'Perhaps you'll be more forthcoming at the next interview.' She picked up the file in preparation for leaving.

For the first time since entering the room, Masterson spoke. 'The detention period is over. Either charge my client or release her.'

'On the contrary, we have been given an extension of twenty-four hours and I intend to interview your client again, by which time we should have more information.'

Despite her statement to the solicitor, she suspected that another twenty-four hours would make little difference and Liz Stewart would walk.

Superintendent Jolly was waiting for her when she returned to her office. He removed his feet from her desk, rose from the chair, and straightened his tunic jacket.

'What did you get out of her?'

'Nothing. She hasn't confirmed or denied anything I've put to her, although I spotted a reaction when I revealed we knew her identity.'

'Have you spoken to the procurator fiscal?'

'Briefly, but she needs more information before deciding whether to charge her. The fiscal's opinion is that we don't have enough.' Kate consulted her notes. 'One of my team is contacting Glasgow for more information about the suspect. We think she might be connected to the leader of a criminal organisation there, name of Jimmy Matthews. Once I have the information, I'll interview her again and see if we get anywhere.' Given the responses Liz Stewart had already given her, Kate wasn't holding her breath.

'Yes, yes, I'm aware of that.' He paused in the doorway. 'See that you keep me informed.'

Kate stared at the door for several moments after Jolly left her office. Something was going on with him and it didn't smell right. But what could she do about it? She was only an inspector and Jolly was a superintendent. That meant she would have to go along with him, but he wouldn't like it when she had to let Liz go.

She lifted the phone from its cradle. It was time to talk to the procurator fiscal. Although she knew in her heart there wasn't enough evidence for a charge, at least it would set the process in motion. Her finger had only pressed three numbers when a tap at her door made her look up. Jenny stood on the threshold. The apologetic look on the girl's face didn't quite mask her air of excitement. Kate replaced the phone. She would call the fiscal later. Jenny evidently had some information for her.

'Come in and sit down, Jenny.'

She leant forward with an encouraging smile.

'What have you got for me?'

Jenny held out a printed piece of paper. 'I've been in touch with my contact in Glasgow and I've noted the information in my report.'

'Go on.'

'Liz Matthews, who we know as Liz Stewart, is the daughter of Paul Matthews, a brother of Jimmy Matthews. Her father, Paul, was killed last year in a gang-related attack. He was shot on the doorstep of his house. Liz has some convictions for shoplifting which go back for several years but she also has convictions for fraud and is known to be violent.'

'Good work, Jenny. That information will come in useful.'

A pink flush crept into Jenny's cheeks and Kate sensed her pleasure at the praise.

Jenny rose from the chair. 'Is there anything else you want me to do?'

'Yes, I think there is.' Kate's thoughts focused on the alleged confrontation between Angel and Jimmy Matthews. Was there a connection?

'It's a long shot,' she said. 'But email a photograph of Angel to your Glasgow contact to see if she's known there.'

Jimmy Matthews dug his phone out of his pocket. 'About time,' he growled. 'What's happening?' His scowl deepened as he listened. 'You said they'd nothing on her. That's why I'm on my way to Dundee now.' He listened again. 'Make sure of it,' he said. 'That's what I'm paying you for.'

'Trouble, boss?'

'Bugger said they'd have to release Liz today because they have nothing on her unless she confesses and there's no way she'll do that. But the cops are keeping her another twenty-four hours.'

'You want me to tell Jo Jo to turn back?'

'Naw! We'll keep going to Dundee and collect her tomorrow. Masterson says they'll have to release her when the time's up, and if she keeps up the no comment answers they won't have enough to charge her.'

He settled back in his seat and watched the scenery whiz past. The plan to take over Tony Palmer's operation in Dundee had become a shit show, but he wasn't going to give up. He'd just have to consider new tactics.

Jimmy's plans for expansion hadn't included Glasgow. He wasn't a big enough face there, and he didn't want to rile the crime families entrenched in the city. They were vicious bastards, even more vicious than Mad Dog, and they didn't pull any punches if anyone encroached on their territory.

No, his plan was better. It had already worked in Edinburgh where he'd taken over Georgio's organisation. The man had put up a good fight, but after they'd threatened to mete out the same punishment to his son, Georgio had signed the legal papers transferring everything, and now Jimmy was the proud owner of a nightclub empire in Edinburgh.

He'd intended to do the same in Dundee. All he had to do was plant the drugs, grab Tony's wife, and the man would have been history. It had been working until Angel got herself killed and Liz was arrested, which left him with no one on the inside at Teaser's or Tony's house.

But it could still work. It would just need more muscle.

'What you thinking, boss? We still going to grab Tony's wife?'

Jimmy smiled at Mad Dog. The man had this knack for knowing what people were thinking. Most folks kept their distance from him and wrote him off as a mad bastard. But Jimmy had known him when he was Billy Jones before he earned the Mad Dog title. The two of them had grown up together, and Jimmy never underestimated Billy's intelligence. Others had and lived to regret it.

'Not today,' Jimmy said. 'Not while the cops are sniffing around. Too risky. We collect Liz as soon as she's released, and we return to Glasgow. We'll take it from there after that. Once the heat dies down, we'll come back. And, you never know, the cops might make it easy for us by arresting Tony.'

'Yes, boss.'

Jimmy patted his knee. 'Don't worry. Our time will come, and you can have Tony all to yourself.'

The big man's eyes narrowed, and he stretched his lips in a smile, although there was no humour in it.

Luigi found Fabio waiting for him on the staircase.

'Jimmy Matthews is on his way. I spotted the tracker's movement on the road between Perth and Dundee about half an hour ago, but you were with Tony. They're probably here by now.'

Luigi followed the boy upstairs.

The room Fabio rarely left and which he'd turned into a workroom for his electronic pursuits was dominated by a large monitor. Fabio enlarged the map on the screen and pointed to a red arrow. 'It looks like they're booking into the Apex City Quay Hotel again.'

A grim smile flickered over Luigi's mouth. 'You got the stuff we need?'

'Of course.'

'Is it traceable?'

Fabio laughed. 'Think I'm stupid? I got it on the dark web. Nothing's traceable there.'

'How long will it take for you to assemble it?' Luigi was careful not to say what it was.

'It's ready. I just have the finishing touches to add.'

'Good. With a bit of luck, we'll plant it tonight.'

44

Tony blinked. His head ached, his tongue stuck to the top of his mouth, and he had no idea what time of day it was. He glanced at his watch. Dammit, was that the time? How much had he drunk and how long had he been out? It had been years since he'd been on a bender like the one last night.

He stretched to rid himself of the stiffness in his body and sat up. It took a few minutes for him to realise he was lying on the leather sofa in his office. He hadn't gone home last night. He'd been too wasted. Besides, there was nothing to go home for when Madge wasn't there.

The events of the day before returned, and he groaned. What a bloody mess.

He hefted himself out of the sofa and crossed the room to look through the window side of the mirror to the club below. Light filtered down, from the small windows set high in the ceiling, doing little to disperse the shadows and the gloom of the deserted nightclub.

So much had happened over the last few days. Angel's death had started it all off, although he was sure he had nothing to do with that. But who would believe him if they knew he'd woken up lying beside her blood-soaked body? It was still a puzzle why they hadn't killed him as well. And why Angel? Why not him? He was sure he must have more enemies than Angel. But Angel wasn't Angel, was she? She was Lesley Matthews, wife of that pillock, Kevin Matthews. He would lay bets that one or other of the Matthews was responsible for her murder. And they'd set him up to take the fall.

Then there was the little matter of the incriminating photographs locked up in his safe at home. There had been no blackmail demand. But maybe whoever sent them didn't want money. Maybe it was all part of the setup. He shuddered. He needed to get home. Find out who delivered the envelope and confront them.

His mind made up; he lifted the phone. 'Come and get me,' he said when Brian picked up. 'I'm still at the club.'

It was mid-afternoon when Tony entered the house through his private entrance at the side and went into his office. He fished the envelope out of the safe and emptied the photographs onto his desk. Turning the envelope over in his hands he searched for any clue to the sender, but there was nothing. Only his name, Tony, scrawled on the front. Likewise, the photographs offered no clues, although they seemed genuine and there was no mistaking Angel's bedroom and Tony lying in the bed beside her.

He leaned back in his chair and pursed his lips. The photographer must have used a flash to get such a clear picture. Why hadn't he woken when it went off?

A pang of regret struck him. He'd disposed of the whisky bottle and the glasses they'd used. The only proof he'd been drugged.

With a sigh, he replaced the photos in the envelope and, taking it with him, walked through into the main part of the house.

Luigi appeared from the direction of the kitchen. The man seemed to have a second sense and was always on hand when Tony arrived.

'Can I help you with something, boss?'

'You can. This envelope came yesterday, and it appears to have been hand-delivered. I want to know who sent it.'

'No problem. It should show up on the CCTV footage.'

Luigi turned and led the way to the small room at the rear of the house where all the security equipment was installed.

A small bank of monitors showed different views of the outside of the property.

Luigi settled in front of a keyboard and opened a folder containing masses of files. 'What time do you want me to start checking the footage?'

'I'm not sure, but I'm assuming it must have been

delivered early before anyone was up and about.'

Luigi prodded the keyboard and opened a file. 'I'll start at midnight then.'

Images on the monitor in front of him raced past as he fast-forwarded the footage. It didn't take as long as Tony had anticipated before movement was detected at the front door.

Luigi stopped the file running and backtracked until just before the movement. He then inched it forward until the person stooping to post something through the letter box was visible.

Recognition was instantaneous, making Tony draw in a sharp breath while his hand tightened on the envelope.

The urge to dash out and confront his blackmailer was overwhelming but he restrained himself. He needed all his wits about him first. So, he spent the rest of the day recovering from his hangover.

After a shower, a short time in the gym, and a dinner he didn't want, he felt more alive and ready for the fray.

He'd deliberately waited until Teasers opened for business before he made his appearance. Now he was here he watched the activity below through the one-way mirror. His eyes fixed on one of the dancers. The one on the pole to the left of the main stage. She was good. There was no doubt about that. But she'd betrayed him, and Tony didn't forgive betrayal.

At midnight the interval music played, and the dancers left their poles one at a time to walk through the punters to the dressing rooms, avoiding seeking fingers and accepting the money tucked into their G-strings. The ten-minute break allowed the dancers to freshen up and the punters to spend their money at the bar.

After a few minutes, Tony left his office and made his way to the dancers' dressing room. This was where he planned the confrontation to take place. Not in his office, because that would finger him if anything untoward took place, and he hadn't decided how to handle the situation.

The gabble of voices silenced when he reached the door. He lounged against it and met the girls' curious eyes with a smile. 'Don't let me hinder you.'

CHRIS LONGMUIR

His eyes sought the person he was seeking. Did she know why he was here? She gave no indication of it as she stared into the mirror in front of her and applied fresh lipstick.

When the music from the clubroom started up again a flurry of movement rippled through the dancers as they rose to filter out of the room.

Tony met their sidelong glances with amusement and inhaled their perfumes when they passed him in the doorway. But when Candace drew near to him, he reached out and grasped her arm.

'Not you. I want a word with you.'

She tried to shake his hand off, but he tightened his grip and pulled her to the side to allow the rest of the girls to pass.

Once they were alone, Tony said, 'Those photographs.'

'What photographs?'

'Don't come the innocent. You know what photographs. And you weren't very clever when you left them. Did you think your visit wouldn't be recorded?'

'I don't know what you mean.'

A spurt of anger made Tony want to shake her. 'You know perfectly well what I mean.' The menace in his voice was unmistakable. 'Is it money you want because I can assure you blackmail doesn't work with me?'

'Not money. Revenge for what you did to Angel.' Her voice was defiant, and she met his eyes with a glare.

'I did nothing to Angel. What happened to her was not done by me.' A lump rose into his throat threatening to choke him, as a vision of Angel, covered in blood, seared into his brain.

'You were there that night.'

'So were you, or you wouldn't have been able to take those photographs. How do I know you didn't kill her?'

'You can't pin that on me.'

Tony met her scowl with a measured look. His heart was thumping so loudly he thought she might hear it. It wasn't impossible. He was certain he hadn't killed Angel, and she had been there.

'You going to kill me as well?' Her voice penetrated his

thoughts. If she had been a man, he might well have arranged something of that nature, but he had an aversion to harming women.

'I don't kill women.'

'Tell that to Angel.'

Defiance shone from her eyes, and her body stiffened. Her fingers tried to prise his hand off her arm, leaving scratch marks on her skin.

The menace left his voice and tiredness crept over him. 'If it's money you want?' He left the question dangling.

'I told you, I don't want money. Besides, it's too late for that. I've already posted the photos to the police.'

Despair made Tony sigh. 'You'd best get back to work.' He let go of her arm.

Her eyes widened. 'You're not going to sack me?'

'Not yet,' he said.

With a look of disbelief, she ran up the corridor to the clubroom.

Tony sagged against the wall. He'd been tempted to send her packing, but that would signal to the police that she was the sender of the photographs. Somehow, he thought she wouldn't want that known. Particularly as it would place her on the scene during the night Angel died.

Once again, he wondered what part she had played in Angel's death. But thoughts of the photographs in police hands pushed those thoughts out of his mind. There was a more pressing problem. How would he react when the police came knocking?

45

Jimmy Matthews cradled the whisky glass, but his eyes never left the door he'd seen Tony vanish through.

One by one, the dancing girls returned to take their positions on the small circular stages scattered between the tables, but the one nearest to him remained empty and there was no sign of Tony.

His glass was empty by the time the last girl appeared and he had enough time to notice the angry expression on her face before she replaced it with the empty smile with which all the dancers greeted the customers.

A few seconds later, Tony emerged. He ran a hand over his immaculate hair and nodded to men sitting at the nearest table. He stopped for a quiet word before he moved on.

Jimmy kept his eyes fixed on him and when Tony drew near, he stretched his lips into a smile.

'I must say you serve a decent whisky. And you run a tight ship.' He nodded towards the dancer who had recently arrived. 'Not giving you any trouble, is she?'

Tony towered over him, but Jimmy met his stare with a bland look.

'I never have trouble in my nightclub.'

'There's always a first time,' Jimmy said.

'Not ever. I trust you are not about to prove me wrong.'

The menace in Tony's voice made Jimmy smile.

'I wouldn't dream of causing trouble.' Not tonight, Jimmy thought, but it won't be long. When it happens Tony won't see it coming.

Luigi and Fabio watched the moving arrow on the screen.

'They're leaving Teasers now.' Luigi's pulse beat faster.

The time to act was approaching fast.

'Heading for the hotel.' Fabio squirmed in his chair. 'That's them entering the car park now. We've got them.'

He rose from his chair and grabbed his jacket.

Luigi placed a restraining hand on his arm. 'We've got all night. Besides, we need to wait for Tony to come home before we leave.'

'But he didn't come home last night. He slept at Teasers.'

'That's true, but it doesn't hurt to be careful, and we have all night.'

It was an hour later before Tony entered the house. Luigi met him in the hallway. 'Can I get you anything, boss?'

'No, Luigi. I'm fine, just a bit tired. I'll be fine after a sleep.'

'If you're sure, boss. I could bring you a coffee?'

'No, no. I won't need you again tonight. I suggest you retire as well.'

'Yes, boss.'

Luigi waited for half an hour before he alerted Fabio. It was time to go.

They slipped out of the house by the side entrance using a key to the office area which Tony didn't know Luigi had. But Luigi hadn't worked for Georgio all those years without acquiring various skills.

'You got everything we need?' he asked Fabio as he rolled the motorbike down to the main road where he could start the engine with no one in the house hearing.

'It's all in the bag.' Fabio mounted the pillion placing it in front of him.

Conscious of the bag pressing against his back and knowing what it contained made Luigi hesitate before starting the engine. 'You sure it's safe?'

'Yes. It will only go off if someone rings the mobile phone I've attached to it. And as I'm the only one who knows the number, I hardly think that's likely.'

'I hope you're right.' The rumble of the motorbike's engine muffled Luigi's words.

Within a few minutes they arrived at their destination, and

once again, Luigi parked the bike in Chandler's Lane.

They soon reached the hotel and Luigi gestured to Fabio to follow his lead. 'Keep low and make sure you don't get caught by the cameras.' He pointed to a slowly moving CCTV camera on the edge of the building. 'Follow me and do what I do and you'll be all right.'

Luigi slid into the car park in the same way he had on his previous visit, closely followed by Fabio. Once in, it didn't take them long to identify the car and Luigi kept a lookout while Fabio attached the device to the undercarriage.

'That's it done.' Fabio stood and dusted the knees of his trousers with his hands.

'Keep down.' Luigi pulled the boy's arm. 'We don't want to be detected now.'

'Sorry, I forgot.'

'You can't afford to forget. Now keep low and follow me. It's time to get out of here.'

Luigi remembered his promise to Georgio about keeping Fabio safe. What they'd done tonight hadn't been safe and Georgio would never forgive him if Fabio wound up in prison. But the boy had been adamant he wanted to be involved and that Jimmy Matthews deserved all he got.

His nerves were on edge as they retraced their steps to where he'd parked the motorbike and he didn't breathe easily until they were clear of the waterfront and heading home.

46

Wednesday

The photographs hadn't left Tony's possession since he'd removed the envelope containing them earlier in the day. Their sharp edges had prodded him several times during the evening, reminding him they were in his inside jacket pocket, sited just over his heart.

If the police had copies, as Candace claimed, they would come for him, and he needed to be ready with some answers. But the photos were incriminating. How was he going to talk his way out of this?

Tony knew full well he had escaped justice for many things he'd been involved with, and his hands were not clean. But to get banged up for something he hadn't done was ironic, although he supposed some would say it was justice of a sort.

He took the photos out, spread them on the top of the dressing table, and angled the desk light onto them.

The images, gleaming in the reflected light, looked even more incriminating. There was no denying it was him in the bed beside Angel.

But there was no date or time stamp. He scrutinised them to see if there was anything in the images that would show when they were taken. Satisfied there was nothing, he sat on the edge of the bed to think.

The night hours passed slowly as he brooded on his problem. At one point he thought he heard movement on the landing outside his room, but it was probably Luigi who never seemed to sleep, so he ignored it.

By the time early morning light crept into the room he knew how he was going to handle the police enquiries into the photographs, and he sat back to await their arrival.

Kate yawned while she waited for her computer to jump into life. She hadn't been getting enough sleep over the past few days. It was this damned case which seemed to be going nowhere. And Superintendent Jolly poking his nose in didn't help. She could have done without that.

The ping of an arriving email jolted her out of her lethargy, and she opened her inbox. Scrolling through the emails, she deleted the obvious spam ones, left the admin ones until later, and opened the ones that looked promising. The third email she opened had image attachments. She hesitated a moment because opening attachments could be risky, but the email header was 'Angel' and what scammer would know that name. What the heck. If it was dodgy the IT guys would just have to sort it, but she had a feeling in her gut the images could be important.

Clicking on each image file, her eyes grew wider with each photograph displayed. Was this a breakthrough at last? If it was, she knew a certain superintendent who wasn't going to be happy.

A few clicks later and the images were winging their way to the colour printer in the team room. While she waited her fingers drummed on the desktop until the last one printed. Then, ever mindful of security, she logged out of her computer.

Her office door slammed shut behind her as she strode to the printer to collect the photographs.

The team was already congregating at the end of the room to wait for the daily briefing. At least she hadn't needed to summon them today, maybe they were getting the message she wouldn't put up with any shit from them.

She pinned one of the photographs onto the whiteboard. 'I received this today, and I think it may be the breakthrough we've been waiting for.'

Bill came forward for a closer look. 'We've got him. Let's see him wriggle out of this one.'

Kate suppressed a smile at the satisfaction in Bill's voice.

'We don't know when these photographs were taken,' she

said, 'let's not be too hasty in our assumptions.'

A look of disappointment passed over Bill's face.

'But we need to consider them. So, I'll need you and Sue to go out with a couple of uniforms and bring Mr Palmer in for questioning.' She'd considered sending someone else, but she didn't want to deprive Bill of the pleasure of doing what he'd always wanted to do.

'Do we charge him?'

She thought she detected a note of longing in Bill's voice. He'd been waiting a long time for this opportunity.

'I know you'd love to do that, Bill, but we hold off for the time being. Ask him to come into the office to help us with our enquiries, and if he refuses use the powers you have under Scots law to arrest him. I think he'll see sense.' At the back of her mind was Superintendent Jolly's reaction, and she didn't want to stir up a hornet's nest if this lead fizzled out.

'In the meantime, we still need to continue our questioning of Liz Matthews. Jenny has received more information from our Glasgow colleagues. We'll use that to break her down. But if we can't get anything else from her, we may have to let her go. Blair and Sid, I want you to do the interviews. Consult with Jenny for the additional information and get started. Remember, the time extension runs out at eleven o'clock.'

She turned to Jenny. 'Angel's photograph. Have you sent that to Glasgow?'

'Yes, they're checking it and promised to have something for me this morning.'

'Good. Now we've all got lots to do so I suggest you waste no time in getting down to it.'

Kate headed back to her office to have the long-delayed chat with the procurator fiscal and to work out how she was going to present the photographs to Superintendent Jolly. She reckoned she knew the response of the fiscal, but she dreaded the one from Jolly.

Downstairs the duty room was a hive of activity. Phones rang, computers beeped and the duty sergeant he was talking to seemed frazzled.

Bill sighed with frustration. 'There must be a couple of uniforms available. They can't all be out on emergencies.'

'Sorry, Bill, but there are all sorts going down this morning. We've got a major accident at the Forfar Road roundabout on the Kingsway. A threatened suicide on the road bridge. A guy going bananas at Ninewells Hospital, and a hostage situation at Kirkton. Some bloody guy armed with a crossbow and a sword has a woman, her two children, and a social worker locked inside a flat with him. He's threatening to top anyone who tries to get inside.'

'What's the social worker doing in there?' Bill's curiosity overcame his annoyance.

'Went in to take the woman and kids out and landed up locked inside with them.'

The ringing phone interrupted the sergeant mid-flow. 'Bloody hell. Not another emergency. I can't stand it.' He grabbed the phone and listened. 'Sure, sure.' He scribbled on a piece of paper. 'It might be a wee while before I can get anyone to you.' A cackle of noise erupted from the phone, and he held it away from his ear for a few moments. 'Yes, sir,' he said. 'I'll make sure that's understood.'

He consulted a computer screen before turning back to Bill. 'There's a patrol car about half an hour away. I'll call it in. Just keep your fingers crossed the damned car doesn't get diverted to another bleeding emergency.'

'Just our bloody luck,' Bill said to Sue. 'We get the chance to arrest Tony Palmer, and there are no bloody uniforms available to accompany us.'

'Half an hour won't make much difference. It'll give us a chance to catch a cuppa,' Sue replied.

'You can go back upstairs and be blasted out of the water for not being out on the job, but I'll stay down here to wait.'

'Don't be such a sourpuss. I'm sure the sergeant won't mind if we use the machine down here.'

'Bloody liberty,' the duty sergeant said. 'Just don't forget to put a couple of quid in the tin beside it. And use the paper cups, the china ones are all spoken for.'

'Will do, Sarge.' Sue picked her way through the proliferation of computer stations to the rear of the room.

She returned a few minutes later and shoved a cup of coffee into Bill's hands. 'Get that down you while we wait.'

Bill nodded his thanks, although the scowl didn't leave his face. He was itching to get out there to bring Tony Palmer in.

47

Luigi hadn't slept since they'd planted the device and neither had Fabio. From time to time he looked in on the boy who never seemed to have moved position since their return, his eyes fixated on the computer screen in front of him, watching a red arrow that never moved.

The house was waking up when an unwelcome thought crept into his mind. He'd been so involved with setting things up and making sure the plan was working, he'd forgotten to ask Fabio if there was anything in his room that would point to them.

Luigi paused on his way to the kitchen where he could hear Bet clattering dishes. He cast his eyes towards the stairs. Fabio was young, not much more than a boy. Maybe he'd expected too much from him and he'd promised Georgio he would look after him. He'd been mad to involve him in this plan. But what else could he do? Fabio was the one with the expertise.

He changed direction and mounted the stairs.

Nothing had changed since his last visit. Fabio still sat in the same position; his eyes fixed on the computer screen.

Luigi glanced along the corridor before pulling the door shut behind him. It closed with the softest of clicks. He crossed the room and placed his hands on the boy's shoulders.

'Nothing happening so far.' Fabio didn't look up. 'The car hasn't moved all night.'

'You look tired. It's a wonder you can keep your eyes open.'

'I'll sleep when this is all over.'

Luigi shook his head. What had he got the boy involved in? If they were caught, he'd spend years in prison instead of joining the other students at Abertay University.

He looked around the room at the conglomeration of plugs,

wires, and computer components. Half of them were a mystery to him. He had no idea what they were for or what to do with them.

'The stuff you used to make the device. You sure there's no trace of it left here?'

Fabio removed his gaze from the computer screen and cast Luigi an amused look. 'What d'you take me for? Of course, there's nothing here. It's all at the bottom of the dock. I dropped the bag in the water while you were wheeling the bike out of Chandlers Lane.'

The morning light grew brighter and the air in the bedroom more stifling, but Tony didn't have the energy to open a window. The wait for the police to arrive seemed interminable, and he spent the time either staring into space or pacing the room.

He was tempted to phone his solicitor but decided against it. That would have indicated he knew the intentions of the police in advance of their arrival.

By nine o'clock his stomach was growling in protest, and he went down to the kitchen in search of breakfast. If they came while he was eating, he would make them wait. But when Bet dished up the plate of bacon and eggs, he couldn't eat it. 'Just a piece of toast this morning.' He pushed the plate away.

Bet didn't comment but he could see she was thinking he'd had a night on the bevvy, and maybe she wasn't far wrong.

Luigi appeared at his side while he was buttering his toast. 'Phone call, boss. It's on your private line.'

'Yes,' Tony said, as he listened to the voice on the other end of the line. 'Thank you for letting me know. I'll get on to my solicitor and make the arrangements.'

It was half-past ten before the police car drew up outside the house. He watched from a window while two uniformed cops got out and joined the two plainclothes officers on the pavement. One of them was Sergeant Rogers. Sue, he thought her name was. But the other one was that bloody Bill Murphy.

It had to be him. That bugger had been the bane of his life for as long as he could remember.

They looked towards the house and then approached the front door.

Tony straightened his tie, buttoned his jacket, and waited for them to be announced.

Bill braced himself as Luigi ushered him and Sue into the house. He was looking forward to this moment and hoped Tony would put up some resistance so he could arrest him. Nothing would give him greater pleasure.

'Mr Palmer is waiting for you in the drawing-room. Follow me and I will take you there.'

Bill wasn't sure what Luigi did for Tony although he'd remembered his name. Was he the butler? A manservant? Or one of Tony's bodyguards?

As if he guessed what Bill was thinking, Luigi smiled at them as he opened the door. It was a polite smile, although Bill wondered if there was the slightest hint of menace behind it.

Sue returned his smile, apparently less suspicious of the man.

Tony stood in the window recess. He had been watching their approach, and at their entry he crossed the room to meet them.

He held out his hand to Bill. 'I've been waiting for you.'

Taken aback, Bill responded. The handshake was firm, but not too firm. The shake one friend would give to another. But Tony wasn't his friend, so what was the bugger playing at? And besides, why was everyone smiling like damned Cheshire cats?

'I understand you have some questions for me and would like to do it at Bell Street.' He gestured for them to sit. 'Unfortunately, my solicitor is not free until after eleven o'clock, so I've made arrangements to attend at a quarter past. I trust that is a convenient time for you?'

Bill couldn't stop himself from asking. 'How did you

know?'

'Ah! Superintendent Jolly phoned with a request for me to attend an interview. In the meantime, I can offer you refreshments if you want to wait to take me in, or I can get there under my own steam. Whichever you prefer.'

'Bugger enjoyed that,' Bill said after they left. He slapped the steering wheel in annoyance. What was it with him and the super? He'd love to know.

Luigi closed the door behind the two police officers. Their presence had unsettled him, and he hadn't been able to relax until they left. What if they'd come to search the house? How would he have explained the tracking software on the computer? It didn't bear thinking about.

'Problem, boss?' he said when he turned to find Tony standing behind him.

'Not really. Nothing I can't handle.' But there was something in Tony's expression that implied the opposite.

Out of the corner of his eye, Luigi saw Fabio leaning over the bannister at the top of the stairs. The boy looked anxious, and he made a beckoning motion before disappearing back along the corridor.

That meant the car must be on the move. Prickles of unease rushed through him, but he couldn't walk away from Tony without good reason.

'You need me for anything, boss?'

Luigi resisted the urge to hold his breath and tried to maintain a calm exterior while he waited for an answer. But his mind churned with ideas of what he would do if Tony did need him for anything.

'Not at the moment, Luigi. I have several things to attend to in my office and then I'll be out for a time. I'm not sure how long. The police want me at Bell Street for questioning.'

'Trouble?'

'I'm sure Simon will make sure I'm all right,' he said. But the worried look was back on his face.

Relief surged through Luigi as he watched his boss walk

through the connecting door to his office, but he did not relax until the door closed behind him.

Afraid Fabio might trigger the device prematurely, he bounded up the stairs. They had to be certain the timing was right, and Fabio's impatience might wreck the whole thing. He was out of breath by the time he reached the boy's room and he stood panting on the threshold before drawing a chair over to the computer to observe the red arrow on the screen.

Fabio's face bore a frown. 'They left the hotel fifteen minutes ago, but the car is now outside Bell Street Police Station.'

'That's where Tony's heading.'

Luigi's thoughts raced. Was there a connection? Tony wouldn't have risked taking any of his enforcers to a police station, so he would be vulnerable. Did that mean he was walking into an ambush? But that wasn't possible. How would Jimmy Matthews know Tony would be there? It would be a strange place for them to have a confrontation.

'Is it time?' Fabio's hand reached for the mobile.

'No. It's too public. Too many people around. Besides, if the car is still in Dundee, we don't know for sure that Jimmy Matthews is in it. We can only be sure once they're on the road back to Glasgow.' Luigi bit his lip. He hoped his decision was the correct one and that Tony was in no danger.

It was almost an hour later before the car moved again and they watched the red arrow as it tracked the journey through Dundee. The car was well on its way to Perth before Luigi gave the signal.

'Now,' he said.

Fabio's finger speed dialled the number and the two of them sat back in their chairs and smiled. Job done.

48

Simon Pegg was waiting for Tony at the bottom of the steps leading up to the police station when Brian dropped him off.

'I'll phone for you when I'm finished here,' Tony said before turning to greet Simon.

The solicitor was immaculately dressed in a dark grey suit with an accompanying waistcoat, white shirt, and bow tie. His slicked-back hair and olive complexion suggested he came from a sunnier country, although Tony knew he was Dundee, born and bred. He held out a hand, and a smile softened the supercilious expression which he presented to the world.

'Good to see you, Tony.' They shook hands. 'We'll soon get this business sorted.'

A woman emerged from the door at the top of the steps followed by a tall man dressed similarly to Simon.

Tony's eyes narrowed when he recognised her. It was that bloody Liz Stewart who had been feeding Madge drugs. He'd thought the cops had her banged up in a cell, but here she was, walking towards him. She stopped when she saw him, and he thought for a moment she intended to say something. But she turned away and walked towards a waiting car.

Jimmy Matthews got out of the car to welcome her. He stared at Tony and nodded before helping Liz into the back seat.

Unable to believe his eyes, Tony swore under his breath. Why the fuck had the cops let her go?

He clenched his fists to stop his anger from exploding in a torrent of abuse. If the cops weren't going to charge her, he'd make sure she paid for what she'd done.

Simon touched him on the arm. 'Shall we go inside and get this over with?'

Tony sensed the unasked question in Simon's quizzical

expression, but he simply nodded and headed up the steps to the entrance.

A uniformed cop led them to the interview room, pointed to where they should sit, and then left closing the door behind him.

It was a bare room with cream painted walls which were grubby in places, a functional table, and four chairs strategically placed, two at each side of the table. And it stank of body odour and vomit. A red light blinked high in the room's corner, and Tony was sure they were being observed.

'I see they've honoured us with the executive suite.'

Tony reckoned the choice of room had been deliberate, but he wasn't prepared to show it bothered him. Nor would he give any sign he found the chair uncomfortable even though it pressed painfully on his thighs. And no amount of wriggling would relieve the hardness of the back, which forced him into a rigid position he was sure would do wonders for his posture. The chairs weren't designed for comfort. Another deliberate choice, he was sure.

The minutes ticked by and despite Tony's resolve to remain calm, his stomach clenched and sweat gathered under his armpits. His hands pressed on his trouser legs so any dampness would be dispelled. He was damned if he'd let the buggers get to him.

Simon sat beside him with an expensive-looking gold pen in the hand that rested on the legal pad in front of him. He met Tony's eyes with a smile.

'It's a ploy,' he said. 'They want to unsettle you.'

'It will take more than that to unsettle me.'

Tony regulated his breathing. Several deep, slow breaths later, his stomach unclenched, and his anxiety decreased to a tolerable level. He was ready for them. At least, he hoped he was.

Upstairs in the team room, Kate, Bill, and Sue clustered around the monitor with the direct feed to the interview room.

'Most people look worried when they're waiting to be

interviewed, but he looks quite relaxed. As if he didn't have a care in the world.'

'He's always been a confident bastard. Thinks he can get away with anything.' Bill itched to knock the smile off Tony's face. Those photographs should do the trick.

Kate glared at him. 'Sorry, boss, but he's got off with so much in the past I can't help swearing.'

'I hope you keep it under control when you're interviewing him, or you'll get nowhere.'

'Yes, boss.' Bill resolved to be at his most professional even though the bastard provoked him.

'I see Mr Palmer has arrived for his interview.'

Superintendent Jolly's approach had been silent. Bill wondered if that was a deliberate action on the super's part to catch them out. Although what the bugger thought he would gain by that was beyond Bill.

'Yes, sir,' Kate said, 'we were planning how to handle it.'

Jolly pulled a chair over and placed it in front of the screen. 'I'll join you to watch the proceedings. Another pair of eyes might be helpful.' He removed his peaked cap, brushed the top with his arm, and placed it on the desk in front of him. 'Let's not keep Mr Palmer waiting. I'm sure he's a busy man.'

'During the interview my officers will ask Mr Palmer to explain some photographs. I trust you've had time to study them.'

Bill's eyes flicked between Kate and the super wondering how he would react to her confrontational stance. But the man seemed unperturbed.

'Of course.' He settled himself into a more comfortable position in his chair. 'Which of your officers will be conducting the interview?'

'DS Murphy, and DS Rogers. I thought, given Mr Palmer's standing in the community, it warranted the attention of two of my sergeants rather than constables.'

Jolly gave no indication he recognised the sarcasm in Kate's voice although Bill was sure it had not gone unnoticed, and he wondered if Kate would pay for that at a later date.

The super's voice was smooth as he focused on the

monitor. 'Perhaps we should get on with it then and not keep Mr Palmer waiting any longer.'

'We are waiting for the procurator fiscal to arrive before we start. She thought it would be useful to observe the interview to help her decide whether there are legal grounds to pursue Mr Palmer further.'

Superintendent Jolly frowned, and Bill got the impression he would prefer to continue without her. The fiscal often insisted on a high standard of evidence and didn't always agree with police decisions a prosecution was necessary. Something that didn't always go down well with the top brass.

'Ah, here she is now.' Kate turned to welcome the tall, slim, unsmiling blonde woman who had entered the team room.

Jolly stood. 'You're new to Dundee and I don't think I've had the pleasure.' He held out a hand for her to shake.

'Astrid Christensen,' she said with a tight-lipped smile. 'And I've been the fiscal here for over a year.'

Bill noted her tone of reproof and Jolly's discomfiture. It amused him that the man had just been taken down a peg. Served him right.

'I suppose now you have arrived we can get on with the interview.' Jolly waved a hand at Bill and Sue. 'Well, get on with it. What are you waiting for?'

'I was with Kate when we interviewed Palmer at his home,' Bill said as they made their way to the interview room, 'I'll take the lead.'

'Don't forget the super's watching the interview.'

Sue didn't need to say it, but Bill knew she meant, 'Don't get stroppy with him.'

'Don't worry, I'll keep my cool.'

49

Despite Tony's attempt to remain calm he wasn't as ready as he thought he was, and anxiety gnawed at his insides. He knew it was imperative to maintain his composure, but as the time dragged on with the passing minutes feeling like hours, keeping a calm exterior was becoming more difficult. He wanted this done and over with so he could get on with his life.

When the door finally opened, the knot in his gut tightened.

The cop entering the room was that bloody Bill Murphy, the one who had it in for him and had sworn to see him behind bars. The attractive, redheaded cop, Sue Rogers, followed him. At least, that was better. He hoped Sue would be the one asking the questions, but he doubted it. Murphy wouldn't miss his chance to stick the knife in.

The two detectives took their seats opposite Tony and his solicitor, Simon Pegg. Sue leaned over, switched on the recorder, and recited the date and names of everyone present.

Tony hoped that meant she would conduct the interview, but his hopes were dashed when Bill Murphy spoke.

'For the record. Can you confirm your name is Anthony James Palmer?'

'Yes, but I prefer to be called Tony.'

Bill ignored him and continued, asking him to verify his date of birth and address. Following Tony's confirmation, he started to read the caution.

The knot in Tony's stomach tightened. 'Hang on a minute. I'm here voluntarily to help you with your enquiries. Am I under arrest?'

'I'm afraid that in accordance with the Criminal Justice (Scotland) Act 2016, I am required to read the caution, but you are not under arrest and are free to go at any time you wish. However, I would not advise it, otherwise, we might have to consider arresting you.'

'Does that mean I am a suspect?'

'During an investigation, everyone connected with the victim is a suspect until proven otherwise and, as the last person to see the victim alive, that means yes to your question.'

Simon bent towards Tony. 'It's normal procedure. Nothing to worry about.' Simon cast an amused glance at Bill Murphy. 'My client has nothing to hide, therefore he has decided he will answer any questions you care to put to him.'

Tony caught a flicker of disappointment in Bill's eyes. No doubt the cop had been expecting him to respond to his questions with no comment. Tony always thought this kind of response was incriminating and meant the person responding might be guilty. He had no intention of giving the impression of guilt.

'Take us through your movements on Friday night, the 20th of August until Saturday morning, the 21st of August.'

'I explained all that to you when you interviewed me before.'

Before Bill could reply, Sue leaned towards him. 'It's for the tape. I'm sure you'll understand. We need to get everything on record.'

Tony's anger subsided. 'It's a drag, but if you feel you need a record of any information I can provide, that's fine.'

The interview continued without incident and Tony recited all the information he'd previously supplied.

'You maintain you only knew Angel under her performing name. Do you stand by that?'

Tony couldn't prevent the slight hesitation before he replied. 'Yes, I only knew her as Angel Golding.'

There was no way he was going to tell the cops he'd found out Angel had been the wife of Kevin Matthews. If they knew he was aware she was Lesley Matthews, they could use that against him. They already knew of his run-ins with the Matthews' gang and would probably conclude he had killed

Angel because he found out she was spying for them.

'These photographs.' Bill laid the photos in front of Tony, spreading them out so the detail was clear. 'If, as you say, you left the victim's flat after you inspected it for intruders, how do you explain these?'

Tony had been expecting the photographs to be produced at some point, but he raised his eyebrows in feigned surprise.

'Where on earth did you get these? I haven't seen them for several months.'

'Several months?' There was a note of surprise but also disbelief in Bill Murphy's voice.

'Yes, it was a clumsy attempt to blackmail me at the end of last year, but it didn't work. My wife knew I sometimes strayed but that I always returned to her. So, I told the blackmailers to fuck off and do their worst.'

'I notice you have not previously mentioned having an affair with the victim.'

'I'd hardly call it an affair. A dalliance, maybe. My dancers are very attractive women. It's hard to resist. However, after what happened to my daughter at the beginning of the year, other women lost their charm for me.'

The expression on Murphy's face changed from triumph to disappointment, and Tony wasn't sure how much of his explanation the cop believed.

It was some considerable time later before the questioning ended and Bill Murphy stood up.

'We may want to interview you again. Do not make any plans to leave the area.' He left the room without a backward glance.

Sue Rogers rose from her seat and prepared to follow Bill out of the room.

'Thank you for your help, Mr Palmer. We'll let you know if we need to see you again.'

Simon heaved his briefcase onto the table and placed his legal pad and pen into it. 'That was a bit of a marathon, but I think it went well.'

Tony wasn't so sure. The interview had lasted over two hours and had felt more like an interrogation. Meanwhile, Bill

Murphy's knife felt as if it was firmly planted between his shoulder blades. He would have to do something about that man. And he would have to do it quickly.

Kate, Superintendent Jolly, and the procurator fiscal sat in a huddle in front of the video link monitor. Looking up at their entry, Kate beckoned Bill and Sue to join them.

'We've been discussing the interview and it would be helpful to get your general impressions.'

The fiscal laid a pen on top of her open notebook. Her grey eyes were steady and her tone matter of fact.

Bill considered her with wary eyes. He hadn't sussed out Astrid Christensen yet. All he knew was she liked to do things by the book and wouldn't agree to prosecute unless she was sure the evidence was unshakeable.

'He was too smooth. He had all the answers, and I'd swear he knew about the photographs before we produced them. I'm also sure he has more information about the victim than he's admitting. My gut feeling is he was lying.'

'I'm afraid courts do not convict on the basis of gut feelings.' The fiscal closed her notebook and rose. 'Currently, there is insufficient evidence to charge Mr Palmer with anything. Let me know when the forensic results come through. In the meantime, I have to leave to attend to another matter.'

Superintendent Jolly, looking smug, also took his leave.

Bill waited until he was alone with Kate and Sue before he spoke. 'I'm damned sure he's guilty.'

'Then we need to prove it,' Kate said. 'We should have the forensic results back within a day or two and if we find Tony's DNA on the bedding, that should clinch it.'

'He's a slippery bugger,' Bill said, 'but if his DNA is there, he'll have a hard job wriggling out of this one.'

He returned to his desk to record in his notes the date and time of the interview and his impressions of it.

'This time,' he said to Sue, who was sitting at the desk next to him. 'I'm going to get that bugger.'

'I've heard that before.' She reached into her drawer, removed a packet of salt and vinegar crisps and threw it to him.

'This time it's different. We have more evidence and I'd lay bets on there being Tony's DNA on the bedding. Let's see him dodge that one.' He rammed a handful of crisps into his mouth and crunched them. Tony's time was almost up, and Bill didn't intend to let him off the hook.

50

Tony stood outside the police station basking in the midday sun while he waited for Brian to arrive with the car. His stomach growled, reminding him he had only eaten a piece of toast earlier in the day, but he had things to do before he could take time off to eat.

When the car arrived, he instructed Brian to take him to Candace Morgan's flat. It was time to have a talk with her and by the time he was finished, he was sure she would reconsider her position and refuse to give evidence against him.

Tony remained in the shadows while Brian rapped on the door.

'You took your time,' the girl who opened the door said. She peered out at Brian. 'Oh, I thought you were Candace coming back. She's not here.'

Tony caught his breath. The girl standing in the doorway had brown hair scraped back in a ponytail, but he would have recognised her anywhere.

He walked forward out of the shadows. 'Well, well, isn't this a surprise?'

The girl retreated into the flat and Tony followed her. She reached for the heavy-framed spectacles sitting on the table and perched them on her nose to peer more closely at Tony.

'I'm afraid I don't know you, but if you're looking for Candace, she won't be long.'

'Good try, Angel.' Tony reached out and removed the glasses. 'But I'd recognise those eyes anywhere, and that nose, and that mouth.'

She backed away from him.

'But the question I now have is who was the body lying beside me in the bed when it wasn't you?'

'You're mistaken.' Defiance flared in the girl's eyes.

'Candace always said I looked a bit like Angel, but I'm not Angel. I'm Linda Taylor.'

The door behind them burst open. 'What the hell are you doing here?' Candace faced up to them. 'And what are you doing threatening Linda?'

Tony regarded her with amusement. 'You forget I own this building. I can enter it any time I wish. As for threatening Linda.' He looked around the room. 'I see no Linda here. But what I do see is a very much alive Angel.' He lowered his voice to its most menacing tone. 'And now, perhaps the pair of you would be wise to tell me what you've been up to and who the hell was the body in the bed?'

Bill attacked the keyboard with vicious finger stabs. If there was one task he hated it was having to document everything he did. Bloody paperwork was killing proper police work. That and procedures. Having to do everything by the book. He was sure it must have been easier in the old days when you kicked shit out of a suspect until they confessed. How he would have loved to kick the shit out of Tony in the interview room.

After he'd typed the last word and sent the report to the printer, he became aware Kate was gathering the team around the display boards. Something must be up. Maybe the forensic results were back.

A surge of elation rippled through him. If the forensics proved what he thought they would, Tony would have nowhere to turn, and they'd get him. With mounting excitement, he joined the group in front of the boards.

Kate acknowledged him with a nod of the head.

'I think we can get started now that we are all here. Jenny has been following a line of enquiry with some of our colleagues in Glasgow Division and she has come up with some interesting information. Over to you, Jenny.' Kate moved away from the board.

Bill focused on Jenny who had moved to the front of the group. He was pleased she was getting a bit of attention because she was so often overshadowed by Blair and Sid. Probably deliberate on their part. Today, she looked more confident. Her posture was more erect making her seem taller, and her eyes sparkled behind her oversized spectacles.

'A brief update first,' Jenny said. 'We already know that the car stalking Angel was owned by a Glasgow detective, name of Denzil Rafferty, who has connections with a gang in Glasgow run by Jimmy Matthews. The woman named Liz Stewart who has been under investigation has been identified as Liz Matthews, a niece of Jimmy Matthews. She has convictions for fraud and is known to be violent.' Jenny paused for a sip of water before continuing.

'That name, Matthews, kept on coming up in connection with our investigation of Angel Golding's murder and, as we suspected she was using an alias, I sent her details to Glasgow. This included a photograph. Glasgow Division was unable to match her fingerprints or any of the details we sent, but they had more luck with the photograph. According to them, it has been identified as that of Lesley Matthews, wife of Kevin Matthews, and daughter-in-law of Jimmy Matthews. She has had some involvement with police in the past, mainly minor offences. Glasgow Division is sending us her physical file as it contains more information than the electronic version.'

'Thank you, Jenny. Good work.' Kate stood and touched Jenny's arm. 'I'll take it from here.'

Head down and pink with embarrassment, Jenny scurried back to her seat.

'This raises some new questions in our investigation. Why was she in Dundee? Why was she working for Tony Palmer if she was part of the Matthews' outfit? And above all, why were the fingerprints of our victim not found on the database if Lesley Matthews had a record?

Our first task is to examine the file which is being sent. It wouldn't be sensible to assume anything until we've seen that, and hopefully, it will be here by tomorrow.'

'What about this detective fellow, Denzil Rafferty?' Bill had a vague recollection there had been some follow up into him, although he hadn't been involved in that part of the investigation.

'Jenny, where are we with that?'

'He's gone to ground. When Glasgow Division checked on him, they found his offices had been subject to a fire which destroyed a large part of the building, and there have been no recent sightings of him. They said they'd contact us once he surfaces.'

Bill mulled the information over in his mind. He didn't like loose ends, and there seemed to be a multitude in this case.

'Just a thought,' he said. 'We know, or at least think, that the Matthews' outfit is making a move on Tony Palmer's interests in Dundee. If this Liz woman, who we now know is a Matthews, was a plant in Tony's house to spy on him, does that mean they planted Angel in Teasers to spy on Tony? And, if so, does that give him the motive to kill her?'

Kate turned thoughtful eyes on Bill. 'That's a possibility, although there is one flaw in that argument.'

'And that is?'

'He didn't kill Liz Stewart alias Matthews, who was harming his wife. So why would he kill Angel for spying on him?'

Bill clamped his mouth shut. He had no answer, but he remained convinced Tony was responsible for Angel's murder.

51

Tony had to admire Candace as she stood in front of him, spitting fire and fury.

'You are going to tell me everything, so it might be better if you sat down and made yourself comfortable. I'm sure Brian will help you if you have a problem with that.'

Brian took a step forward, and after a glance at his imposing bulk Angel seated herself on the sofa. Candace followed suit.

'That's better,' Tony said.

'Now, I'm sure you won't want to look at Brian while we have our little chat, so I don't think he will object to standing behind you.'

Tony pulled a chair over and sat in front of the two girls. Candace flinched and drew back, but Angel stared at him with a look of contempt on her face.

'Shall we start by you telling me which one of you murdered that poor girl upstairs? I assume she must have been the real Linda Taylor?'

'I'm telling you nothing.'

'My, you're a little fireball, aren't you, Candace? What about you, Angel, or should I call you Lesley?'

A fleeting look of alarm crossed Angel's face at his use of her real name. But she said nothing.

'Cat got your tongue, Angel?' Tony sighed.

'Perhaps I should tell you what I've deduced. Correct me if I'm wrong.'

It hadn't taken him long to guess what had happened once he realised Angel was still alive. It didn't take a genius to work it out.

'As I see it, you prevailed upon my good nature to accompany you to your flat and once there, you drugged me, undressed me, and placed me in your bed. You then invited Candace and her friend, Linda, to the flat, killed Linda and placed her in the bed beside me. Have I got it right so far?'

He knew by the look on their faces he had.

'What I don't know is which one of you killed the girl and I am unsure of the motive. At a guess, I'd say it was because you wanted to escape the clutches of your husband and his father.' He paused and looked at Angel. 'Ah, I see by your expression I'm right.'

His voice deepened and became more menacing. 'But the thing I can't figure out was why you wanted to frame me for the murder.'

'What are you going to do with us?' Candace shrank back on the sofa, the anger she'd displayed earlier gone, replaced by fear and resentment.

'Ah, that is the problem?'

He'd never had any compunction about dealing out retribution to men, but there was something within the core of his being that was reluctant to apply the same punishment to women. But he couldn't let them off with what they had done.

'You could let us go. We could vanish. We've done it before.' Angel looked at him, a mute plea in her eyes. 'I don't think I could hack prison.'

'Why would I do that? It would leave me on the hook for your murder and I'm not prepared to take that chance.'

'But you're not a grass, are you, Tony?'

'No. But neither am I a martyr. I have no intention of taking the blame for something you did.'

'What will you do?'

The tremble in Angel's voice sent a pang of pity through him, but he resisted it. In trying to frame him for murder she had done something unforgivable.

'I haven't made my mind up yet, but I need you to stay here while I think.'

It was obvious what was in Angel's mind when he finished speaking. Once he left, the two of them would be gone. He smiled. It gave him pleasure to dash her hopes.

'I'll arrange for someone to keep you company to ensure

your safety.' His eyes narrowed. 'And your compliance.'

He turned his attention to Brian and instructed him to send for Ken to guard Candace and Angel while he put the next stage of his plan into action. He couldn't risk the two girls running before it all played out.

Bill sat longer in Donovan's pub than he'd intended, and it was dark when he left to walk along the quiet street to the car park.

He brushed aside the thought it might not be a good idea to drive in case he was over the limit, but he'd only had one beer.

Anyway, whose damned idea was it to make the legal driving limit in Scotland so low even one beer was too much?

He stuck the key into the ignition. It wasn't far to drive, he would take his chances.

The Victorian villa where he lived was in darkness when he parked in front of it. The downstairs flat opposite his, was vacant waiting for a new buyer, while the upstairs tenants were probably still out on the town.

He stumbled on the steps leading to the front of the house, cursing under his breath because the light was out. Damned bulb was always popping. But the hall lights were out as well. He felt the way to his door, turned the key and entered.

A rustle of movement broke the customary silence. Someone was here, waiting for him. His first thought was burglars, and he crept to the lounge door prepared for battle. What he didn't expect was the nozzle of the gun prodding his back.

'It's loaded,' a voice whispered in his ear, 'don't do anything foolish.'

'What do you want? If it's money you're out of luck, there's nothing here. And, as you can see, I don't possess many worldly goods.'

'I'm afraid it's not that simple.'

Rough hands gripped his arms, and a hood was pulled over his head. Other hands went through his pockets and removed his mobile phone.

'We need to take you somewhere,' the voice continued. 'Tony wants a word with you.'

Candace's grip tightened on Angel's hand as she looked at Tony. This wasn't playing out the way they meant it to. By this time Tony should have been locked up and facing a charge of murder, while they would have had money in their pockets and a new life to start. But the plan had backfired, and they were caught between a rock and a hard place.

Tony smiled at them, but his eyes remained flat and menacing.

Candace shuddered. The bugger was taking pleasure at their discomfort, and the more her fear increased the more he seemed to enjoy it. If she had ever doubted Tony was capable of anything, she didn't doubt it now.

The door behind him opened to admit a large muscle-bound man. This must be the Ken he'd sent for. She'd seen him before at Teasers and knew he was one of Tony's enforcers. Her heart rate increased, and her hand tightened even more on Angel's. She didn't rate their chances under this man's watchful eye.

Tony rose and buttoned his jacket. 'Ken will stay with you while I consider what to do next.'

He walked to the door but stopped on the threshold to turn and smile at them. 'I wouldn't advise you to leave. Ken really doesn't know his own strength. In the meantime, you will have time to reflect on your actions. Plus, you'd better hope my decision will be to turn you over to the police because the alternatives will not be pleasant for you.' The menace in his voice was unmistakable.

52

Thursday

Rough hands pushed Bill, and a door slammed behind him. His breath came in hot, steamy gasps inside the rough hood, which smelled of something oily. Where had they taken him? Judging from the echo of the door and their footsteps on the stone floor it must be somewhere big and empty. It didn't bode well for him.

Hands forced him onto a chair before they tore the hood from his head. He gulped in mouthfuls of air and glared at his captor. Phil stood in front of him with his hands on his hips and hatred spoiling his too-perfect features.

'Why am I here, pretty boy?'

Phil's scowl deepened. 'Shut that smart mouth of yours.'

'That's enough, Phil.' Tony sauntered over and sat on the chair facing Bill. 'We mustn't annoy our guest.'

Bill looked around, taking in the barn and the empty animal stalls at the far end. Country then, not city. No doubt the place was remote with no help anywhere nearby. How long would it take them to find his body? His face remained expressionless. No way was he going to allow them to see his fear.

'Do you always treat your guests so lavishly?' He didn't bother to hide the sarcasm in his voice.

Tony leaned over and patted his knee. 'I only want to talk without any interference from your colleagues.'

'You could have talked when we had you at the station.'

'Ah, yes. Such a lovely interview room. The ideal place to have a nice private chat.' His face hardened. 'All you wanted from me was a confession to the murder of Angel. Considering her murder was nothing to do with me I wasn't really tempted to accede to your request.'

'I'm expected to believe that, am I?'

'I know perfectly well you want to believe I'm guilty. We have a history, you and I, and there is no doubt in my mind you would like to lock me up and throw away the key. But I also know you believe in justice. And if you continue trying to pin Angel's murder on me, justice will not be served.'

Bill snorted in disbelief but couldn't stop a worm of doubt creeping into his mind. What Tony said was true. He wouldn't rest until he'd seen the man incarcerated in prison for more years than he had left to live. Was that colouring his investigation? Was he trying to fit Tony up?

'The evidence all points to you. You were with Angel the night she was murdered. You can't deny it. No one else entered or left the building during the time it took to kill her. And you're a murderous bastard. We all know that.'

Phil moved behind Bill. He held his breath as he waited for the final blow to land. There was nothing he could do to stop it.

Tony held up his hand and shook his head. Phil moved further away.

Bill let out his breath.

'I may be a murderous bastard.' Tony sounded amused. 'But I have never killed or been responsible for a woman's death. I draw the line at some things. Besides, why would I kill Angel? She was my top dancer. It wouldn't be good business. Angel was the reason many of the punters came to Teasers. They wanted to see her perform. I'm afraid the one thing you are lacking in your investigation is motive.'

Bill shifted on the hard chair. Tony had a point. They hadn't been able to find a motive.

'I'm sure the motive will become obvious as the investigation proceeds. And it will proceed with me or without me.'

Tony ignored him and continued to speak. 'I did not murder Angel and the evidence you have is weak. You say I was the only one to enter and leave the building during the period the killer struck?' He leaned forward and brought his face close to Bill's. 'Don't you see what that means? The killer was still in the building.'

'That's not possible. The only people in the building were your tenants. Your dancing girls. Why would any of them want to kill Angel? I'm damned sure we'll find your DNA all over Angel's bedding and once we find that, you're done for, mate.'

'Perhaps it might help your thinking processes if I told you a story.' Tony settled back in his chair, narrowing his eyes and appraising Bill. 'You need to understand my story is hypothetical and does not incriminate anyone.'

'I'll be the judge of that.'

Tony laughed. 'It doesn't matter, anyway. Under Scots law, anything I say needs to be corroborated and who is going to do that?'

Bill stared at him. The man was right. Without corroboration, anything he was told wouldn't stand up in a court of law.

'Once upon a time there was a dancer, let's call her Angel. She was being threatened by some Glasgow mobsters, let's call the main man Jimmy Matthews. He instructed one of his thugs, let's call him Mad Dog, to bring Angel to his table at a nightclub. Angel didn't want to go, but Mad Dog forced her.' Tony's eyes narrowed. 'And there was this man who observed everything and rescued Angel from the clutches of Jimmy Matthews. To ensure her safety he escorted Angel to her flat. His intention was to leave her there and return home to his wife. However, Angel insisted he accept a drink of his favourite whisky as a reward for protecting her.' Tony stared at Bill. 'You following it so far?'

Bill nodded, wondering what Tony was getting at because the man was obviously Tony himself.

'The man accepted the drink, and he knew no more until he woke up in bed with the bloody body of Angel lying beside him. After his initial confusion, and once he'd had time to think about it, the conclusion he came to was the drink Angel gave him must have been drugged. That poses the question. Why would Angel want to drug him?'

He leaned forward to stare into Bill's eyes. 'Then the plot

thickens when an envelope of photographs is sent to the man.' Tony inspected his fingernails before buffing them on the front of his jacket. 'These photographs show him sleeping beside Angel. Somewhat compromising, I'd say. But that poses another question. Why did he not wake up when the photographs were taken? The flash would be enough to wake even the heaviest sleeper. Unless, of course, the man was in a drug-induced sleep. You following me so far?'

Tony's composure was slipping, and Bill wondered if the man was as confident as he sounded. What did he have to gain from telling this story?

'I can think of only one reason. Angel knew the man was afraid of losing his wife, so she planned to blackmail him. But the problem is that Angel was also in the bed. She must have had an accomplice.'

Despite himself, Bill's curiosity surfaced.

'Just for interest, we'll call this accomplice her friend, Candace. Angel gets into the bed with the man and the subsequent photographs are sent to the man, but they are also sent to the police. Now, ask yourself what benefit that would be to the photographer other than to incriminate the man.'

Candace. She was the one with purple-streaked red hair who claimed to be Angel's friend. The one who had identified her body. Bill remembered her.

'Why would Candace want to kill her friend?'

'Ah, now this is where it gets interesting.' The smile on Tony's lips did not reach his eyes. 'How sure are you it was Angel's body in the bed?'

Bill's thoughts flashed back to the previous day. The information Jenny had acquired from Glasgow about Angel. Her identification as Lesley Matthews whose fingerprints didn't match those of the murdered girl.

Tony leaned back in his chair with a satisfied look on his face. 'I see you have doubts.'

'Candace identified the body. We have no reason to disbelieve her.'

'Not unless Angel is still alive.'

'If Angel is alive whose body is lying in the mortuary?'

'That is for you to find out, but I suggest you don't have far to look. Perhaps Candace's partner, Linda Taylor, might supply you with the answer.'

Doubts swirled through Bill's mind, and although he wasn't sure what Tony was suggesting the implications were disturbing.

'This is all too far-fetched.' Even as he said it, Bill knew his reluctance to believe Tony hinged on his need to get something on him. Get a conviction that would send the man away for a long time and this was the nearest he'd ever come to that.

Tony heaved a sigh. 'I see I'm going to have to spell it out for you. Angel is alive. I've seen her with my own eyes. I knew her too well for her change of appearance to fool me. You will find her in Candace's flat. It's up to you to find out why they killed the poor girl they left in Angel's bed.'

'Why are you telling me this?'

'To get you off my back and because I believe your sense of justice will outweigh your desire to have me banged up.'

Tony stood. 'We're done here.' He turned his back on Bill and walked away. 'Take him home,' he said to Phil.

53

Tony's sense of unease increased during the drive home. Had he made a colossal mistake in the way he'd handled Bill Murphy? By giving him the lead to solving the mystery of Angel's supposed death, had he also delivered enough evidence for him to pursue a different trail which could wind up with Tony's incarceration?

He shivered. He'd trodden a fine line for years, skirting the edge of criminality even though he sometimes got his hands dirty. But he'd always been careful and ensured nothing led back to him. Why had he now handed Bill Murphy enough ammunition to enable the detective to come after him? All he had to do was ignore the facts as Tony had presented them, turn them around so they meant something else. If he did that, Tony was finished.

When he reached the house, he headed for the lounge. There was no point climbing the stairs to his bedroom. Madge wasn't there, and he had no inclination to sleep, plus his mind was too busy buzzing over his lack of judgement in tackling Bill Murphy. It could only result in an increase in the guy's dislike of him and his need for revenge.

Revenge? Where had that thought come from? He lifted the decanter and splashed whisky into a glass before slumping into an armchair. Was it revenge Bill Murphy sought? And, if so, for what?

Never before had he stopped to question the cop's motives, although over the years Murphy's suspicions of him had grated. Other cops came and went, but Murphy always seemed to be on his tail.

He turned the glass around in his hand contemplating the amber liquid. Murphy had mentioned being at school at the same time as Madge, but Tony couldn't remember him. There had been a weedy kid who'd followed Madge around like a dog in heat and he remembered duffing him up a couple of times because he was annoying her. But surely that couldn't have been Murphy, or could it?

No. He shook his head. It wasn't possible. Whatever it was, Murphy had his knife in him, and he loved to twist it.

Bloody hell, there was no way the guy was going to allow his sense of justice to prevail over his desire to sink that knife even further into his back.

Tony swallowed his drink. There was no doubt about it. He had just made the biggest mistake of his life.

The smell of oil inside the hood filled Bill's nostrils and turned his stomach. He'd lost all sense of time and had no idea how long it was before the buggers wrested it from his head and bundled him out of the car. He landed on the pavement with a thud, banging his knee and elbow when he landed. Dazed by the impact he wasn't quick enough to get the number plate of the car. Not that it mattered. He knew Phil and Gus had driven him home.

He didn't feel safe until he closed the door of his flat and let the welcoming darkness inside swallow him. Bile rose from his stomach into his throat, and it felt as if a drummer was beating a tattoo in his head. There was a packet of paracetamol in the kitchen. Maybe that would relieve it. But first, he needed to turn the lights on. Luckily, the cupboard with the master switch was on the wall behind the door, making it easy to find in the dark.

His guess was right: the buggers had thrown the master switch and once he clicked it the hall light flared into life. He stood, blinking in the sudden glare, before heading for the kitchen and the welcome paracetamol.

With the pill bottle in his hand, he bent over the sink and retched. Acid burned the back of his throat forcing him to swallow mouthfuls of cold water from the tap. Tears pricked his eyes and cold shivers engulfed him. He reckoned he was lucky to be alive. But what to do? He was so close to nabbing

Tony Palmer and now the man had spun him a story which he found difficult to take in. Should he believe him? Or should he continue his campaign to get Tony locked up?

Unable to make his mind up, he reached for the phone in his pocket, but it wasn't there. He staggered to the lounge and spotted it perched on the coffee table. Grabbing it, he punched in the number.

'I need to talk. Can I come round?' The sleepy voice at the other end grunted with displeasure, but Bill paid no attention. 'Yes, I know what time it is, but I don't know which way to turn, and I need to run this past you.'

Ten minutes later, after abandoning his car on the double yellows in front of the house, he was banging on the door.

'No need to break the door down.' Sue beckoned him inside. She was wearing a white towelling bathrobe and hadn't had time to run a comb through her hair.

'You look like shit and in need of a strong coffee. I'll put the kettle on.'

Bill followed her into the kitchen. 'I feel like shit.'

His mind raced. He wanted to tell her everything, but where to start?

'We've worked together for a long time, and you know me better than anyone.'

Sue poured water on the instant coffee in a mug and handed it to him. 'Seems to me we haven't been paired up quite so much recently.'

Bill shrugged. 'Not my fault Kate likes to poke her finger into the pie and get involved. When Andy was the inspector, he was happy to leave it to us. But I'd rather run this past you before I do or say anything to Kate.'

'I suggest we get comfortable first.' Sue led the way through to the lounge and pointed him towards an armchair.

Bill brooded over his coffee before he spoke, but once he started everything that had happened poured out of him.

'Apart from the fact Palmer kidnapped you, which is an offence, what do we have?'

'No collaboration,' Bill said gloomily. 'He would just deny it and say I was imagining things. And no doubt he'd have a convenient alibi.'

'Yes, there's that.' Sue's voice was thoughtful. 'It seems to me your desire to get something on Tony is clouding your thinking and getting in the way of examining the facts. Let's compare Tony's story with the facts we already have.'

Bill gulped the last of his coffee. His head was clearing now.

'The dancer known as Angel was found dead on the morning of Saturday, 21st of August. The last known person to see her alive was Tony Palmer on the evening before. She was being stalked by Denzil Rafferty; a Glasgow detective who has not yet been traced. An unidentified caller arriving by car was observed. His car has not been traced. Another resident heard water in the pipes in the early morning which indicated someone was showering. Since then, Angel has been identified as Lesley Matthews, estranged wife of Kevin Matthews, son of Jimmy Matthews.' Sue paused for breath. 'Strange how that name keeps popping up.'

'None of that lets Tony off the hook and I reckon we can take it for granted he was the one in the shower which confirms he was in her flat after her murder.' Bill was hanging on to his belief that Tony was guilty.

'There is one thing though that could make the story he told you hold up.'

Bill knew what she was going to say, and he didn't want to hear it. He didn't want Tony's story confirmed because that meant he would slither out of this mess in the same way he always did.

'The fingerprints of Lesley Matthews don't match those taken from the body.'

'But the body was identified as being Angel Golding.'

'That only adds more confirmation to Tony's story because the person who identified her was Candace Morgan and I defy you to say she's not in this up to her neck. Anyway, if I know Kate, she'll already have forensics on it.'

Bill's shoulders slumped. He'd been so close to getting something on Tony Palmer, and now it was all slipping away.

54

Tony woke with a crick in his neck and a numb arm. Chairs weren't designed for sleep and his head had slumped to an awkward angle. He flexed his shoulders and stretched his arms until a pins and needles sensation heralded the return of feeling.

The sounds of movement and creak of floors signalled the house waking up. Luigi would be checking everything, wee Morag would be scuttling about with her brush and dustpan, and Bet would be in the kitchen getting ready to prepare the day's meals.

His stomach growled, reminding him he hadn't eaten since the day before. He rose and, bypassing the breakfast room, headed for the kitchen to see what was cooking.

Bet and Luigi, bending over the *Dundee Courier*, which was spread out on the massive kitchen table, turned at the sound of his approach.

'Something interesting in the news?'

Flustered, Bet turned away from the newspaper, grabbed some bacon from the fridge and slapped several rashers into a frying pan.

Tony spotted an open tin of bannocks and grabbed one before peering over Luigi's shoulder.

'A car exploded near The Horn on the Perth dual carriageway. The paper reckons it was a bomb, and the cops have closed off the whole road.'

Tony shrugged. Exploding cars and bombs were of no interest to him, but he thought he heard something more than just interest in Luigi's voice.

'The paper says there were casualties, although the numbers still have to be clarified. But the car had Glasgow number plates, so it's possible that's where they were from.'

'How do they know that?'

'The roadside cameras captured the car's registration number before it blew up. I wouldn't be surprised if the cops have traced the owner already.'

Tony swallowed the last crumbs of the bannock. 'I need to make a phone call.'

He returned to the kitchen within ten minutes, having found out all he needed to from Superintendent Jolly. Jimmy Matthews wouldn't be bothering him again, and he had a perfect alibi for the time the car bomb exploded, one that Detective Sergeant Murphy would be obliged to confirm. That would stick in the bugger's craw.

For the first time in his life, Bill arrived before the rest of the team. A light reflected out through the open slats of Kate's blinds, and she seemed unaware of their approach. Her elbow rested on the desk and one hand cupped her chin while the other sorted through the pages of the file in front of her.

Bill moved restlessly while Sue tapped on the door. It had been Sue's idea to come here at this unearthly hour.

'Kate's always in early and you have to tell her everything,' she'd said.

But Bill wasn't so sure. Once Kate knew, she was bound to share it with the team, and that would open him to ridicule. The cop, kidnapped by gangsters, who lived to tell the tale. He could just imagine the rumours that would spark.

'Come.' Kate's voice sounded weary as she invited them in. Had she been here all night? It wouldn't surprise Bill if she had.

He shuffled into the office behind Sue, painfully aware he was wearing yesterday's shirt. Not that there was anything unusual about that, but he imagined he'd caught a whiff of oil from the collar. A reminder of last night's embarrassing events.

Kate was bound to notice. She was always on at him to smarten up and although he was apt to shrug her comments off, this time it was different.

'There has been a development we thought you should be aware of,' Sue said.

Kate closed the file in front of her and regarded them with eyes that were sharper than Bill liked. 'I take it this is something that couldn't wait until the team briefing?'

'After Bill makes his report, you will understand why we came to you first.'

'Go ahead,' Kate said. 'I'm listening.'

Bill kept his eyes fixed on the wall behind Kate's left shoulder while he related the previous night's events. It was less embarrassing than meeting Kate's eyes. Once he'd finished, Kate sat in silence for a few moments, and he shuffled his feet nervously waiting for her reaction.

At last, she spoke. 'Do you want Palmer charged with abduction?'

Bill cringed. It was the last thing he wanted. He could never face any of his colleagues again and the press was bound to get hold of it.

'No, I don't see the point. How would we prove it? I don't know where they took me which means there is no physical evidence, and it needs corroboration by two people to prove the charge in court. Given that the only people who could do that are employed by Tony there is little chance of that. And I have no doubt Tony will have an alibi.'

'If we trace the car they used to transport you we could get forensics onto it.'

'That's probably a non-starter. They would have boosted a car to use and by this time it will be a burnt-out wreck in a lay-by or field. Tony's too smart to be caught that way.'

Kate drummed her fingers on the desk, deep in thought.

'I'm inclined to give credence to Palmer's story. We now know that Angel Golding was an alias for Lesley Matthews and that her fingerprints do not match those of the victim. I forwarded those fingerprints to the forensic team yesterday, and they confirmed the presence of Lesley Matthew's fingerprints at the locus. That led me to question the identification of the body by Candace Morgan. I've been puzzling over that for most of the night. And now, you appear to have supplied the answer. I think we need to bring these two women in without delay.'

Bill's last hope of incriminating Tony Palmer vanished. The evidence was now pointing in a different direction.

'Meanwhile,' Kate continued, 'I don't suppose it reflects well on our team that a known gangster hijacked one of our officers.' She picked up her pen and scored through a section of her notes, making them unreadable. 'I will treat the information about Candace Morgan and Lesley Matthews as intel from a confidential source, and you are charged with going out and bringing them in for questioning and fingerprinting. That should supply the answers we need.'

She laid her pen on the desk. 'Don't let me keep you. Get on with it.'

55

Candace had lain awake all night, worried about the presence of Ken watching them from a corner of their bedroom. Now, with daylight filtering into the room, she wasn't sure whether to be relieved or more scared.

Angel lay cocooned within her arms, and although her eyes were closed Candace was sure she hadn't slept either.

'You were crying during the night,' she whispered into Angel's ear.

'I keep imagining what Tony will do to us. He's not a forgiving man.' Tears rolled down her cheeks. 'I know what he did to the man who murdered his daughter.'

'What did he do?' Candace wasn't sure she wanted to know but couldn't resist asking the question.

Angel shuddered. 'I don't want to think about it, but that man died in agony. Tony called it justice.' She turned her face into the pillow. 'What if he does the same to us?'

'He wouldn't dare.'

Candace hoped she was right, but she'd seen the expression on Tony's face when he'd told them the alternative to police involvement wouldn't be pleasant. An icy shiver ran down her spine.

It was another three hours before anything happened. Three hours of mounting fear, trying to avoid Ken's eyes, and dreading the reappearance of Tony.

Silence cloaked the room, only broken by the sound of Ken's footsteps when he paced to the window to look outside. So, when the hammering on the door echoed through the room, Candace's nerves already at fever point, went into overdrive. Angel clutched at her in desperation, and she felt the girl's body shaking, while the look of fear in her eyes intensified.

'The waiting is over, and it will be all right,' she said, although she wasn't sure if she was trying to convince herself more than Angel.

Candace drew the girl into a tighter embrace, only loosening her grip after Ken opened the door to reveal two plainclothes and two uniformed cops.

A sigh of pent-up relief whispered through her lips. At least now they knew their fate.

'The ladies have been waiting for you,' Ken said as he stood back to allow them entry.

One of the cops read them their rights and asked if they understood. Although she hadn't heard a word, Candace nodded assent. Angel did the same.

The man who'd cautioned them looked worried. 'You do understand you are being arrested on a charge of murder?'

Candace looked at Angel and squeezed her hand.

'Yes, officer, we understand,' she said.

Accompanied by the procurator fiscal, Kate spent much of the day watching the interviews of Candace Morgan and Lesley Matthews on the video link. Both agreed there was sufficient evidence to charge the two women with the murder of Linda Taylor.

With a sense of satisfaction, she gathered the papers and reports on the arrest and subsequent interviews, and although it was late in the day, she pulled the team together for an update.

'I want to thank you all for the good work you have done on this case, and I'm pleased to say we have a satisfactory conclusion and are going forward with a prosecution. As some of you know, we arrested Candace Morgan and Lesley Matthews this morning for the murder of Linda Taylor. Both women have been interviewed at various times throughout the day and they are currently blaming each other for the murder. I think we can rest assured we will get a conviction.'

'What about Tony Palmer? I thought he had an involvement.'

Kate looked around the room to identify the speaker. 'Thank you for that, Blair,' she said. 'You are quite correct. The DNA results have been returned and they identify him as being present. However, he has provided information that upholds the evidence we have gathered regarding the two women we have charged. Naturally, he will be required to give evidence when the case comes to trial.'

'What about yesterday's car explosion? My understanding is that Jimmy Matthews was one of the victims and there was a direct connection between Matthews and Tony Palmer.'

'Yes, and why are we not involved in the investigation?'

'I'll answer you first, Blair. They have brought in a counter-terrorist squad to deal with the explosion which has been identified as the result of a car bomb. This is normal procedure and will only involve us in a liaison capacity. As for you, Bill, you are right. There is a connection, and I've fed that to the investigating officers. The problem is that the evidence points to the bomb being triggered by a mobile signal and Palmer has an alibi.'

'What's new?' Bill looked disgruntled.

'Unfortunately, his alibi is impeccable. He was being interviewed by you and Sue at the time of the explosion. I've watched the video footage back. His hands were in view for the entire interview and at no time did he handle his phone.'

'One of his thugs could have set the bomb off.'

'I'm sure the investigation will prove that one way or the other. In the meantime, I think we should congratulate ourselves on having solved our current case.'

56

Four weeks later

Madge laid the opened book on her knee and relaxed into the deckchair. Her concentration was improving, although she felt herself drifting off as she read. She turned her face up to the sun to enjoy its warmth as it dappled her skin. Scotland's unusual heatwave had now passed, leaving behind warm, balmy days, which were more enjoyable.

Silence reigned in the garden, broken only by bees buzzing around the roses in the border. She was at peace with herself, enjoying the slower pace of life in this rural setting, although, to be truthful, she missed the noise and vitality of Dundee.

A hand touched her shoulder, and she turned to see Marlene.

She smiled at her. A slow, peaceful smile that relaxed her face and crinkled her eyes.

She picked up the book. 'I forgot to thank you for bringing this,' she said. 'I've never read poetry before, but I'm enjoying it. Some of the poems are so full of emotion they touch my heart.'

Marlene sat on the grass beside her. 'It's Tony you have to thank. He bought the book and asked me to bring it to you.' Marlene plucked a blade of grass. 'He's missing you.'

Madge wasn't sure whether to believe her. When she was admitted to this place, she'd been furious with him for sending her away. Convinced he wanted to replace her with one of his fancy women. Now, she wasn't sure, although she had no doubts that over the years Tony had cheated on her many times. But after they lost their daughter – she closed her eyes as the ghost of Denise invaded her mind – he'd seemed different. He'd come home every night when he finished at Teasers until that last night. The night the dancer was killed.

That was when everything went wrong.

'If he misses me so much, why did he send me here?' Her voice was husky, reminiscent of the hoarseness of her speech when she was first admitted. Drugs could affect voices like that, the doctor told her. But she was much better now, and the hoarseness had lessened.

Marlene reached out and grasped her hand. 'It was to protect you. As long as Jimmy Matthews was hanging around, you were in danger. He couldn't forget what Matthews did to Georgio and what he threatened to do to Fabio. It made Tony afraid Matthews would hurt you to get at him. And he almost succeeded because Liz, who was supposed to be looking after you, was his niece. Her name was Liz Matthews, not Stewart.'

Madge watched a bee buzzing around a rosebush. She wanted to believe Marlene, but the doubts lingered.

'Won't you at least see him?'

Would she? In her heart, she wanted to but feared her resentment would spill over and damage their relationship so badly it would never recover. Which, she supposed, meant she wanted their relationship to continue.

Thoughts swirled around her brain, adding to the confusion already there. Maybe she wasn't as well as she thought she was.

Marlene's grasp on her hand tightened. 'He's waiting in the car. You just have to say yes.'

Her throat tightened and her mouth refused to form the word, but she nodded her head.

Tony wiped his hands on his trousers. Although every window in the car was rolled down it was stifling inside. But if he got out that would put him in Madge's line of sight, and he wasn't sure how she would react. If she was still angry with him, then all Marlene's persuasive powers would be for nothing.

The minutes, feeling more like hours, ticked past before Marlene approached the car.

'Well?' His heart thumped the way it used to when he was

a teenager waiting to see if Madge would go out with him.

'I've told her you're here. She's waiting for you in the garden. But she's still fragile so tread carefully.'

Emotion welled up within Tony and tears pricked his eyes. He nodded, afraid to speak and afraid Marlene would see the tears. Men didn't cry. It was a sign of weakness.

He stepped out of the car, and ignoring the sweat trickling down his back, buttoned his jacket. With a last look at Marlene, he strode across the lawn to where his wife sat in the deckchair.

Strands of her hair fluttered in the breeze, and she raised a hand to remove a wisp from her face before looking up at him. He ached to reach out for her, smooth the hair back from her face, and touch her. But he restrained himself.

'You suit your hair longer.'

A slight smile trembled at the corners of her mouth, but her eyes were wary, and he couldn't tell what she was thinking.

He lowered himself to sit on the grass at her feet. 'The house is quiet without you and Dr Davidson thinks you've responded so well to treatment here that maybe it's time you came home.' He waited a moment for her response, but when she didn't answer, he added, 'I've missed you.' Unaccustomed to voicing his feelings the words were barely audible, and he wasn't sure if she heard them.

'The dancer, the one they thought had been killed. Did you care for her?'

The misery in Madge's voice was unmistakable and added to the guilt Tony felt about all the times he had betrayed his wife.

He turned his head and stared up into her eyes, wanting to grasp her hands but afraid to in case she rebuffed him.

'Only in the same way I care for all my employees.'

She nodded, but her hands gripped her book so hard her knuckles whitened.

'It was a difficult time, Madge. I know I've neglected you, but I was afraid. The cops thought I'd killed her, and I couldn't see any way of convincing them otherwise. Then Jimmy Matthews and his thugs were breathing down my neck and I knew he wouldn't think twice about harming you to get to me. The only thing I could think of was to get you out of harm's way.'

Tears trickled down his cheeks, forcing him to brush them away with the backs of his hands. What was happening to him? He'd never been an emotional man. Never cried before. Never pleaded before. But he was pleading now. He couldn't lose Madge.

'You do see that, don't you? I couldn't lose you.' He stopped short of saying he loved her, although that was what he thought. There was just so far a man like him could go.

Madge's expression softened, and she placed a hand on the top of his head.

'There is one proviso,' she said, 'no more dancers, no more women, otherwise I walk.'

Relief surged through him. 'It's a deal,' he said, and he meant it.

Books by Chris Longmuir

DUNDEE CRIME SERIES

Night Watcher
Dead Wood
Missing Believed Dead
Web of Deceit

KIRSTY CAMPBELL SERIES

The Death Game
Devil's Porridge
Death of a Doxy

SUFFRAGETTE MYSTERIES

Dangerous Destiny

HISTORICAL SAGAS

A Salt Splashed Cradle

NONFICTION

Nuts & Bolts of Self-Publishing

CHRIS LONGMUIR

Chris Longmuir was born in Wiltshire and now lives in Angus. Her family moved to Scotland when she was two. After leaving school at fifteen, Chris worked in shops, offices, mills and factories, and was a bus conductor for a spell, before working as a social worker for Angus Council (latterly serving as Assistant Principal Officer for Adoption and Fostering).

Chris is a member of the Society of Authors, the Crime Writers Association and the Scottish Association of Writers. She writes short stories, articles and crime novels, and has won numerous awards. Her first published book, Dead Wood, won the Dundee International Book Prize and was published by Polygon. She designed her own website and confesses to being a techno-geek who builds computers in her spare time.

http://www.chrislongmuir.co.uk

Ingram Content Group UK Ltd.
Milton Keynes UK
UKHW010635260723
425801UK00003B/30